La

R. Raj Rao is the aut   *id*,
soon to be made into   picture, as well as of
the technically accomplished novel *Hostel Room 131*, and the
collection of short stories *One Day I Locked My Flat in Soul City*.
His other work includes poetry, plays, biography, translation
and much non-fiction. One of India's leading queer theorists,
Rao teaches Indian literature, LGBT literature and creative
writing at the University of Pune.

LADY LOLITA'S LOVER

R. Raj Rao

HarperCollins *Publishers* India

First published in India in 2015 by
HarperCollins *Publishers* India

Copyright © R. Raj Rao 2015

P-ISBN: 978-93-5177-478-5
E-ISBN: 978-93-5177-479-2

2 4 6 8 10 9 7 5 3 1

R. Raj Rao asserts the moral right
to be identified as the author of this work.

HarperCollins *Publishers*
A-75, Sector 57, Noida, Uttar Pradesh 201301, India
1 London Bridge Street, London, SE1 9GF, United Kingdom
Hazelton Lanes, 55 Avenue Road, Suite 2900, Toronto, Ontario M5R 3L2
and 1995 Markham Road, Scarborough, Ontario M1B 5M8, Canada
25 Ryde Road, Pymble, Sydney, NSW 2073, Australia
195 Broadway, New York, NY 10007, USA

Typeset in 11.5/15 Adobe Devanagari Regular at
Manipal Digital Systems, Manipal

Printed and bound by RRD, UK

For Sandeep

ONE
Royal Video Parlour

Royal Video Parlour was situated at a bustling intersection in central Bombay. To its north was the famed neighbourhood of Dadar, the corolla of the city from where it stemmed in all directions and where the central and western lines affably met. To its south was Parel, a mill area inhabited largely by industrial labour that would migrate to the city from villages in the state of Maharashtra and indeed the rest of India.

Royal Video Parlour had been established, according to its signboard, in 1970 by Daulatrao Jadhav. He was the father of the present proprietor, Ashok Jadhav who, as an only son, inherited the store from his father. Then, the name 'Royal Video Parlour' pointed to a future where people would watch movies, not in cinema theatres, but in their own bedrooms on low-priced VCRs. Ashok Jadhav had renovated the store when he took over, changing the gaudy pink oil paint of its walls to sober off-white distemper with matte finish. He saw no reason to meddle with the name of the store, even though there were several Royal Video Parlours all across the country that bore no connection to his outfit.

In the beginning, Royal Video Parlour had stocked gramophone records in 33 and 45 RPM speeds. It even had a few 78 RPM classics dating back to the days of Kundanlal Saigal and Pankaj Mullick. The 33 RPM 'long-playing' records of Bollywood films had been especially popular among the long-haired collegians of the day and sold like bestselling novels. Two such LPs, of *Johnny Mera Naam* and *Amar Akbar Anthony*, broke all records and brought in tons of lolly for the Jadhavs. That was when Ashok Jadhav and his wife decided to air-condition the store.

In time, however, audio and video cassettes pushed the long-playing LPs into oblivion. Ashok Jadhav ordered these cassettes by the hundreds from wholesalers in the suburbs, and built wall-to-wall shelves all around his 20x20 store to stock and display them. This gave the store the appearance of a bookshop, and more than once he toyed with the idea of calling it Royal Video Library. This would have worked as, in addition to selling its wares, the store had begun to lend out video cassettes in keeping with the demands of the day.

Alas, the days of audio and video cassettes too, were short-lived. By the turn of the century, they were beginning to come to an end. Ashok Jadhav now filled his wall-to-wall cabinets with VCDs and DVDs that flooded the market, the majority of which were pirated and sold at the notorious Ded Galli. A new film released on Friday and by Saturday morning, a pirated DVD of it, a theatre print surreptitiously recorded, could be bought for the price of a single ticket, or even less. Nor were there police raids worth their name that could deter him from buying the stuff.

But it would be incorrect to suggest that all Royal Video Parlour stocked were Bollywood flicks. There were English films too, and then there was the pornography that was indispensable, for everyone asked for it. The rich and poor, young and old, men and women, though in the end only the men got it. Ashok Jadhav occasionally had qualms, wondering if it was okay to desecrate the store his father had founded with so much zeal. But if he said no to porn, he would lose his clientele to neophytes in the trade, like VCD Express and Movie Den that had mushroomed in the vicinity.

The customers themselves made for a wide spectrum of humans. Predominantly, the Dadar – Parel belt was a working area replete with chawls that were built in the nineteenth century. Its inhabitants served in factories by day and spent their evenings at Royal Video Parlour, borrowing Hindi films, Marathi films, Double-X and Triple-X DVDs, and whatever else was on offer. Ashok Jadhav did not mind their presence. It indicated to the competitors that his was the more popular store.

If it was men who frequented the store after sunset, it was middle-aged housewives who went there in the daytime to ask for the newest tearjerkers. Ashok Jadhav enjoyed flirting with them, although marriage had rendered most of them shapeless, like pumpkins. However, many of them insisted on dropping in post-lunch when they were done with their household chores. That was usually the time he left the store in the charge of his boys and dashed off home for a siesta, his own healthy wife snoring beside him on the bed. By the time he returned to the store at five, the women had all gone back home to cook the evening meal for their husbands.

There was another side to Dadar – Parel. Mill land situated here had been sold to the builders' mafia (and the Thackerays) at throwaway prices after Datta Samant's incessant strikes had closed down the textile mills once and for all. Flamboyant high-rises, many of them architectural wonders that resembled Dubai's seven-star hotels, had come up here. They boasted extravagances such as temperature-controlled swimming pools and helipads.

The occupants of the overpriced flats may have been fed gold, but they came to Royal Video Parlour all the same. Snootily, they turned their noses up at Bollywood blockbusters. Instead, they asked for English films, dropping names like Tom Cruise, Tom Hanks, Brad Pitt and Sean Penn, with which good old Ashok Jadhav could not say he was familiar. He obliged them nonetheless, never one to scuttle a good business proposition, by dutifully jotting the names of the films down. He would then bug the Ded Galli godfathers to smuggle them for him from Hong Kong and Singapore.

In this age of home deliveries, where everything from a pizza to a motor car was handed over to the consumer at his doorstep, Ashok Jadhav had to ensure that his customers got their DVDs at home if they did not feel like trekking to his store in the incinerating Bombay heat. For this, he employed boys in the age group of fifteen to seventeen, most of them from Marathwada like himself. The boys were poor and only too glad to leave their villages behind to make money in Bombay. They were school dropouts who hadn't even made it past class 10, for conditions in their homes were hardly conducive to romancing with books. Ashok Jadhav employed them and paid them a monthly salary of Rs 1200. He also rented a room nearby to board and lodge them, and bought them Atlas bicycles on which they ran errands. Rather than treating them as servants, he thought of them as his sons and indulged them. Whenever he went shopping with his wife to Dadar market, he bought them shirts and pants, caps and shoes. They had to look smart, he insisted, since they went into people's homes. Of course, his largesse did not burn a hole in his purse, for at any given time he hired no more than three, or at the most four of these boys, saying sorry to others who appeared at the store to ask if there were vacancies. In Bombay, even a delivery boy's job was coveted.

Bombay's glamorous ethos, the liberty that Ashok Jadhav gave them, the trendy apparel that became a part of their everyday lifestyle, and the fact that they were forever smothered by images of Bollywood heroes during their time in the store, got into the boys' heads. They began to fancy themselves as local Salman Khans, Shahrukh Khans, Hrithik Roshans and Vivek Oberois.

Lolita ambled into Royal Video Parlour one sultry evening. She had moved into the neighbourhood about a fortnight ago and was mentally noting the names of all the shops in the locality that she would have to frequent. There were grocery stores, takeaways and a beauty salon that she visited before spotting the Royal Video Parlour and stepping in for no apparent reason.

'Yes, madam?' Ashok Jadhav obsequiously greeted her, brushing aside the other customers who pestered him with their queries. 'May I help you?'

'Thanks,' said Lolita curtly. 'Just looking around.'

Lolita's perfume reached Ashok Jadhav's nostrils. She wore a yellow dress with purple flowers and had tiny jhumkas in her ears. She was fair, wore her hair short like Princess Diana, and had gold nail polish on her fingernails and toenails. The most distinctive feature of her personality was her height. Lolita was tall. Her height made her look slimmer than she was and her green-mango breasts, though small, stood out. All in all, Ashok Jadhav thought she was a beauty, the kind of woman one saw in movies and magazines. Not in real life.

Lolita toured the store for half an hour, aware that its proprietor would cast lustful glances at her every now and then. She returned with a handful of DVDs and asked if she could borrow them.

'Madam, you will have to become a member first,' Ashok Jadhav informed her and ordered Sandesh, one of his star delivery boys, to give her the membership forms.

Sandesh stood waiting as Lolita filled out the forms. Her handwriting, he noticed, slanted naughtily towards the left. Furtively eyeing what she wrote, as he did in his exams when he wanted to copy off of someone else's paper, Sandesh discovered that Lolita was twenty-nine years old, though she looked younger, and lived in Jannat, Dadar's poshest high-rise.

'Madam, you will giving also address proof and photo,' Sandesh said to Lolita in broken English, when she handed him the forms.

'Oh, I'll get those tomorrow,' Lolita replied, smiling. Her teeth were like those of the women in Close-Up toothpaste ads. 'Don't have them on me right now.'

The smile unnerved Sandesh and he perspired. He was all of fifteen, lanky and high cheekboned. This was his first job. 'Okay,' he said to Lolita, and opened a dog-eared register to jot down the names of all the DVDs she borrowed. They were a mixture of Bollywood and Hollywood films, including *Titanic*.

Ashok Jadhav was busy with a cantankerous customer. He came back to Lolita after disposing of the customer and indicated to Sandesh with a flicker of his hand that she was now his business. Lolita's displeasure at this was visible on her face in no uncertain terms: she preferred to transact with Sandesh than his master, who she was sure had a dirty mind.

'Madam, you will have to give us a security deposit of Rs 500,' the man was now saying to her, hassling her further.

Lolita opened her handbag and slapped the dough on the counter.

'Receipt,' she sternly demanded.

Ashok Jadhav called out to Sandesh. He was the only delivery boy present in the store. The other two, Darshan and Aniket, were loafing somewhere.

'Write out a receipt for madam,' he brusquely said.

'Yes, sir.'

Sandesh fetched the receipt book from a cupboard and tried to imitate Lolita's handwriting as he wrote. He found he did this very well. Lolita put the receipt into her handbag but did not leave the store immediately. Instead she hung around, examining every DVD on display.

A whole hour passed. Closing time was approaching and Ashok Jadhav had no choice but to politely tell the lady to come back tomorrow.

'Please come early,' he ingratiatingly said. 'Spend the whole day here if you like. We are having many interesting DVDs that will amuse you.'

Sandesh looked at his watch and Lolita looked at hers. It was past nine. Lolita left the store, as both master and servant went to see her off. Her car, a black Zen Carbon, was parked just a few yards from the Royal Video Parlour. This was a two-door model, Ashok Jadhav told Sandesh, that Maruti Suzuki had introduced in India on an experimental basis, along with Zen Steel in metallic silver. At one time, he had thought of buying it himself.

As Lolita turned on the ignition and drove off, Sandesh wondered why anyone would want to buy a two-door car. He had no idea how people would get into the back seat of Madam Lolita's car.

Sandesh and Darshan manned the store when Lolita appeared the next afternoon, around three, in a red dress.

'Hi,' she addressed Sandesh, trying to catch his eye, as he averted hers. He was pleased to see Lolita again, but had been trained not to look her, or anyone above him in station, in the eye.

Lolita admired the way Sandesh combed his hair, parting it at the centre and letting it fall over his forehead at both ends in bewitching curls. She thought his sartorial taste superb, the white cotton shirt and black jeans that he sported suiting him perfectly. As she gave him a once-over, her eyes froze at his crotch for a second before resuming their downward journey towards his fake Woodland shoes. He was dark in complexion, ebony, but that did not take away from his beauty, his taut muscular body and sumptuous butt atoning for every other flaw, including a few pimples that marred his forehead.

The only blemish, the way she saw it, was his height. Sandesh wasn't tall, and when they stood side by side, she dwarfed him.

Lolita was about to frame the question, when the sight of Sandesh's sweaty body made her heady. 'Do you stock porn?' she bluntly asked, coming to the point without ceremony.

It took Sandesh a while to realize that what the lady wanted was a blue film. Never in his time at the Royal Video Parlour—and he had worked there for six months—had a woman been so *bindaas*. To top it all, her breath smelt of rum.

Sandesh ensured that Darshan wasn't within earshot. He wished he could ask the guy to go out for a smoke, for which he would gladly have paid.

'Yes, madam,' he said to Lolita, conspiratorially lowering his voice. 'We stock porn.'

He used her very words, as if he were her parrot. He took Lolita to one end of the store and gave her a handful of Double X DVDs, afraid that Darshan would snoop. But Darshan was a guy who minded his own business.

'Good,' said Lolita, returning the DVDs she'd borrowed the previous day and putting the new ones into her handbag. She left the store, smiling her thanks, when Sandesh suddenly remembered that he hadn't made an entry in his register or obtained her signature. This was mandatory.

'Madam, madam,' he ran after her as she unlocked the door of her Zen Carbon.

'Such a pain,' Lolita grumbled when, back in the store, she was made to sign. The date and the names of all her DVDs were duly recorded. 'Is this really necessary?'

Sandesh kept mum. He slyly slid his hand to his crotch and found he had a hard-on.

Upon Lolita's exit, Darshan approached Sandesh for dope. 'Who was that chick?' he asked in Marathi. 'Do you know her?' Although Darshan was a guy who kept to himself, Lolita proved too much for him as well.

When Ashok Jadhav got to the store that evening, Sandesh told him nothing. He did not report to his boss that yesterday's madam had showed up in his absence. He did not say that what she borrowed were not innocuous Hindi films, but pornography. Nor did he disclose that he voluntarily gave her many Double X DVDs, getting a kick out of it, when he could have politely said, 'Sorry, madam, we do not stock porn,' for porn was meant for men and Madam Lolita was a lady.

Lolita called again in the afternoon.

'There's less traffic in the afternoon,' she explained, fanning herself with a newspaper. Then she realized that neither of the two boys she spoke to was Sandesh.

'Where's the guy who's been attending to me?' she asked them.

'He's on leave,' Darshan replied. Aniket nodded.

'When will he be back?'

'Tomorrow.'

Lolita left without another word and Darshan shrugged.

'What kind of creature is that?' Aniket asked, as Darshan gave him the low-down. The next morning, Darshan panted when he saw Sandesh.

'Madam was here,' he feverishly said. 'Only for you.' Sandesh waited till Ashok Jadhav left for his siesta that afternoon, then went to the cupboard to fish out Lolita's phone number. It was on her membership form.

'Hello, madam,' he found himself calling her. 'Sandesh here.'

'Oh, hi,' Lolita exuberantly said. 'I've got to ask you something private, my dear, so tell me when you are around.'

'Come now.'

'I'll be there in no time.'

In five minutes flat, they heard Lolita's Zen Carbon pull up outside their store. She was wearing a blue chiffon sari with a low-cut blouse.

Lolita took Sandesh to one side and whispered into his ear.

'Those Double-X DVDs, or whatever they're called, aren't sexy enough for me, I'm afraid. Don't you have hard-core porn? You know, scenes of actual fucking?'

The words 'actual fucking' were enough for Sandesh. He knew at once what to supply her with.

'We are having Triple-X DVDs also, madam,' he quivered.

'Then give me those,' she ordered. 'And make it snappy. I have an appointment at four.'

Ashok Jadhav kept his Triple-X DVDs under lock and key; one never knew when there could be a raid. Sandesh, as the senior most delivery boy, had unconditional access to all the keys in the store. But before unlocking the drawers in which the Triple-Xs were hidden, he sent Darshan out on an errand. Aniket was absconding as usual.

'Buy some Manickchand for you and me,' he said in Marathi, handing him two tenners from the cash counter. 'And don't tell sir.'

No sooner did Darshan leave than Sandesh placed all the Triple Xs on the cash counter for Lolita to choose from. Their covers had explicit sex scenes. 'I'll take all of them,' Lolita said, unsettling him with her direct stare. Sandesh brought out his register. 'Your red tape will land me in trouble,' Lolita complained as she signed. 'Can't you dispense with the formalities?'

This was too bombastic for Sandesh.

When he got to his room after dark, he unzipped his jeans and wanked. Lolita had inhabited his fantasies completely.

As he got out for fresh air, he perambulated the streets. Bombay was, after all, a city that never slept. With his hands in his pockets, he strolled into a beer bar and occupied a table. The waiters ignored him, pointing to a sign on the wall that said patrons had to be twenty-one-years-old to be served alcohol.

'What's your age?' they asked him.

'Twenty-one,' he nonchalantly answered.

'But you don't look it.'

'*Gaand maro.*'

Thrown out of one shady bar, Sandesh found his way to another that wasn't as strict. At least not at this late hour. They were in this business for the money. They let Sandesh order a Canon 10,000 beer and gulp it down, before he ordered a second and a third and then a fourth. He stayed in the bar till the wee hours, drinking and smoking, and then puking all over the sidewalk on his way back home. He never made it that night, passing out on the road instead.

When the morning sun blinded his eyes, Sandesh woke up, brushed the dirt off his T-shirt and jeans, and ambled homewards. His head bounced like a yo-yo. He did not report for work that day and when Ashok Jadhav questioned Darshan and Aniket, both of whom shared his digs, neither knew of his whereabouts.

'You mean he's missing?' Ashok Jadhav asked half seriously, half in jest. *Aapan hyana pahila ka?*

Nursing his hangover with black tea into which he squeezed an entire lemon, Sandesh surrounded himself with pencils, crayons and sheets of foolscap paper. In school, drawing was always his pet subject. He scored well, once bagging a silver medal at a village-level competition. Portraits were his speciality and the sketches he now drew as he sipped his tea were those of Lolita. Lolita as he knew her. Lolita in her yellow dress with purple flowers that she wore the first time he set eyes on her at the Royal Video Parlour. She scouted the shelves for porn DVDs. On the other side was Ashok Jadhav, struggling to curry favour with the lady though she cold-shouldered him. Lolita clothed in red, standing next to him, cheek-by-jowl, almost kissing his ear as she whispered, 'Do you stock porn?'

'Yes, we stock porn.'

Lolita in a blue sari, opening the door of her black Zen Carbon. The combination of black and blue made the sketch very pretty and Sandesh decided to frame it and hang it up on his wall. Then he looked at the other sketches and concluded that they were beautiful too, so he would frame and hang them all up on his walls.

After drinking some more lemon tea, his art materials strewn all over the shabby room, Sandesh lapsed into a fitful slumber and dreamt his *Dil Chahta Hai* dream. He had seen the film with his wastrel friends for the hundredth time just the other day.

Darshan, Aniket and he are three friends in love. However, while Darshan (Aamir Khan) and Aniket (Saif Ali Khan) love women their own age, he (Akshay Khanna) loves Lolita (Dimple Kapadia), a woman twice as old as him. Yet, neither Darshan nor Aniket are as serious about their girlfriends as he is about Lolita. Everyone dissuades him from dating her: she's abandoned, they argue, addicted to booze. But Lolita is Sandesh's obsession. He wants to marry her because life without her is hell.

One day Lolita walks into the Royal Video Parlour and sees Ashok Jadhav and he are engaged in a fight.

'You can't marry a woman old enough to be your mother,' he exaggeratedly says. To this Sandesh's retort is: '*Gaand maro*.'

Lolita overhears their verbal duel and walks out of the store in a huff. Then they hear her start her Zen Carbon and speed off. After that, Lolita never returns to the Royal Video Parlour. She has, in all probability, left Jannat, Dadar, the city of Bombay itself. Separation from Lolita is a terrible wrench and no one knows if she's alive or dead.

Sandesh woke up from his dream and began to sob. There was no one around to comfort him. He went to the bathroom to sprinkle cold water on his face, but the taps had run dry. Songs from *Dil Chahta Hai* played in his head:

> '*Dil Chahta hai, kabhi kabhi to …*
> *Koi kahe, kehta rahe, kitna bhi humko diwana …*
> *Tanhai, tanhai …*'

For a week afterwards there was no trace of Lolita. Sandesh was certain that the dream he had dreamt in the aftermath of his binge drinking was prophetic: she had vanished. He thought of dialling her number, which he had memorized, but then got cold feet at the last minute: what ostensible reason did he have for calling? People couldn't be disturbed in their homes just like that.

Things came to a head when Ashok Jadhav announced that the Royal Video Parlour would be closed for three days, as he had to scurry to his village in Marathwada to sort out a land dispute. Some of his cousins were trying to usurp agricultural land that belonged to him and if he did not take appropriate action, it would be too late. His cousins, he told his boys, were no less vicious than the Kauravas.

While Darshan and Aniket emulated their boss and journeyed to their villages to see their folks, Sandesh, always the odd man out, stayed behind in Bombay and sulked. However, Darshan and Aniket did not travel in the same air-conditioned bus as their boss, for he flatly refused to pay, saying 'nothing doing' to their proposal to be his bodyguards. Instead, they caught a *lal dabba* State Transport bus from the Parel depot, not far from the Royal Video Parlour, which took much longer to get them to their destinations than Ashok Jadhav's private, air-conditioned Volvo. The upshot? When Ashok Jadav returned to Bombay and reopened his store, having dealt with his errant cousins to his satisfaction, Darshan and Aniket were tucked away in their villages still.

Lolita chose to stage a comeback at this inexpedient time and throw a tantrum.

'Mr Manager,' she said to Ashok Jadhav with bloodshot eyes, 'I demand a full refund. All the DVDs I borrowed from your store the other day are defective. They've ruined my player, and it's a Sony.'

Ashok Jadhav's ears cocked up at the word 'refund'. Though he called the money he charged his customers a security deposit, it was really non-refundable. Otherwise he would have to close the shop.

'Sorry, madam, we do not give refunds,' he said, trying to keep his cool. He had no idea that the DVDs Lolita had borrowed were Triple-Xs. 'However, I don't think my DVDs are defective. They are of the best quality. Perhaps you were unable to work them on your player. That is a man's job.'

Lolita let the sexist remark pass because Ashok Jadhav was now offering to send his 'man' to her flat to fix the problem.

'Fair enough,' she said. 'But send him right away.'

Ashok Jadhav looked at his watch. It was 7.30 p.m. and customers thronged the store while two of his boys were still playing truant. 'Impossible, madam,' he pleaded. 'It's rush hour and I have just one chap with me in the store today. The other two are on leave. But I promise to send someone first thing tomorrow morning.'

Sandesh, who slyly witnessed the exchange from a corner, prayed that his boss would capitulate and let him visit Madam Lolita's flat then and there. His prayers were answered. Lolita, unused to letting anyone else have the last word, did not relent till Ashok Jadhav, sick of the scene she was creating, ordered Sandesh to accompany the lady to her house, figure out what was wrong, and return post-haste.

'Take my scooter,' Ashok Jadhav shouted out to Sandesh as an afterthought, just as he was about to get into the back seat of Lolita's Zen Carbon. Sandesh knew now that to get into the back seat of a two-door car, one had to thrust the front seat forward. Sandesh did as he was told. He returned to the store to fetch the keys of Ashok Jadhav's Bajaj Chetak.

'If you ride with her, how will you get back, you fool?' Ashok Jadhav chided him, not knowing what he was getting into by parting with his scooter.

Sandesh followed Lolita's Zen Carbon, but she was such a rash driver that he lost her more than once in the peak-hour traffic that was made up of cars, taxis and BEST buses. He saw her, and then he didn't, till finally a traffic cop hailed out to him and asked for his licence.

Sandesh did not have a licence, so he bribed the traffic cop with the petty cash that Ashok Jadhav always left with his boys and secured his release.

However, by now Lolita was nowhere on the horizon. When Sandesh reached Jannat (everyone knew the building), the elaborate security arrangements that required him to fill out a thousand personal details in a giant-sized register intimidated him. As if this wasn't enough for the non-matriculate, he was made to speak to Lolita on an intercom before stepping into the elevator.

'Where did you get lost?' Lolita laughed. 'I've been going bonkers looking for you.'

She then told him to take the elevator up to the forty-ninth floor.

Lolita opened the door of her duplex to Sandesh even before he could ring the doorbell. He entered and was transported to Byzantium. The mauve and lavender walls were covered with original paintings by world masters. Kashmiri carpets, the child labour that went into their manufacture notwithstanding, covered every millimetre of floor while ornate Persian vases majestically stood in nooks and corners.

'Come in,' said Lolita, and directed him straightaway to the master bedroom upstairs where her DVD player sat. En route, he lost count of the number of rooms he saw, some open, others padlocked. The lighting everywhere was sepia: fancy lampshades, chandeliers and Chinese lanterns illuminated the rooms. Potted plants in varied hues gave the house a forest feel.

'May I have a glass of water?' stammered Sandesh.

Lolita went to the fridge in the modular kitchen and poured him a glass of water from a silver jug. Sandesh quenched his thirst, nervously spilling some of the water on his shirt in an attempt to drink without putting the glass to his lips, and wiped his mouth with the back of his hand.

'Relax,' Lolita put him at ease. 'This is a home, like any other.'

'Thanks, madam,' Sandesh mumbled.

It was a short walk from the kitchen downstairs to the air-conditioned master bedroom on the first floor. As soon as Sandesh got there, he busied himself with extension wires, plugs, sockets and remote controls, all in a bid to fix Lolita's DVD player. There seemed to be nothing wrong with it, and when Sandesh tried out a sample DVD (not her Triple Xs, but a collection of Kumar Sanu songs), it was evident that the machine was in perfect condition.

Sandesh joyfully arose to report the matter to Lolita, but she was in the living room downstairs, jabbering on the telephone. He killed time by inspecting the master bedroom and was shocked to see a wedding photograph of Lolita and her husband in a gilded photo frame on a side table. Lolita looked even prettier in the photo than she really was, but when Sandesh scrutinized the picture of her husband, he found him to be not just older than her, but also plumpish and balding. Altogether, he thought the man wasn't smart. He wondered why Lolita would marry a man like that. Moreover, if Lolita was married, where was her husband now? Was she divorced, like Dimple in *Dil Chahta Hai*? Or was he dead? Wasn't Lolita afraid to live in such a large apartment all by herself?

Yawning, Sandesh left the master bedroom and sauntered into the study. There were wall-to-wall bookcases all made of rosewood. Though he was no book lover, he attempted, with much difficulty, to read the titles of some of the books aloud: *My Story, Love's Labour's Lost, Giovanni's Room, The God of Small Things, Hamlet, Lady Chatterley's Lover, Sons and Lovers, Midnight's Children, Mother of 1084, The Guide, Leaves from a Policeman's Diary*. One book even had madam's name as its title: *Lolita*. The name of its author was Vladimir Nabokov, but he did not know how to pronounce the author's name or surname.

Sandesh let the books be when he noticed an expensive laptop on a carved console that served as a writing table and fingered its keys. Lolita startled him by coming up from behind, the cordless phone still in her hand.

'Is the problem sorted out?' she smiled.

'DVD player is okay,' Sandesh said. 'No problem …'

'Let's have some coffee,' Lolita declared. 'And then we'll test the Triple-Xs we got from your store the other day.'

'Okay,' said Sandesh. His heart pounded.

She instructed him to sit in the drawing room and browse through old *Filmfares* while she got the coffee ready. Sandesh had barely made himself comfortable on a colourful Sankheda sofa when his eyes fell on Lolita's well-stocked lounge bar. In it were all the premium brands of whisky, brandy, gin, rum and vodka. On the bar counter was a bottle of Martini with an empty crystal glass by its side. There were also several packs of More and Dunhill cigarettes. Sandesh felt like helping himself to a Dunhill, but decided against it: what would madam think if she saw?

Lolita entered with two cups of cappuccino. 'Thanks for coming,' she said, as both of them sipped their coffee.

Sandesh became aware of the keys he absent-mindedly jangled in his hand and suddenly remembered that Ashok Jadhav's scooter was in his custody. His boss would be fretting, both at his absence and at the disappearance of his scooter.

'Do you want to phone the store to say you'll be late?' Lolita asked him, when she found him repeatedly looking at his watch. Sandesh did not think that necessary. He was much better off here than at the Royal Video Parlour.

The doorbell rang, alarming Sandesh. A maid walked in with a baby no more than a year old. Lolita took the baby in her arms and kissed her. She did not introduce her to Sandesh, but he figured from the way she fussed over the child, as also from her facial features that resembled Lolita's, that she was her daughter. Her name, he gathered, was Tanu.

The maid handed Lolita Tanu's milk and she began to feed her. Why can't she breastfeed the baby, Sandesh thought, still seated in the drawing room while Lolita paced the floor with Tanu. As she did so, she talked to the maid about myriad household chores: dinner, gas, the bazaar, morning milk. She dug out a wad of notes from her handbag and paid the maid, who felt the money was insufficient and asked for more: *itna paisa me itna hi milega*. But unlike the memsaab in the Channel V promo, Lolita wasn't the haggling kind. She paid the maid whatever she demanded, as if she wished to be rid of her at the earliest.

The maid, however, would not leave Lolita alone. She was now asking for a four-figure advance from her salary because someone in her extended family was to be married off, while another was sick and had to be hospitalized. Lolita seemed exasperated by the maid's litany of woes. She stormed into the master bedroom upstairs, the maid in tow, opened her safe and give the maid her advance. They were closeted in the bedroom for very long, the maid, Tanu and Lolita, as if it were a *zenana*, during which Sandesh switched on the TV in the drawing room and surfed the channels. The news channels were full of pictures of the charred Sabarmati Express at Godhra station.

Sandesh heard voices. The female trio had emerged from the master bedroom, and was now stomping about the house. The maid peeped into the drawing room, saw him, and gave him a look that said: I know exactly why you are here.

'Kamalabai,' Lolita shouted out for the maid and Sandesh knew, finally, what her name was. Why must maids always have names like Kamalabai, Shantabai or Sakhubai? He was reminded of his own mother.

'Ji, memsaab?' Kamalabai responded, her hands behind her. She wore a blue-and-gold nine yards Maharashtrian sari and was chewing paan.

'Put Tanu to sleep and then you may leave,' Lolita instructed her.

'Ji, memsaab.'

Kamalabai disappeared with Tanu into one of the apartment's many anterooms. This was the baby's room, full of toys, where Tanu was being trained to sleep by herself in the manner of Western babies, unlike Indian offspring who clung to their daddies and mummies until their teenage years and even beyond.

Lolita joined Sandesh in the drawing room. Together they watched an episode of *Kahani Ghar Ghar Ki* which wasn't exactly Lolita's favourite—she pulled a face when the serial came on—but endured it because Sandesh had the remote in his hand and she liked his thin, long fingers.

In the baby's room, adjacent to the master bedroom, Kamalabai softly hummed a lullaby and rocked Tanu's cradle till she fell asleep. Then she came to tell Lolita she was off.

'Be on time tomorrow,' Lolita said, as the front door closed shut.

'More coffee?' she then asked Sandesh, who politely refused. He hated tea and coffee because he thought they gave him acidity.

'Something stronger, then?' she ventured, shocking him with the question. He remembered the night he got drunk and lay sprawled on the streets of Bombay, bowled over by her.

Sandesh did not answer. Instead, he asked Lolita, 'Where is baby's papa?' He could not bring himself to say 'your husband'.

'Oh, he's in the merchant navy,' Lolita laughed. 'He's away at sea in big ships for most of the year. He comes home every few months, stays for a few days, and then leaves. But why do you ask?'

'Just ... '

Sandesh attempted to put the man he saw in the picture in the master bedroom in a sailor's uniform with a crew cut. That redeemed him somewhat. The phone rang again and Sandesh turned down the volume of the television. Lolita picked up the cordless and spoke in a language unfamiliar to Sandesh, though he was able to make sense of a few words. She interspersed her talk with whole sentences in English. As she spoke, she rose from her perch and paced the large apartment, unable to sit in one place while talking on the telephone. Sandesh could hear her coughing, laughing and crying, all in the course of a single conversation. When she returned to the drawing room, she poured herself a glass of Martini.

'That was him, my husband,' Lolita informed Sandesh, 'calling from a ship.'

The Triple-X was typical hard-core porn. It showed a naked white man, with a dick almost a foot in length, fucking a blonde woman who moaned and groaned in ecstasy as he penetrated her. She had oversized boobs that the white man kneaded with his hands while he screwed her, adding to her noisy sighs. The woman parted her legs wide to let the man get to her core till all one saw were his balls. His mouth was on top of hers as they copulated so that, Lolita noted, contact between them was simultaneously established at three places: his dick and her cunt, his hands and her breasts, his lips against hers. Is that why it's called a Triple-X, she wondered?

In another sequence, the man sat astride the woman and wanked all over her bare back and buttocks. The quantity of cum he ejaculated befitted a bull rather than a human being.

There was a third sequence in which a black man joined the white man and the blonde. Together they performed acrobatic feats in bed with the two men, at one stage, being deep inside the woman: the white man in her cunt and the black man in her asshole.

The DVD went on for a whole hour. Lolita's intentions were not just to be a spectator but a participant who initiated sex between Sandesh and herself. The sight of Sandesh's upright dick in his tight black jeans got her into a frenzy. On his part, even though Sandesh had seen the DVD before, seeing it in Lolita's company with just the two of them in the posh flat and Tanu fast asleep in the same house made him sweat. He decided to take Lolita up on her offer and ask her for a glass of beer.

'Strong or mild?'

'Strong. Canon 10,000. My favourite.'

Lolita regretted that she did not have Canon 10,000 (it was a brand that ruffians drank), but served him Heineken beer in a large beer mug. She herself was on her third Martini and was somewhat tipsy.

'Cheers,' they clinked their glasses and continued to watch the DVD, though they were beginning to lose interest in it. In the sequence that they now saw, the white man and blonde woman had assumed the position of pariah dogs and, like dogs, they were unable to disengage. The man bade his time playing with the woman's nipples, twisting them out of shape while she let out a bittersweet howl.

Lolita inched closer to Sandesh. She slipped her hand into his and massaged his bony fingers. His heart rate rose. He aped Lolita's actions, and soon they were playing tug of war with each other's fingers. Neither knew when the DVD ended.

Lolita and Sandesh rose. She went up to him, took his hands and put them around her narrow waist. Then she put her own arms around his shoulders and they hugged. Lolita stooped a little to bring her mouth at par with Sandesh's and touched her lips to his. She tried to push her tongue into his mouth, but Sandesh was reluctant to part his lips. Lolita licked them, as if her tongue were lipstick, starting from his upper lip and then coming full circle till she reached his lower lip. After several such Max Factor rounds, Sandesh was worked up enough to part his lips a little and Lolita took advantage of this by thrusting her tongue into his mouth where it met his own moist tongue. For Sandesh, this was absolute bliss. Now he didn't want to let go and Lolita thought they should be in the *Guinness Book of Records* for the world's longest kiss. Next, Sandesh began to bite Lolita's lips and though he hurt her, she endured it in the name of love. She guided his hands into her maxi till they reached her breasts which he instinctively fondled. So passionately at times that, like the woman in the DVD, Lolita was obliged to yell. But her screams only motivated him to persevere. Then the inevitable happened: he felt a wetness and stickiness on his fingers and knew he had lactated her, as if he were her son and she his mother.

'Naughty boy,' Lolita indulgently said to him, without intending him to stop. Sandesh wished he could put his mouth to her breasts and suck.

Lolita reciprocated Sandesh's manhandling of her breasts by gripping his butt in a tight squeeze. She unbuttoned him, shirt, jeans and all, down to his Jockeys, which were red of all colours. The celebratory angle of his dick drove her crazy and she dragged him to the enormous double bed. He was seeing a fully unclothed female body for the first time in his life and felt dizzy. His head began to spin and the aerial view of Bombay that Lolita's bedroom afforded aggravated his feeling of being in a revolving restaurant, like the one on Marine Drive, though he'd never been there.

Lolita made Sandesh lie on top of her. She examined the shape of his elongated dick, which though not of very great length, broadened out at the tip, giving it that bulb-like quality that she found electrifying. Lolita knew that Sandesh had never screwed a woman before: he was too young for that. He thus became the passive penetrator, as Lolita expertly placed his dick in her cunt and got ready to consummate their love. Unpredictably, however, Sandesh suddenly sat up.

'Madam, do you have a condom?' he asked her.

The question irritated Lolita, but she quietly opened a chestnut drawer and threw him a scented condom. She had to teach him how to wear it. They resumed their positions in bed and, at last, Sandesh was able to successfully screw Lolita like the actors in the porn DVDs. Like the actresses, she too moaned and groaned, but not without reason, for in his frenzy he did not realize that he hurt her. Then he climaxed. Lolita prompted him to get off her, her principal concern now being his semen-filled condom that had to be disposed off discreetly, lest Kamalabai find it the next morning and gossip with the other servants of the neighbourhood. Sandesh was sated when Lolita yanked the condom off his private part and held it in her hand, as if to examine the quantity of cum he had discharged.

Lolita left the master bedroom to chuck the condom down a chute. When she returned, Sandesh asked her for a cigarette. Both of them lit up in silence and puffed away, satisfied with their maiden sexual encounter. Sandesh looked at his watch: it was past midnight. It was possible that Ashok Jadhav would throw him out of his job in the morning. But he'd cross that bridge when he got to it, he thought. He stubbed his cigarette into a tortoise-shaped terracotta ashtray and got up.

'Goodnight, madam,' he said as he left.

TWO
Lolita: Bio

Lalita Birendra Mukherjee was born in Calcutta in the early 1970s in a joint family. They lived in an ancient ancestral mansion with a courtyard and coconut trees, midway between Tollygunje and Ballygunje. The family was what one would call the 'Bhadralok': Conscious of its Brahmanical identity on one hand, but simultaneously nurtured by the egalitarian teachings of Ram Mohan Roy's Brahmo Samaj. Lolita was the only offspring of Birendra Mukherjee, an economics professor at Presidency College, and Moshumi, who taught at a convent school. Needless to say, her parents doted on her.

When Lolita was born, Calcutta still reeled under Naxalite havoc. The movement itself was officially launched in Naxalbari in May 1967. An uncle of Lolita's was stabbed to death on the streets of the city for wearing a pure gold Rolex watch. Yet, as she came of age, her sympathies were with the Naxalites who, under the tutelage of Charu Mazumdar and Kanu Sanyal, abided by the teachings of Mao Tse-tung: rob Peter to pay Paul.

By the end of the decade in which Lolita was born, Mother Teresa would win the Nobel Peace Prize and become Calcutta's

second Nobel laureate after Tagore. The newspapers would hail
her as Calcutta's 'noble' mother for bringing succour to the lives
of destitutes, or the poorest of the poor as she thought of them,
all in the name of Christ, whom she had seen during a train
journey.

These events had a profound effect on Lolita as she grew up.
She was unable to see eye to eye with her status quo-ist folks for
whom society was stratified in terms of princes and paupers,
literate and illiterate, fair and dark.

Then there was the business of her name, Lalita, which she
loathed because it was the name of Lalita Pawar, the arch-
matriarch of the Hindi films her family religiously watched
every Sunday evening on their black-and-white television
set. But her name also repelled 'Lolita' because of a famous
television commercial for Surf detergent where a woman in a
white sari by the name of Lalitaji put her index finger to her
forehead and cried: *Bhaisaab, Surf ki kharidari me hi samajhdari
hai.* (Brother, there's wisdom in buying Surf.) The ad, like all
other ads, irked her because of the crass commercialization it
represented. It paved the way for multinationals like Hindustan
Lever to set up shop in India and in this case, to add insult to
injury, it used her very own name!

Of course, Lolita couldn't do much about her name until
years later when, as an English Honours student at St. Xavier's,
she was introduced to the works of Nabokov by her professors,
and resolved to modify her name to Lolita because it was
better-sounding than Lalita. Moreover, the unconventional
love story of Nabokov's *Lolita* appealed to her. Her folks tried
their best to dissuade her from changing her name, arguing

that the Bengalis pronounced 'Lalita' as 'Lolita' anyway. But with a name like Lolita the State wouldn't recognize her as their daughter and she would be disinherited after their death, for her name in all official records, and indeed in their will, was Lalita. But she was adamant. Her rejoinder to her folks was that she would only be too glad to be dispossessed; such was her abhorrence of wealth.

By the time she completed her MA, Lolita had seen all the films of Satyajit Ray. The *Appu* trilogy, however, remained her favourite. She thought Ray, the only Indian to win an Oscar, had lost some of his spark in later films where he attempted to shift focus from rural to urban India, obviously to woo the box office.

But more than films, it was books that influenced her, the Calcutta University English literature student, in a city where every paanwallah is reputed to be a poet. English literature in Lolita's youth, of course, was not just Shakespeare and Shelley, but it encompassed a whole host of contemporary writers from all over the world, including India, writers like Kamala Das and later Arundhati Roy, whom she adored. Lolita must have read *My Story* and *The God of Small Things* at least a hundred times each. The former autobiographical narrative eventually led her to Kamala Das's poems and she memorized one of them, *An Introduction*, as if she were a schoolgirl preparing for an oral examination:

> *When I asked for love, not knowing what else to ask*
> *For, he drew a youth of sixteen into the*
> *Bedroom and closed the door.*

The God of Small Things, published when Lolita was in her final year at university, taught her its notorious love laws, 'that lay down who should be loved, and how. And how much.' Lolita was glad the book won the Booker Prize in a year which happened to be the golden jubilee of Indian Independence.

D. H. Lawrence's *Lady Chatterley's Lover* drove Lolita nuts on account of its sexual candidness, but on a more serious note, 'for challenging the deadening restrictiveness of middle-class conventions'. These conventions, according to the learned critic who made the statement that Lolita crammed for the exams while burning the midnight oil, were 'challenged by forces of liberation often represented by an outsider—a peasant, a gipsy, a working man, a primitive of some kind, someone freed by circumstance or personal effort from the distorting or mechanizing world …'

In the case of *Lady Chatterley's Lover*, the outsider in question was gamekeeper Oliver Mellors with whom the middle-class heroine, Constance Chatterley, had an adulterous affair and got pregnant.

Lolita's readings of these texts foreshadowed the course her own life would take and it is absurd to speculate if this happened merely by accident or design or a combination of both. In the past, women were, ironically speaking, kept away from books for good reason: books turned their heads. They ceased to be dutiful daughters and wives and mothers after that, who kept house, cooked and cleaned for their menfolk, but entertained rebellious ideas instead. Books are the temptation to which women must never be allowed to succumb, the way Eve succumbed to the temptation of the apple and Sita to that of the golden deer.

When she was twenty-five, Lolita's parents thought that rather than let her do a Ph.D as she had wanted, it was time she got married. 'No,' she stunned them with her vehement refusal, leaving them tongue-tied.

Lolita detested arranged marriages that abounded in everything but love. The couple was of the same caste and the same religion. Their degrees and bank balances were similar and the girl invariably ended up paying dowry in some form to the boy. Yet the two of them, who took holy vows to spend the rest of their lives together, were strangers who knew nothing of each other's attitudes and values. In these circumstances, what passed off as marriage was a little like a property deal.

'Fair enough,' cried her father, the professor, who refused to rise to the bait. He proposed a scheme. Lolita would be given precisely a year to look for a groom of her choice. If she failed to find one in the stipulated time, she would have to marry the man they chose for her.

'Fair enough,' said Lolita verbatim, mimicking her father.

For the next one year, Lolita struggled to fall in love. She went to parties. She went to discos. She went to coffee shops. She went to underground Naxalite dos. But alas, Mr Right was nowhere in sight. Not that she wasn't pretty. But Calcutta in the 90s was no different from the Calcutta of the 70s. The youth had no time for romance which they dismissed as a bourgeois pastime, fit only for philistine television channels like MTV and Channel V.

By the end of the year, Lolita had no choice but to consent to the idea of advertising for a husband in the matrimonial columns of The *Statesman* and *Ananda Bazaar Patrika*.

Her father drafted the following advertisement and took it personally to the offices of both newspapers.

> *Fair, slim, tall, pretty, intellectual girl, age 25,*
> *with MA (English Literature) seeks groom*
> *who is likewise with five-figure salary.*
> *Caste no bar. Contact PO Box No. 1614.*
> *Brokers please excuse.*

While the ad awaited publication in the Sunday supplements of the newspapers, which were full of classifieds of all kinds, Lolita went online and logged on to new Internet sites like Shaadi.com and Swayamwar.com to try her luck there. But there were no profiles that excited her. Everyone looked boring. Lolita's mother suggested going to a marriage bureau, but Lolita rejected the advice on the spot.

'Ma,' she said, combing her hair, 'give me a break, will you?'

The first person to respond to Professor Birendra Mukherjee's ad in the *Ananda Bazaar Patrika* was the man who would eventually become Lolita's husband, making the scores of other replies that followed redundant. He introduced himself as Captain Aroop Sengupta, aged thirty-two. Mr Sengupta was a sailor in the merchant navy who'd worked for different international companies, but was presently employed with the US-based Mariners' Compass International. 'You ask for a five-figure salary,' he quipped, 'but mine is seven figures. Does that disqualify me? Also, unlike your daughter, I am no intellectual.'

His letter had provided them with his background. He was a Bengali, like Lolita, but of a different sub-caste. His parents lived in Jamshedpur where his father was an officer in the Indian Forest Service, posted in the Dalma range. His mother kept house. They owned a bungalow in Jubilee Park. Mr Sengupta had received a management degree from the famed Xavier Labour Relations Institute, Jamshedpur before training to be a sailor and joining the merchant navy. He had a younger brother, Anoop, who was studying medicine in Ranchi.

'You won't find a family as illustrious as ours,' he claimed.

All Lolita wryly said when her folks asked for her opinion was, 'Why couldn't the goddamn guy enclose a photograph? He could have buck teeth for all I know!'

To prove he did not have buck teeth and was a Suitable Boy, Mr Sengupta accepted Professor Mukherjee's invitation to lunch in their decaying mansion house, midway between Tollygunje and Ballygunje. He came on the Steel Express one Sunday morning and left in the evening by the same train. When the Mukherjees expressed surprise that Mr Sengupta did not bring his parents along, for they would've liked to meet them, he addressed Professor Mukherjee and said, 'You will meet them, sir, but I am my own person who takes his own decisions.'

'My daughter is exactly like that,' Professor Mukherjee replied.

Lolita put her foot down when her mother advised her, shortly before Mr Sengupta's arrival, to enter the room in a sari, the pallu covering her head, with a tray of Bengali sweets.

'Cut the crap, ma,' she screamed. Now, as she marched into the room in a T-shirt and faded jeans and no tray of Bengali sweets in her hands, she observed that Mr Sengupta looked older than thirty-two, and was something of a fatty for the navy.

'Hi,' she said to her future husband.

'Hi,' he grinned, almost from ear to ear. 'You are beautiful.'

'Thanks.'

'As far as I'm concerned, it's love at first sight,' he ventured, trying to break the ice.

Lolita wished she could show him a mirror.

Professor Mukherjee intervened. Father, mother and daughter sat on a long sofa while Mr Sengupta sat on one of the smaller ones. The sofa set looked as if it were made of empty matchboxes, the craftwork of a kid.

'Our daughter doesn't want to be called Lolita Aroop Sengupta after marriage,' Professor Mukherjee said. 'She prefers to be known as Lolita Mukherjee-Sengupta. Any objections to that?'

'Oh, none whatsoever,' Mr Sengupta ingratiatingly said. 'I'm a feminist too.' He looked at Lolita and continued, 'If you like, I'll call myself Aroop Mukherjee.'

'Very funny,' Lolita muttered under her breath. If the man went on like that, he'd soon get on her nerves.

'What is your monthly salary?' Lolita's mother bluntly asked Mr Sengupta.

'Ten lakhs.'

'Ten lakhs!' Lolita exclaimed.

'That's right,' Mr Sengupta replied, trying to curry favour. 'And five out of that will be yours, no questions asked.'

'Oh really?'

'It's a gentleman's word.'

'Is it ten lakhs gross or net?' Professor Mukherjee laughingly asked. He was trying to tactfully fathom if Mr Sengupta paid his taxes, or was a defaulter from whose vaults spilled black money.

'It's ten lakhs after deduction of income tax at source,' Mr Sengupta shrewdly answered. It was a white lie. Merchant navy men were known to evade income tax by declaring themselves to be NRIs.

Mrs Mukherjee went into the kitchen and returned with a tray of sweets. 'Here, sweeten your mouth,' she said to Mr Sengupta, almost stuffing a piece of *sandesh* into it. He took it from her at the last minute and bit into it.

'You have a lovely heritage house,' Mr Sengupta congratulated the Mukherjees, relishing his *sandesh* and asking for a second helping.

And you are not getting it by way of dowry, Lolita thought to herself.

Mr Sengupta stayed for lunch. Professor Mukherjee opened a few cans of beer and the three of them drank. (Lolita's mother, like all 'good' Indian women, was a teetotaller.) After lunch, Mr Sengupta was directed to the guest room for a short nap. Then Lolita's mother made him a cup of masala chai and the three of them saw him off at the entrance of their house. Mr Sengupta hopped into a cycle rickshaw bound for Howrah.

After he left, Lolita informed her parents that she was agreeable to the match. The clinching factor—though she didn't disclose this—was that their marriage wouldn't enchain her by encroaching on her personal space. With Mr Sengupta away at sea, she was free to do as she pleased. Would marriage to any Tom, Dick or Harry guarantee her such independence?

The wedding took place soon after. Time was of the essence, for the sailor had to go back to sea. The Mukherjees and the Senguptas divided all the expenses between themselves, fifty-fifty, including the dough spent on wedding cards.

During the nuptials, both Aroop and Lolita offended the old Bengali priest by facetiously requesting that he chant his mantras in English.

'We need to know what we're getting into,' they argued. 'Sanskrit to us is mere mumbo jumbo.'

But the priest wasn't amused. He gave them his sourest look and continued with his job.

To make matters worse, the sacred knot that fastened Aroop's dhoti to Lolita's sari came undone as they took their seven rounds around the fire. This upset Mrs Sengupta, who regarded it as ominous. Aroop, his father and the Mukherjees did their best to set her mind at ease, urging her not to be superstitious. But she was convinced the wedding had gotten off to a bad start and didn't augur well for the future. As it is, the family had disregarded her advice to have the couple's horoscopes read, and now this …

In the end, Mr Sengupta and his younger son Anoop hastily retied the knot, and the bride and bridegroom resumed their rounds around the fire.

However, further complications arose when they were unable to remember how many rounds they'd already taken. Aroop thought it was three, but Lolita swore it was four. The horrified priest ordained that they would have to start from scratch, take their seven rounds all over again, or else the wedding wouldn't be solemnized and they would live in sin.

Mrs Sengupta sat through all this in a tempestuous state.

The wedding was held at the Taj, Calcutta's priciest five-star hotel on Park Street. There were guests from both parties and there were fireworks, coloured lights, *shehnai* music, *mehendi*, soft drinks and ice cream. But for a select group, the Senguptas and the Mukherjees had organized a banquet that began with the finest liquor available in the market, and then saw piping hot deer meat grace the table.

The venison, which made everyone's mouths water, came from the Dalma forests where Mr Sengupta Sr, the Indian Forest Service officer, misused his position by ordering his subordinates to take his service jeep and hunt down the deer. 'So what if they're a protected species?' he had said, when his subordinates looked askance at him. 'A wedding happens only once in a person's life.'

At the end of the sultry day in April 1999, when temperatures soared to 45 degrees centigrade, Lolita and Aroop were too drained to make love on their maiden wedding night. Both of them slept in the Taj's honeymoon suite that was booked for them for the next three days.

Lolita did lose her virginity, but not in the honeymoon suite of the Taj, which at any given time of day—and night—was full of uncles and aunts and cousins who wanted to make the most of the wedding they'd travelled thousands of miles to attend. Instead, she lost it in an air-conditioned first class coupé of the 2 Up Howrah – Bombay Mail on their way from Tatanagar to Bombay, a fortnight or so after the *bidai*. Rather than living with his parents in Jamshedpur, Aroop Sengupta had booked a sprawling flat in Bombay's latest high-rise and intended to live there in style with his new bride.

Their lovemaking began soon after the train left Tatanagar around midnight and continued till they reached Bilaspur early next morning, when a black-jacketed ticket collector knocked on their door to see their tickets, and a pantry-car attendant served them their English-style breakfast made up of cornflakes, toast, poached eggs, cutlets, yoghurt, fruit and coffee.

Interruptions came only at mealtimes and when their tickets needed to be checked. Every new railway division they passed through necessitated a change of staff, with new ticket collectors voyeuristically knocking on their door to ensure they weren't travelling ticket-less like our politicians.

There was a second night's journey as well which witnessed heightened sexual activity among the newlyweds, both of them stark naked on the extra-wide lower berth, their baggage stashed away on the one above. The entire cabin smelt of spunk. Lolita was certain she'd get pregnant before they reached Bombay.

What's marriage if not a licence to have unprotected sex?

The Mail train caught them unawares by arriving at its destination, Chhatrapati Shivaji Terminus, formerly Victoria Terminus, when it was still dark outside and they were not yet ready to alight. Red-uniformed porters banged on their cabin door: '*Saheb, last station hai.*' (Sir, this is the last station.)

Two months after they arrived in Bombay, Aroop and Lolita had moved into their own flat on the forty-ninth floor of Jannat, a swanky high-rise in Dadar built by the Rahejas. During the interregnum, they stayed in the Royal Bombay Yacht Club at the Gateway of India while the builder gave the finishing touches to their flat. Aroop would have preferred a neighbourhood less middle-class and less Maharashtrian than Dadar, say Pedder Road, Carmichael Road, Warden Road or Napean Sea Road, not to speak of Marine Drive and Malabar Hill. However, what clinched it for him was that the fifty-storeyed Jannat was Bombay's tallest building. It had spacious duplex apartments which fostered the illusion that one lived in a bungalow. The apartment had a terrace from which Bombay looked as if viewed through the windows of an airplane, and there were such high-velocity winds coming directly from the sea that there was a real danger of being swept off one's feet.

'You can bathe with water if you wish,' Aroop said to Lolita picturesquely, 'and you can have breeze baths as well.'

The first few weeks were spent furnishing the flat with the basics: beds and chairs and utensils.

'You can do it up as elaborately as you please after I'm gone,' Aroop said to Lolita. 'You will have all the time in the world and I'll write you a blank cheque.'

Aroop hated the nitty-gritty of shopping, of having to deal with carpenters and plumbers and the like. It bored him to death. He told Lolita that he had full faith in her judgement and her taste, and that he wouldn't crib about anything she did to make their apartment cozy.

'Hire the best interior decorator in town and send me the tab,' he told her.

Afterwards, they looked at cars. Aroop, who had an international driver's licence, insisted that Lolita hone her driving skills by taking daily lessons with the Janjira Motor Training School.

'You've driven your dad's old Ambassador,' he told her, 'but modern cars are very different, with floor-shift gears.' When it came to choosing a car, though they could afford a Mercedes, both of them flipped for the limited edition two-door Zen which had been introduced by Maruti Udyog Ltd on an experimental basis.

'Two-door cars are very popular in Europe,' Aroop explained to Lolita, who'd never been abroad. 'But Indians hate them because they know not what intimacy is. That's why, according to my father, the Standard Herald did not click.' Saying this, he kissed Lolita on the lips in front of the salesman who had just given them a demo. Aroop's own preference was for the metallic silver Zen Steel, but he yielded to Lolita's craze for the jet black Zen Carbon.

'Your choice is my choice, darling,' he whispered into her ear, as he wrote out the cheque and they drove out of the showroom to buy *pedas* and garlands to commemorate their purchase. Aroop told Lolita that the child who would form in her womb any day now would be safe in their car, for there were no back doors that could open suddenly and throw it out. Nor could anyone open the back door and kidnap their child.

'We can now make out in the front seat as we drive. Without a care,' he said. Then he kissed Lolita again and fondled her breasts, which he privately thought of as his *mehboob's* boobs.

Their honeymoon, which they kept procrastinating, eventually took place during the rains. Aroop's merchant navy buddies recommended Matheran, a hill station a hop, skip and jump away from Bombay, whose speciality was that it was free of automobiles of any kind.

'The only vehicle allowed into the town is an ambulance,' the couple was told.

Aroop and Lolita, both Bengalis, had been to Darjeeling (Gorkhaland) in north Bengal, and as kids, they had gone on excursions with their families to Simla, Mussoorie and Nainital. Aroop's personal favourite, however, was Patnitop. *On top of wife*. These Himalayan getaways, at very high altitudes with the snows gracing them in winter, were not as novel as Matheran nonetheless, discovered in the late nineteenth century by an Englishman.

'*Mathe raan ahe,'* the locals are believed to have said to him as he climbed to the summit in Maharashtra's Sahyadri range, made famous by Shivaji who built forts on many of the peaks. There is a forest on top. That is how the picturesque hill station, with dirt tracks carved through the woods, derived its name. Then in 1901, a Muslim by the name of Adamji Peerbhoy constructed a narrow gauge railway line that took tourists up to Matheran from Neral, the base station on the Bombay – Poona route. The cream-and-blue mini train, hauled by a steam engine that huffed and puffed, came to be known as the toy train and matchbox train, and was a great hit with children and adults alike. It went through a tunnel known as One Kiss Tunnel, long enough for lovers to have just one kiss.

However, the Senguptas realized to their dismay that the matchbox train went into hibernation during the monsoons because it could be blown off the tracks. They were left with no choice but to take a taxi from Neral where the early morning Deccan Express deposited them. The Premier Padmini, with five passengers on board excluding the driver, zigzagged through the hills in first gear, its engine always threatening to stall. Aroop and Lolita, who sat in front with the driver on a long seat, held hands as the taxi knifed through the mists, a heavy drizzle wetting them. 'So romantic,' Aroop said to his wife, unperturbed by the presence of three burly men in the back seat who were constantly asking the driver where they could buy booze.

The taxi dropped them at Dasturi Naka from where they would either have to trek to Matheran or ride on horseback. They chose the latter, selecting two very handsome horses, a white stallion-like creature for the husband and a silver-grey steed for the wife. Unlike other holidaymakers, the Senguptas did not haggle with the *ghodawallahs* over prices and agreed to pay them whatever they demanded. Lolita found some of the *ghodawallahs*, barely seventeen or eighteen in smartly-ironed khaki uniforms, hot. She harboured prurient thoughts in her mind, trying to imagine what it would be like if she were locked in sexual union with those young men. Her reverie was broken by a group of unruly monkeys who audaciously climbed down a tree trunk and grabbed a packet of biscuits from someone's hands, leading to all-round pandemonium.

The five-star hotel where they had booked a honeymoon package (six days, five nights) was once an old colonial bungalow owned by a wealthy Parsi industrialist who inherited it from the British after Independence. It was converted into a forest lodge when scions of the family, settled in the US, sold it to a hotel chain. It comprised a series of high-ceilinged rooms around which ran a verandah with massive easy chairs where one could rest their arms and legs. Teakwood beds, tables and chairs in walnut finish adorned all the rooms, which also boasted an array of lampshades and chandeliers that supplied diffused lighting after sunset. But the highlight of the place were its meals; the Western-style breakfast and lunch buffet served on the verandah, and the banquet-type supper in the dining room late evening.

Aroop and Lolita found that there were mainly foreigners in the hotel. They ran into them at mealtimes, or when they lazed away on the hammocks in the hotel's abundant garden where a fortune-teller unsuccessfully pestered them to have their futures read.

Matheran had its share of sightseeing spots like Panaroma Point and One Tree Hill from where one got breathtaking views. But the damp weather deterred honeymooners like Aroop and Lolita from venturing out of the hotel, except to go to the bazaar or the Charlotte Lake nearby. They spent the rest of the time ensconced in their hotel suite where Aroop made fervent love to his bride for six days and five nights, and Tanu was conceived.

'Give me five years,' Aroop said to Lolita, 'and I'll make enough money to quit the merchant navy and set up a business. Then we'll never be separated.' The clock ticked as the hour for his departure approached, when a van would come to fetch him.

The parting proved to be tougher for him than for Lolita, who busied herself with homemaking and preparations for the baby that had already been conceived. It would arrive in three-quarters of a year. Entrusted with a plethora of cheque books and credit cards once he left, Lolita shopped in Bombay's trendiest stores for furniture, furnishings, drapes, carpets, wallpapers, cradles, chandeliers, antiques, air conditioners, refrigerators, clocks, telephones, paintings, music systems, kitchen equipment, bar counters, ceramic tiles, stained glass and potted plants to transform her spartan apartment into a cozy nest which oozed luxury. She appointed Rajasthani carpenters who sat in the parking lot forty-nine floors below and built her wall-to-wall cabinets, much to the chagrin of the society's secretary whom Lolita dismissed with the flick of a hand.

'I couldn't care less about what you think,' she said to the double-chinned Sindhi gentleman when he reprimanded her for using a common area of the building as if it were her private property.

She went everywhere in her Zen Carbon which she learned to drive with élan, guaranteeing that the black beauty, which she got polished once every month, did not have a single scratch or dent.

To recruit household help, Lolita interviewed scores of maidservants and a couple of boy servants too before zeroing in on Kamalabai whom she straightaway employed. What went in Kamalabai's favour was that she was middle-aged with no strings attached, her husband having dumped her years ago and her kids all grown up. She was also experienced, having worked as an ayah in the homes of Bombay's glitterati, including the film star Shabana Azmi. Kamalabai lived alone in a shanty not far from Jannat and smelt good, making it a point to spray all her nine-yard saris with cheap perfume bought for Rs 30 per bottle from the Dadar station overbridge. But above all, Kamalabai was a hard worker. Lolita had to show her something only once before she understood it and did exactly as memsaab pleased. On her part, Lolita paid Kamalabai twice the amount of money other ladies in the building paid their servants, and a couple of them grumbled when they met her in the elevator.

'Our servants will also ask for more, baba,' a lady with too much gold on her person said to Lolita, beads of perspiration dotting her upper lip like a moustache. But Lolita, who refused to be drawn into an argument with the woman whom she perceived as Bombay's noveau riche, kept her cool.

'We shall see,' she tersely said to the lady, as the elevator reached the thirty-second floor and the lady got off.

Between Christmas and New Year, Aroop's vessel unexpectedly anchored in the Bombay harbour on its way to Japan and he shocked Lolita by coming home unannounced.

'Darling,' he said, opening his arms to hug her, 'my ship made an unscheduled stop in Bombay. So here I am, dying to usher in the new millennium with my beloved wife.'

Lolita had to cancel an appointment with her gynae to be with her husband, but otherwise it was okay. As she made him a Spanish omelette in her state-of-the-art kitchen, he put his ear to her tummy. 'How's the baby doing?' he asked. 'I can hear it kicking.'

The metamorphosed apartment caught his eye and caused them to pop out.

'You're a genius,' he said to Lolita, 'if you could do all this single-handedly. I'm so proud of you.' Lolita spent the rest of the morning giving Aroop an account of the money she'd spent decking up the flat that ran into lakhs. 'That's peanuts,' he cried. 'You could have spent more.'

Kamalabai arrived, and both Aroop and she gave each other a once-over.

'This is saab,' Lolita introduced her husband to the maid, 'and this is Kamalabai,' she said, looking at Aroop.

'Hello, Kamalabai,' Aroop said to the woman, who shyly covered her face with the pallu of her sari and slipped into the kitchen.

'Let's not call her a servant,' Lolita said to Aroop when she was gone, and they discussed other words that could best describe her: ayah, housekeeper, domestic attendant. The first they instantly rejected because it smacked of imperialism, but the other two, they agreed, were less loaded.

'Why not simply call her Kamalabai?' Aroop finally said, and they both burst out laughing.

'Kamalabai has worked with Shabana Azmi,' Lolita informed Aroop. Naturally, he was impressed.

'You're a one-woman institution,' he congratulated her again.

The New Year's Eve bash at the Royal Bombay Yacht Club, where Aroop and Lolita had stayed while their flat was being prepared, was one of the most licentious dos they had attended in all their lives. That 1999 was yielding to 2000, the Y2K year, became the pretext among sailors for intemperate drinking, debauched dancing and wife-swapping as the music blared. Couples were given numbers they had to match and choose their partners for the night; a Mr Malhotra sleeping with a Mrs Chawla, or a Mrs Patil making out with a Mr Singh. Elsewhere, there were drunken brawls and fisticuffs and many young sybarites, not quite accustomed to the cocktail of alcoholic beverages they had gulped down in the name of revelry, threw

up on the carpeted floors. Aroop and Lolita sat through it all
with glasses of Martini in their hands, reluctant to be a part
of the mayhem that was taking place on the dance floor. Yet
they enjoyed themselves that night, with frenzied mobs at the
Gateway of India just outside the Royal Bombay Yacht Club
noisily welcoming the twenty-first century, and ships in the
harbour casting colourful beams into the sky.

However, the next day, his hangover notwithstanding, Aroop
received an SOS from his shipping corporation, Mariners'
Compass International. It informed him that his vessel was
about to set sail. He hadn't even the time to bid a proper farewell
to Lolita, who had gone to the bazaar with Kamalabai when he
left: Such was the hazardous life of an able seaman.

Unlike most Indian women whose husbands pack them off
to their parents' homes during the last few months of pregnancy
to handle the messiness of childbirth, Lolita stayed in Bombay.

'Let your folks come down to Bombay to preside over your
delivery,' Aroop frequently told her on the phone, calling either
from his ship or a port where his vessel had anchored. 'Our
house is large enough to accommodate them.'

In deference to his wishes, the Mukherjees caught a Jet
Airways flight to Bombay, travelling executive class, for which
Lolita paid. Professor Mukherjee was in urgent need of a knee
replacement surgery, for his knees had begun to give way like
those of Prime Minister Atal Behari Vajpayee. But he told his
wife that his knees weren't more important than his grandchild
who would soon be born. When the matter was reported to
Aroop, he admonished Lolita for not advising her dad to have
the operation done in Bombay.

'Bombay has better medical facilities than Calcutta,' he declared. 'Even Prime Minister Vajpayee had his surgery done at the Breach Candy Hospital.'

But Professor Mukherjee was adamant. He was unwilling to have his body tampered with in a strange city where he didn't know a soul who could come to his aid.

'I'll have the surgery done in Calcutta,' he told his daughter and son-in-law, and that was that.

Meanwhile, Mrs Mukherjee attended to both her husband and daughter, closely monitoring Lolita's diet and physical activity to ensure the birth of a bonny baby. Morning and evening, she accompanied her on walks in Jannat's immense landscape gardens, full of roses, jasmines and chrysanthemums. When necessary, she drove with her to her gynaecologist's clinic, a stone's throw away. The gynae, a Gujarati lady in her fifties, was pleased with Lolita's progress.

'You're doing fine,' she told her patient, 'and your delivery will be hassle-free.'

However, in May, when Lolita went into labour, the gynae alarmingly informed her parents that Lolita needed a Caesarean, if both her life and the life of her baby were to be saved. Lolita wished to contest her doctor's claims, certain that she was out to fleece her. But her parents advised prudence. In the end, she signed on the dotted line, giving her gynae the permission to cut up her abdomen and extract the baby that lay concealed in her womb.

'Congratulations,' the doctor said to her, as the effects of the anaesthesia wore off and painful spasms that gripped her belly subsided in the deluxe ward of a private nursing home where the Caesarean was performed. 'You are the proud mother of a lovely baby girl.'

Lolita's parents were allowed to see her. They were genuinely happy at the birth of their granddaughter, not being the sort who had a patriarchal preference for sons. Lolita's mother massaged her hands to get the blood circulation going, while her father stood benignly by. 'Call her Tanushree,' Mrs Mukherjee told Lolita, gently taking the newborn in her arms and rocking her. The name stayed.

By the time Aroop received the news of his daughter's birth in Plymouth, UK and took the first available British Airways flight to Bombay, hijras were already singing and dancing outside his door. They had a hell of a time persuading the liftman to take them to the forty-ninth floor and he yielded only when they manhandled and molested him. A couple of them grabbed his testicles (he wore no underwear, being from UP and finding the Bombay weather humid) and a few others shoved their grimy fingers into his mouth. The hijras were decked up in all their finery. Once on the forty-ninth floor, they clapped and danced and sang a bevy of Bollywood numbers, including one from *Amar Akbar Anthony* that featured hijras like themselves.

Tayeb Ali pyar ka dushman
Hai hai.

When Aroop arrived, they made way for him, figuring he was the man of the house. But he ignored them and headed for the bedroom where his wife and daughter lay.

'I can't believe I'm a father,' he told Lolita and kissed her all over.

His in-laws, who slept in one of the spare bedrooms, heard his voice and came out to greet him. 'Thank you for being here,' he said to them, to which Professor Mukherjee replied that it was their duty.

The family ignored the hijras. It was left to Kamalabai to pay them a couple of hundred bucks from her kitty before they grudgingly left, choosing to climb down forty-nine floors this time rather than come face-to-face with the irascible liftman. But they bumped into him in the foyer and began punning on the word 'lift', boisterously asking him if they could lift him into the air, and more obscenely, if he had trouble 'lifting' his dick.

Despite earnest appeals to his Yankee bosses and using paternity as an excuse, Aroop could wangle no more than three days' leave to celebrate the birth of his firstborn. And those three days were slothfully spent at home in the company of Tanu, Lolita and her parents.

After his departure, Lolita's mother parked herself with Lolita for a whole month, while her father took off for Calcutta on the Geetanjali Express amid worries on the part of his womenfolk as to how the weak-kneed man would cope. Lolita's mother expertly trained both her daughter and Kamalabai in the art of raising a baby girl, giving them a thirty-day crash course at the end of which Lolita was thoroughly well versed in child management and could probably head a paediatric ward.

Lolita found herself with little to do after her mother's departure. The apartment was fully furnished now and needed little attention. Kamalabai was a dedicated housekeeper who reported for work on time and knew exactly what to cook, or how to quieten little Tanu when she cried. It wouldn't be

hyperbolic to say that Lolita did not have to lift a finger to run
her house: everything happened with clockwork precision.

Lolita spent her time watching TV and reading books, but
the long hours sometimes seemed interminable and she began
to have second thoughts about the kind of married life she
had bargained for. Aroop had warned her before leaving that
he'd always be away for six months at a stretch, and when he
did come home at the end those six months, it wouldn't be for
more than a few days. However, he kept his word and sent her
cheques for Rs 5,00,000 every month, thus making her feel like
a lottery ticket winner.

Lolita was not the kind who liked to hobnob with unruly
neighbours. Two months into her solitary existence, Tanu and
Kamalabai being the only faces she saw on an everyday basis,
Lolita took to heavy drinking. When the reserves in her well-
stocked lounge bar got depleted, she replenished them with the
aid of Aroop's friends in the Indian Navy whom she met at the
Royal Bombay Yacht Club. Services guys, it is well known, get
their quota of whisky, rum and vodka at one-third the market
price. They obliged Lolita by loading cartons of the stuff into
the boot of her Zen Carbon whenever she telephoned them,
deriving a kick on figuring out that Lolita drank without her
hubby's knowledge.

Another two months and Lolita could be classified as a full-
fledged alcoholic. She drank not just after sunset but in the
mornings and blazing afternoons as well, a crystal liquor glass
always in her hand. Kamalabai looked upon this with disfavour,
but couldn't muster up the courage to scold memsaab in the
manner an aunt or a mother-in-law would. She sometimes

thought of telephoning Lolita's folks in Calcutta, but developed cold feet when it came to actually picking up the receiver and dialling their number. She was worried about the effect Lolita's drinking would have on Tanu, health-wise, and was relieved to find that, contrary to her mother's advice, Lolita did not suckle her daughter. But one day something came over Kamalabai; she could take Lolita's drinking no longer.

'Stop, memsaab. It's bad for you,' she screamed at her mistress, shocking her. It took Lolita a few seconds to realize her maid had told her off. Then she exploded.

'Kamalabai,' she yelled. 'You're just a fucking maid. Mind your own business please. If you meddle in my affairs again, you'll be sacked.' The harsh words brought tears to Kamalabai's eyes and she wept into her roach-eaten sari.

But Lolita did not apologize to Kamalabai.

From that day onwards, Kamalabai was no more than a mute witness to the occurences on the forty-ninth floor of Jannat.

THREE
Sandesh: Bio

Sandesh Gaikwad. He was an eighties kid born in Paithan, a taluka in Maharashtra's Aurangabad district, famous the world over for the Ajanta and Ellora caves. Sandesh was born into poverty. A Dalit farm labourer in the fields of wealthy upper caste zamindars, his father, Bajrang Gaikwad, had been duped and dispossessed by his own kith and kin. He had a string of daughters, four to be precise, from his runaway marriage to a poor Brahmin girl. But he was finally blessed with a son, thanks to the benedictions of Lord Khandoba. Bajrang Gaikwad pinned all his hopes on Sandesh. He was the saviour who would educate himself, migrate to the city and liberate his family from drudgery. Hence, when it was time to admit Sandesh to school, a Marathi medium pathshala where only Dalits went, he advanced his age by a year. It was 1992, the year the Babri Masjid had been demolished by Hindu fundamentalists.

'How old is he?' the headmaster, who wore a white shirt over a white pyjama along with a white Gandhi topi, asked. Bajrang Gaikwad made quick calculations. Luckily, he hadn't obtained any of his kids' birth certificates, so there was nothing in writing. Seeing him fumble, the headmaster couched his question differently.

'When was he born?' Bajrang Gaikwad knew that his only son was born in 1987.

'1986,' he blurted out. His wish was that Sandesh should finish school as early as possible and start working.

'That means he is six-years-old,' said the headmaster. 'We will admit him directly to class one.'

'Thank you, sahib.' Bajrang Gaikwad was truly grateful for the favour.

In their makeshift brick-and-mortar home on the outskirts of Paithan town, little Sandesh's mother and sisters celebrated his victory with home-made *sheera* to sweeten everyone's mouth. The sisters themselves went to school sporadically but generally stayed at home to help their mother with the household chores. Yet they were determined to make their kid brother study.

'He'll become a scholar, like Baburao Bagul,' the four of them giggled. Peals of laughter rocked their home.

The next day, Bajrang Gaikwad took Sandesh to Ambedkar Chowk, the main shopping area in Paithan town. Here, he bought him a notebook, pencil, eraser, sharpener and school bag. He placed an order for two sets of school uniforms with a Muslim *darzi*, the uniforms comprising two white shirts and khaki knickers. He looks like a member of the RSS, the latter thought, when Sandesh tried out the uniforms at the *darzi's* some days later. Like a true RSS member, Bajrang Gaikwad decided that his son would go barefoot to school everyday.

'Why does he need footwear?' he asked his wife, who was afraid that the rocky surface of the burning hot path that led to the school would scald her only son's feet. 'Let his feet be in direct contact with Mother Earth.'

On the first day of school, Sandesh wept as his father, whose finger he tightly clutched, led him to his class and handed him over to Mrs Parulekar, the class teacher in whose custody he would be.

'Don't be fooled by his crying,' the teacher, a Maharashtrian lady in her early thirties, advised Bajrang Gaikwad. 'Or else he'll never get used to school.'

Mrs Parulekar was right. From day two, little Sandesh took to school as a fish takes to water. Everyday, he gripped his father's hand as the old man took him to school in the morning and brought him back in the afternoon. When his legs ached or when it rained and the pathway was marshy, Bajrang Gaikwad balanced his son in his arms and carried him all the way home. He often stopped on the way to buy him a Cadbury chocolate or a pack of Bourbon biscuits.

Sandesh's parents, being next to illiterate, couldn't oversee his studies. But his Brahmin mother, Sunanda, had a second cousin, Sadashiv Babu, who was a pathshala teacher in the town. He popped in at the Gaikwad residence twice or thrice a week to help Sandesh do his homework. The Gaikwads were in no position to pay him his tuition fee, which in any case he thought incorrect to demand from them. But whenever he visited them, they made it a point to kill a chicken and treat him to a hearty non-vegetarian meal which was banned in his own home by his god-fearing wife. The lady would burst into tears whenever he expressed a desire to eat chicken, mutton, eggs or fish.

Sadashiv Babu took a keen interest in Sandesh's studies, as if he'd adopted him. As a result, he passed his exams with flying colours and was the cynosure of his teachers' eyes. Then one day, when Sandesh was in class four, Sadashiv Babu suddenly had a heart attack and died.

Deserted by fate, Sandesh's life in secondary school was in stark contrast to his primary school days under the tutelage of Sadashiv Babu. His mind wandered as he couldn't make head or tail of what his lackadaisical teachers taught him. Private tuitions would have helped, but that was beyond Bajrang Gaikwad's means. The pyjama-clad headmaster summoned the farm labourer more than once to caution him.

'Your ward, I'm afraid, will fail if you don't do something soon.'

But what could Bajrang Gaikwad do? He gave vent to his frustration by thrashing his son with the chapatti roller, amid terrified shrieks of his wife and daughters urging him to stop.

The pyjama-clad headmaster's words were prophetic. Sandesh did not let him down: he promptly failed in standard five and lost the advantage of the head start his father gave him by advancing his age by a year. The school stepped in and offered him free tuitions with the help of which he passed standard five, and did not fail thereafter. Though his mark sheets always revealed that he'd barely managed to scrape through in all subjects, except drawing, in which he won laurels. Maths was a particularly bothersome subject that confounded him no end. It so repulsed him that when, as a seventh standard student, a roguish classmate named Somnath invited him to be part of a conspiracy to break into the headmaster's cabin and steal the maths question paper on the eve of the exams, Sandesh jumped at the opportunity, was caught by a night watchman, and suspended for a whole term.

Failure and suspension, however, did not put an end to Sandesh's wayward ways as he entered adolescence. In standard nine, he beat up a teacher who made him remove his shirt and stand on a bench with his arms up for a whole period. The teacher, a Maratha by caste, was known to be prejudiced towards Dalits and had been warned by the school authorities before. Yet, his hatred of 'untouchables' was so deep-rooted that he always looked for excuses to harass students. Sandesh, a long-haired backbencher who drew sketches of his teachers as they lectured, was an easy target. What irked Mr Londe, the teacher in question, was that Sandesh had drawn an outrageously funny caricature of him and passed it around, causing titters among the students. Now, as Sandesh did exactly as Mr Londe ordered, the newly grown hair on his armpits made him go red with shame as he slowly undid his buttons, took off his shirt and raised his arms till they ached. Luckily there were only boys in the school, he consoled himself. Still, after class that day, smarting from the humiliation, Somnath and he followed Mr Londe, who always came to school on foot, accosted him at a forlorn spot and pounced on him. Sandesh struck him on his testicles with his knees, causing Mr Londe to squeal in pain like a pig, while Somnath tightly gripped both his arms behind his back and twisted them. '*Ye hath hamka de de Thakur,*' he said, reciting Gabbar Singh's famous lines from *Sholay*. Then both Sandesh and he burst into maniacal laughter, Gabbar Singh style.

Sandesh did not complete his matriculation. He reached the tenth standard all right, but the prospect of a board exam unsettled him. In January 2002, the year he was to take his board exams and the year he would meet Lolita, Sandesh attended school for the last time. Bajrang Gaikwad had, by this time, written his son off as a bad egg. The two hardly spoke to each other when they met at home late at night. Sandesh's mother and sisters, who were turning ripe for marriage, did their best to effect a truce between the warring factions. But neither father nor son relented.

'What is the son of a bitch going to do in life without a basic degree?' Sandesh's father, who had himself never seen the inside of a school, yelled at his wife.

But Sandesh, who did not open his mouth as his parents bickered, had an answer to his father's question. Somnath and his slippery friends had introduced him to a thick-moustached man in Aurangabad who could procure fake certificates for a fee.

'Everything from tenth to Ph.D,' the man had boasted when Sandesh and Somnath met him at the Paithan ST stand. 'You name it.'

Of course, the thick-moustached man's fees put them off because he demanded Rs 10,000 for a fake tenth standard certificate, Rs 12,000 for a fake twelfth standard certificate, and Rs 15,000 for a fake graduation certificate.

'We can't afford that much,' Sandesh told him point-blank. On hearing this, the thick-moustached man puckered his eyebrows, frowned, and offered them a discount of Rs 1000. Sandesh and Somnath came away without striking a deal.

'We'll phone you if the need arises,' they told him and he gave them his mobile number, showing off his sleek Nokia handset. The guy was one of the few people in the town to own a cell phone at a time when even incoming calls were chargeable.

While at school, Sandesh grew accustomed to cutting classes and frequenting movie theatres where matinee shows ran cheap. He and his mates either cycled or trekked to the theatres and bought their tickets at half the price. Adult films, both Hindi and English, were their favourite; not infrequently, some of them sported a false moustache or beard to prove they were above eighteen.

On quitting school, the group grew more adventurous. They boarded rickety buses or borrowed motorbikes and went to Aurangabad to see scantily clad white women touring the Ajanta and Ellora caves, and the Bibi-ka-Maqbara which they referred to as a 'duplicate' Taj. The cleavage turned them on, prompting some of them to pass lewd remarks and make lascivious catcalls. Sandesh was in his element with these guys and spent most of his waking hours in their company. They hatched plans to molest the Western women and filch their costly cameras. Usually, such plans came to nothing. But a couple of times, the activities of the juvenile gang were brought to the notice of the tourist police who arrested them for a day and then let them off after stern warnings.

The boys soon formed a club which they called Fight Club, after the famous Hollywood film. Members of this club, mostly small-boned lads in their early teens who'd chucked school and had no plans of attempting college, killed time by playing chess, cards and carom for money. The Bombay underworld fascinated them and they excitedly recounted stories of dreaded dons like Dawood Ibrahim and Arun Gawli, who recruited adolescents like them as sharpshooters.

'Wish I could be a sharpshooter,' Sandesh sometimes said. Guns fascinated him so much that he was once on the verge of shoplifting a pistol from a store in Aurangabad, but abandoned plans when he realized that the object he was about to put into his school bag and trigger off the store's burglar alarms was no pistol but only a cigarette lighter. He felt like an ass for a whole day after that and vowed to religiously study the anatomy of a gun to prevent further goof-ups.

'Why don't you join Daddy's gang?' Fight Club members advised him, referring to Gawli, that gangster turned MP whose followers reverentially called him 'Daddy'. 'He has a base in Aurangabad city.'

Sandesh replied that this was a career option he would seriously consider.

One pastime the Fight Club members indulged in that fulfilled Sandesh's desire to fiddle with guns was to go hunting in the jungles around Paithan town. They called it 'shikar'. Someone bought or stole a high-powered air gun, belonging in all probability to a wealthy zamindar's spoilt brat. Another, ostensibly a mechanic by day, got hold of a battered jeep and the party of ten was dustily off. With headlamps that did not work, they drove on rugged country roads throughout the night, some of them taking swigs out of a bottle of Old Monk rum that was being passed around. But in the end, all they managed to gun down were a couple of miserable rabbits. During these

expeditions Sandesh, who remained sullen, fingered every part
of the air gun that closely resembled a rifle: butt, trigger, barrel.
'One day, I'll own a rifle myself,' he would say to his accomplices
in the jeep.

The Fight Club members were in the midst of a fight. Half
of them defended a bespectacled gentleman in his mid-thirties
who met them in a hair-cutting salon and introduced himself
as Mr Ali while the other half swore he was a charlatan.

'Hello, friends,' he had addressed the boys in English. 'My
name is Mr Ali and I'm a Bombay-based investment banker. I
have schemes for jobless youth like you that can make you rich
in no time.'

The boys cocked their ears at the mention of the word
'rich'. Mr Ali, who'd deliberately started off in English, quickly
switched over to Hindi and Marathi.

'Here is my business card,' he said, opening his leather
briefcase. 'My speciality is that I can double your money in
the shortest possible time. Government investments take six
years to double. Private investments double in about five years.
I can do it much sooner than that. It doesn't have to be a large
amount. It can be as little as Rs 500.'

There were rumblings among the boys. The more sceptical
among them openly pooh-poohed the man's claims. '*Dhongi*,'
fraud, they warned one another. The more credulous among
them, however, were inclined to give him a chance. 'These
Bombay guys are magicians,' they argued. 'What do we small-
towners know?'

Sandesh sat on the fence, siding neither with the sceptics nor
the gullible. He hoped Mr Ali was right, for if money could be

doubled that easily, life would be a ball. 'Do you have Mr Ali's visiting card?' he softly asked Somnath, on whose shoulder he rested his arm.

'Here, take it,' said Somnath, fishing out the gaudy visiting card from his tattered wallet. 'I have no use for it.'

All the boys, sceptics included, wanted someone other than themselves to be the guinea pig. If *he* parted with his money and got it doubled, they would begin to have faith in the scheme and patronize Mr Ali. Now, as Sandesh asked for his visiting card, they were pleased that they had found their man.

'Go right ahead,' they instigated him. '*Bindaas.*'

The sceptics exchanged glances. They were sure Sandesh would be conned. But then again, it was *his* dough, and who was he to them?

The next day, Sandesh called Mr Ali from a public telephone, using a one rupee coin.

'In how much time can you double my money?' he bluntly asked him, coming to the point without ceremony.

'Who's on the line, please?' Mr Ali suavely asked. It wasn't unusual for investment bankers like himself to be trapped by income tax and SEBI sleuths.

Sandesh mumbled an incoherent introduction in poor diction that almost caused Mr Ali to hang up on him. Just then, the latter remembered the hair-cutting salon where he'd met the boys while having a facial.

'Tell me your name again, please,' he said to Sandesh.

'Sandesh Gaikwad.'

'Hello, Sandesh Gaikwad. What can I do for you?'

'In how much time can you double my cash?'

'That depends on you. In how much time do you want it doubled?'

'In a day.'

There was a dazed silence. Mr Ali was still on the line. But it took him a few seconds to recover before he could speak to Sandesh again. 'Okay,' he said. 'I'll double your money for you in a day. But you will have to bring me at least Rs 10,000. I'll give you Rs 20,000 the next day.'

'Done.'

Mr Ali told Sandesh to meet him at a vada pav stall opposite the ST bus stand as soon as he was ready with the money.

Ever since Sandesh met Mr Ali at the hair-cutting salon, where the boys often hung out, he had cast his eye on his father's meagre savings that were not kept in a bank, for his old man held no bank account, but were tucked away in a wooden almirah in the house. Relations between father and son were so strained that Sandesh knew it was useless to *ask* his father for the money.

In the circumstances, all Sandesh could aspire to do in order to lay his hands on the cash was to embezzle it without permission. He would filch exactly Rs 10,000, not a rupee less, not a rupee more. And when Mr Ali returned Rs 20,000 to him twenty-four hours later, he would quietly replace the money he had 'borrowed' and keep the rest for himself. If the ends were noble and beneficial to all, how did the means matter? Sandesh vaguely toyed with the idea of taking his mother, or at least his sisters into confidence, but soon gave up on it. They would disapprove of his actions and brand him an *uchlya*, a thief. Would they understand his need to start out in life with a bit of dough to back him up? They who had given him birth but did nothing to guarantee him a life? Sandesh was convinced that what he was about to do was no crime.

The recalcitrant teenager got his chance the very next day when the family went to Aurangabad to attend a niece's wedding. Manufacturing a flimsy excuse for not attending his cousin's marriage, he stayed at home while his parents and sisters left in a Toyota Qualis, driven by an acquaintance.

As a rule, Bajrang Gaikwad never locked his almirah. 'What's in there for anyone to steal?' he would sarcastically ask. The words echoed in Sandesh's ears as he opened the almirah and ransacked it, taking out clothes and papers and strewing them all over the floor. The money he was in search of was kept concealed by his father in an inner safe, and it was with some effort that he located it, almost giving up in despair more than once. Abuses freely came to his lips. 'Damn that *chingus,* stingy, old man,' he swore. 'Why does he have to hide his dough as if it's gold?'

On discovering the lolly and pocketing the amount that Mr Ali had demanded, after which there were scarcely a couple of hundreds left, Sandesh was faced with another chore. He would have to rearrange everything in the almirah exactly as it was, so that no one would notice that something was amiss. The operation lasted nearly an hour and on successfully executing it, Sandesh locked the house and went to Fight Club headquarters to hobnob with his friends. Of course, he told no one what he'd just done. He hid the money he had robbed in a worn-out school bag and laboured to mask the guilt on his face. When his parents returned late that night, they found he was already in bed. This was unusual for the youngster who, on an average night, never hit the sack till well after 2 a.m.

As soon as the first rays of the morning sun illuminated the sky, Sandesh awoke. Unusual again for a guy who never voluntarily got out of bed until mugs of water were poured on his head. He washed his face, scrubbed his teeth with neem twigs and left the house to make a call to Mr Ali.

'Where's the good-for-nothing boy headed for this early?' he heard his father ask his mother as he left.

The public telephone in the vicinity of Sandesh's house was dead. He had to walk half a kilometre before he found one that worked.

'I'm Sandesh, sir,' he said in reply to Mr Ali's groggy 'Hello' when he dialled the number. Like Sandesh, Mr Ali too was a late riser and was surprised that his phone rang before noon.

'Good morning, Sandesh. Have you got the money?'

'Yes, sir.'

'Lovely. Come to Jai Malhar Hotel, opposite the ST bus stand, by 11.30 a.m. with the cash. I'll be waiting for you.'

Mr Ali disconnected the phone and went back to sleep. Sandesh got back home and then went to the village well for a bath. When his mother inquired what he was up to, he told her someone had promised him a job. This gladdened the poor woman's heart. 'Bless you, my son,' she cried.

At the stroke of 11.30, Sandesh was at the Jai Malhar Hotel opposite the ST bus stand. Mr Ali kept his word and was already inside the restaurant eating a vada pav with a green chilli.

'Would you like to have some?' he asked Sandesh, as they met and shook hands.

'No.'

'Then let's get to business straight away.'

Sandesh took out the twenty 500 rupee notes that he carried in his shirt pocket and handed them to Mr Ali. The latter beamed.

'Tomorrow, I'll give you twenty 1000 rupee notes,' he said. 'Same place, same time.'

He then ordered two cups of tea to celebrate. They shook hands again and parted, both going in different directions.

It was difficult to describe Sandesh's state of mind that day. He could neither eat nor sleep. Mr Ali's words, 'same place, same time,' rang in his ears all night. But when he actually trudged to the Jai Malhar Hotel at 11.30 a.m. the next morning, the latter seemed to be nowhere. Sandesh waited till noon before calling Mr Ali on his mobile number.

'The number you are trying to call is currently not reachable,' a voice repeatedly informed him.

Sandesh scrutinized Mr Ali's visiting card and found it had an address on it. But when he boarded a bus and landed up at the address, several kilometres away, a Muslim with a fez cap told him that no man by the name of Mr Ali ever lived there. 'I've had other Mohammedan tenants, like Mr Khan and Mr Shaikh, but never a Mr Ali,' he said. Sandesh then thought of taking the Fight Club members into confidence and telling them what had happened, for hadn't they pledged to swim and sink together? But he decided against it, for it was beneath his dignity to let his buddies know that he had been made a sucker. I'll handle this on my own, he said to himself, as murderous thoughts occurred to him. Ali saab, you're dead. The moment I see you, I'll push a Rampuri knife into your stomach and get it out from the other side, he thought.

The next seven days saw Sandesh hunt for Mr Ali everywhere. He combed every square kilometre of the town looking for the man who made him feel like a bumpkin. Being ripped off was only one part of the story. The other was his punctured pride. His buddies would laugh at him. 'The fellow made you a *chutiya*,' they would joke, when he went to Fight Club. Thus he looked in shops, restaurants, street corners, side streets, public parks, beer bars, bus stops, autorickshaw stands, meat markets, cinema halls and every conceivable place for the man whose head he wished to smash to pulp.

It came to nothing. Mr Ali was anywhere but in Paithan town. His mobile continued to say that he was not reachable, or that he was out of coverage area, or that the mobile had been switched off. Frustration gripped Sandesh. He did not go home that night, but continued to look for his culprit till the wee hours. He had no clue if his father had discovered the loss of his hard-earned money yet. Probably not, for his father wasn't the sort who went to his almirah every so often to see if his money was still there.

But where was Mr Ali? As soon as Sandesh's dough was safely in his custody, he had boarded a private luxury bus and left town. The bus was headed for Bombay and that's where Mr Ali went, sleeping throughout the eight-hour journey through bumpy roads. When he hit Bombay late that evening, he caught a jam-packed local and got to Dharavi, Asia's largest slum, where he lived with his Hindu mistress in a rented shack. 'I had a successful business deal,' he told her, and treated her to beer and tandoori chicken ordered from a nearby kiosk. 'I need a home delivery,' he said to the guys at the kiosk, as he gave them his address and mobile number, which they already had.

After a frolicking night, Mr Ali rose early to go to his bank in the Fort area before the trains got too crowded. Here, he deposited Sandesh's 10,000 bucks and politely asked the lady at the teller to update his passbook. It reflected a six-figure sum, indicating scarily that Sandesh wasn't the first guy on earth whom Mr Ali had duped. His victims included men and women from sixteen to sixty, and to each he offered a scheme that was tailor-made for them.

'What is it that you want?' he would ask them, as he had asked Sandesh. And when they told him what they had in mind, no matter how far-fetched it sounded, he said, 'I can do it for you.' It was as simple as that.

Mr Ali never returned to Paithan again. He knew that Sandesh was too much of a neophyte to report him to the cops. Even so, as a matter of policy, he never reconnoitered. Once he was through with a place, he cast his net elsewhere.

Bajrang Gaikwad wouldn't have discovered the theft of his life's savings had the thought of his daughters' weddings not crossed his mind.

'I have to marry off four girls,' he said to his wife, as she rolled chapattis in their cow dung-plastered kitchen. 'Why didn't you give me more sons?'

On saying this, he impulsively went to his almirah to count his money, as if by counting it the number and the denomination of the currency notes would miraculously increase.

'Put your money in a co-operative bank,' some of his well-wishers had advised him. 'At least you'll earn something by way of interest.'

But Bajrang Gaikwad had no faith in banks. What if they pocketed his cash and denied that he'd ever had an account with them? He wouldn't know whom to approach for redress.

As soon as it struck him, as does lightning, that he'd been looted, Bajrang Gaikwad collapsed. His wife ran to his rescue and sprinkled cold water on his face, allowing her chapattis to char in the process. This revived him, but his first words to her were, 'I want to hang myself from the ceiling fan.'

Without knowing what the issue was, Bajrang Gaikwad's wife wailed and beat her breast, as if he were already dead. Her husband sobbed too and this caused Sandesh who, unimaginably, was present in the house when the drama unfolded, to go up to his parents and confess his crime. 'I stole the money,' he matter-of-factly said. However, he did not tell them why he'd committed the theft.

From his parents' point of view, Sandesh's bluntness, ironically, prevented the truth from sinking in at once. Then his words hit his father like a thunderbolt. He grabbed Sandesh's belt, hanging on a nail nearby, and whipped him all over his bare body (Sandesh always wore shorts at home). Next, he snatched the chapatti roller from his wife's hands and hit his son on the elbows, knees and knuckles. He punched him in the belly with his fists and slapped him across his face so hard that the neighbours thought someone had lit firecrackers. Finally, Bajrang Gaikwad, full of wrath, lifted a giant-sized stone and was about to bring it crashing down on his son's skull when his weeping wife and daughters overpowered him.

'Kill him,' his wife hysterically shrieked. 'But you will have to kill me first.'

While his father beat him up, Sandesh, only a boy still, yelled. Now he moaned and groaned in agony. There was blood on his arms and legs. He couldn't walk. His ears smarted. Tears inconsolably came to his eyes. Bajrang Gaikwad left the house shortly afterwards, as exhausted as his son by the assault. He did not tell his wife where he was headed. Nor did she inquire. Instead, she led her injured son to a *charpoy* in the courtyard and nursed his wounds with turmeric paste. His sisters brought him tea, but he vomited after just the first few sips. 'I'm dying,' Sandesh cried, inducing a fresh bout of hysteria in his mother. 'Take me to a doctor.'

But Sandesh Gaikwad's youthful body had enough resistance to withstand his father's malice. He recovered in a few days and resumed his wanderings around town. He came home only to bed and board.

Eventually, there was nothing for Sandesh to do but to leave for good. He ran away without informing anyone, not even his mother or the Fight Club members. All he took with him in a Kala Niketan bag, which he found on the road, were a couple of worn shirts and trousers along with a childhood photo of him and his parents. Money-wise, he had exactly Rs 200 in his pocket, borrowed from a classmate, and a wee bit of change that he would use to make telephone calls.

Sandesh boarded an early morning Paithan – Bombay ST bus and, like thousands of others before him, came to the city of dreams to try his luck. He had two addresses with him, one of Somnath, who had also gone to Bombay to make a living, though unlike Sandesh he hadn't run away. The other address was that of a distant relative of his mother who had settled down in Bombay many years ago.

When the bus deposited him at the Bombay Central ST bus terminus, Sandesh, looking the perfect villager in a metropolis that thought it was India's answer to New York City, made inquiries from passers-by. While half of them ignored him, he made his way to the chawl in which Somnath lived, in Malabar Hill of all places.

Sandesh did not tell Somnath about Mr Ali. 'You can't put up with me,' Somnath said, alarmed at Sandesh's request to lodge him till he found his feet in the city. '*Yeh hai Bambai meri jaan.* Here it's each one for himself and God for all.'

However, taking pity on his childhood buddy, Somnath consented to let Sandesh sponge off him for a week or so while he looked for a place to stay. 'If you don't find anything, there are always the pavements of Bombay,' he said, giving Sandesh a taste of the hard-heartedness that was Bombay's trademark.

But Somnath was only pulling his friend's leg. During the week that Sandesh was his guest, he proved to be a hospitable host who, apart from giving his Fight Club pal three meals a day and a comfortable bed (while he himself slept on the floor), also took him on a tour of the city that was as good as any conducted by the Maharashtra Tourism Development Corporation!

Their Bombay darshan began at Malabar Hill itself (known alternatively as Walkeshwar and Teen Batti), where Somnath took Sandesh to Banganga, a duplicate Banaras just as the Bibi-ka-Maqbara at Aurangabad is a duplicate Taj.

Here, as they stripped and descended the steps for a holy dip, the skyscrapers that surrounded them on all sides overawed Sandesh. He began laboriously counting the number of floors in each building. In one particularly tall high-rise he counted up to thirty-five and wondered what it would be like to live on the topmost floor.

'It's like living in an airplane,' Somnath explained, eager to display that he was much more conversant with the ways of Bombay-ites than his untutored friend, fresh from the country.

From here, they trekked to Kamala Nehru Park and Hanging Gardens, and passed the awesome Jinnah House and the chief minister's residence. Later, at Marine Drive, they scaled the sea wall and trod all over the tetrapods from Chowpatty sands to Nariman Point. Sandesh recalled scores of Hindi films that had a Marine Drive sequence: *Andaaz*, featuring Rajesh Khanna and *Muqaddar Ka Sikandar* with Amitabh Bachchan. Both heroes had sung songs as they rode past Marine Drive on motorbikes.

Somnath generously treated Sandesh to bhelpuri and kulfi at the Chowpatty Beach. 'Bhelpuri is Bombay's speciality,' he informed his friend. Amazed at the way he freely spent his money, Sandesh asked Somnath what he did for a living. But Somnath's reply was evasive. How could he confess to his childhood yaar that here in Bombay he washed the cars and cleaned the loos and disposed of the garbage of the stinking rich who lived in apartments that cost over a crore? In response to Sandesh's question, all he did was sing his favourite Johnny

Walker number from the old film *C.I.D*: *Yeh hai Bambai meri jaan*, and suggested going to the Gateway of India next.

Sandesh loved the sight of boats bobbing in the water at the Gateway of India. 'Wish I had a camera,' he told his mate. People boarded motor launches and sailed to the Elephanta Caves nearby. These rock-cut caves dedicated to Lord Shiva (of the perpetual phallus) were built between the second and seventh century A.D., and then forgotten about until the British discovered them centuries later and accorded them the status they deserved. Sandesh and Somnath would have loved to ride to the Elephanta Caves in a motorboat, but when they made inquiries and found that the ticket for a round trip was Rs 100, they dropped the idea. 'Shortage of vitamin M,' Somnath said. Instead, they turned their attention to the Taj Mahal Hotel opposite and to the pigeons on the promenade which the public fed with gram. They joined the others and bought two rupees' worth of gram from a peanut seller to hurl to the pigeons. The Taj, they knew, was out of bounds for vagabonds like themselves, who were only permitted to savour its magnificence from a distance.

'Do you know how much a cup of tea costs at the Taj?' Somnath asked Sandesh.

'How much?'

'It costs Rs 500.'

Sandesh stared with open-mouthed wonder at some foreigners who were entering the hotel. When he had seen them at the Ajanta and Ellora caves at Aurangabad, he had no idea they were so wealthy. But if they could stay in a five-star hotel whose tariff was Rs 10,000 a day (as Somnath told him), it surely meant money was like paani to them. Sandesh reflected on his own plight by contrast. He was driven to leave home for Rs 10,000, the daily rent for a room at the Taj.

'I want a ride in a double-decker bus,' Sandesh suddenly said to Somnath at the Gateway of India. They were licking ice-cream cones bought from a roadside vendor. Somnath, familiar as he was with the city of Bombay, had to think for only a minute.

'Got it,' he confidently told his friend. 'Let's go to Haji Ali. Many double-decker buses go there.'

Half an hour later, Sandesh found himself in the front seat of a Technicolour double-decker bus that had an advertisement for Cadbury's chocolate painted all over it in black, blue and yellow. This was fascinating for Sandesh, who was merely used to seeing red-coloured State Transport buses, coated with layers and layers of dust, which the Fight Club members referred to as *lal dabba*. The front seat on the upper deck gave him a bird's eye-view of Bombay as the bus crawled through traffic and drove them through posh areas like Churchgate, Queen's Road and Peddar Road before it deposited them at Haji Ali.

While on the bus, Sandesh heard passengers ask the khaki-uniformed conductor for tickets and wondered why they gave him their names: Babulnath, Haji Ali, Prabhadevi, Sitladevi.

'They're not *their* names, silly,' Somnath corrected him. 'They're the names of places. *Yeh hai Bambai meri jaan.*'

'How is the *dargah* built in the middle of the sea?' a bewildered Sandesh asked, when they got off the bus and saw the Haji Ali mosque from the sidewalk. 'That's a miracle,' Somnath replied. 'But the area is rocky. The mosque is actually built on the rocks.'

They then saw the kilometre-long road that would take them to the *dargah*. Shops, beggars and pilgrims thronged it. 'The road is submerged during high tide,' Somnath explained. 'Those inside the mosque are stranded and have to wait till the tide recedes. A bell rings just before high tide to warn pilgrims.'

They commenced their walk to the shrine. Shopkeepers on both sides of the road besought them to buy their flowers and incense. Maimed and crippled beggars thrust their stumps in front of them, asking for alms. Shoving them aside, Sandesh and Somnath kept walking. On reaching the shrine, they removed their footwear, covered their heads with handkerchiefs as they saw others do and offered their respects at the tomb of Haji Ali.

Sandesh prayed, hoping his mother and sisters back home in Paithan town did not miss him too much. Give them courage, he said to the saint who was the presiding deity of the *dargah*. Once their worship was over, Sandesh and Somnath went to the rear of the shrine, like several other youngsters, and descended the rocks where Sandesh caught hold of a giant-sized crab and placed it on his palm.

'Let's eat it,' Somnath suggested. Both boys were ravenous but neither had the dough to fill their stomachs with all the delicacies that were on sale outside. Shortage of vitamin M. They threw small pebbles into the sea that caused ripples in the water. 'Life is as vast as the ocean,' Sandesh reflected, surprising his friend. 'Are you becoming a philosopher, or what?' Somnath asked him.

After spending an hour at Haji Ali, Sandesh and Somnath went back home, this time by single-decker bus.

A few days later, Somnath plainly told Sandesh that he would have to take his leave. 'I can't let you parasite off me forever, my friend,' he said. However, as a gesture of friendship, he took Sandesh to Fashion Street in south Bombay to buy him a couple of inexpensive T-shirts before they parted.

There were rows and rows of pavement shops at Fashion Street, which stretched from the legendary Metro theatre at Dhobi Talao to the Central Telegraph Office at Flora Fountain. Collegians mobbed the shops that did not have names, only numbers. Each shop had an area of no more than fifty square feet at the maximum. Yet it was incredible how much business it did in the course of a day.

Sandesh was tempted by all the export rejects he saw on display. Never in his life had he seen clothing so trendy. If he had had the dough, he would have bought all the T-shirts and jeans and jackets that were hung on the walls, and had a makeover. But, as it turned out, all Somnath could afford to buy him were two half-sleeved T-shirts for Rs 50 each. Shortage of vitamin M. On one of the T-shirts, the legend read: *You're massive, I'm passive*. Sandesh accepted his present with gratitude, swearing that one day he would return to Fashion Street with a loaded wallet.

'*Yeh hai Bambai meri jaan,*' he said to Somnath. 'Here, anything is possible.' The slogan had already become a sort of catchphrase among them. Bombay's humid weather caused both boys to profusely sweat.

'Why is it so hot here?' Sandesh asked, fanning himself with a newspaper.

'Because Bombay, unlike Paithan, is on the coast.'

'Don't you miss our home town?'

'No.'

Wiping their necks with handkerchiefs, also purchased cheaply at Fashion Street, Somnath asked Sandesh where he was headed next.

'Lower Parel,' Sandesh answered.

'Lower Parel?'

'A relative of mine lives there.'

Sandesh unfolded a soiled piece of paper that he extricated from his pockets. It bore the address of his relative which Somnath read.

'Oh,' he said. 'I'll put you in a bus that will take you there.'

But Lower Parel wasn't an area that Somnath, a resident of Malabar Hill, knew at all. He misguided Sandesh, putting him into the wrong bus with insufficient change to buy his ticket. Sandesh had a harrowing time as bus conductors screamed at him and people on the roads refused to give him directions to get to his destination. '*Malum nahi*,' they said, when he thrust his soiled piece of paper on which he'd scribbled the address of his relative before them. Don't know.

A traffic constable almost beat him up for distracting him with his queries, thus facilitating the escape of a driver who was talking on his mobile as he drove. Doubtless, the guy would have paid the cop a hefty bribe to secure his release.

At last, however, Sandesh reached his relative's home in a slum colony behind the Prakash Industrial Estate. He had no idea how he was related to this greying man with four brats whose noses leaked and whose sex he couldn't determine. Were they boys or girls?

'What brings you here?' the astonished relative asked Sandesh, as he appeared at the door.

'Work,' said Sandesh, resolving not to let the man know that he'd run away from home. 'I have come to Bombay to look for work.'

The brats surrounded Sandesh as he sat down on a chair offered to him and drank a glass of water from a dented aluminium tumbler. Then they climbed over his lap, his shoulders and his head. Sandesh felt as Gulliver might have on first arriving in Lilliput and trampling on the Lilliputians. But, like Gulliver, he couldn't protest. After all, he was his relative's guest and expected the fellow to give him shelter.

Unlike the week he spent with Somnath, Sandesh was bored stiff in his relative's house with little to do. The relative himself left for work at sunrise and returned well after sunset, the reason for this being, as Sandesh soon discovered, his wife, who was a shrew. She nagged him whenever he was around. She harangued her kids. She spoke in a high-pitched voice, as if she were an opera singer, the clanging of utensils providing the accompaniment. Though Sandesh was a guest, she did not spare him either. She asked him, in no uncertain terms, how long he intended to stay with them, and before he could mumble an answer, she bluntly declared that they did not have the 'capacity' to feed another mouth. For the meals that he'd already eaten, he would have to pay, if not in cash, in kind. At first Sandesh did not grasp her meaning, but eventually he realized that what she had in mind was that he would have to sit with her kids to teach them the ABC. Now this was a task he abhorred because it reminded him of his own despondent schooldays.

'No,' he said to her. 'I can't do it.'

His relative got home one rainy night to find Sandesh engaged in a verbal duel with his wife. 'Get out of my house, you good-for-nothing boy,' the woman was saying to him, as Sandesh yelled at her. The relative decided that enough was enough.

'Do you want a job?' he asked Sandesh early next morning, as he made tea for them both on the gas stove while his wife slept.

'Yes.'

'I shall find you one.'

Later that morning, he telephoned Ashok Jadhav, proprietor of the Royal Video Parlour whom he knew well.

'Send him to me at once,' the latter said, when the relative asked him if he could employ Sandesh. 'As it turns out, my business is expanding and I'm badly in need of extra hands.'

FOUR
Forces of Liberation

After their maiden sexual encounter in Jannat, Lolita and Sandesh became lovers. They met the next day, and the next, and the next, and even attempted, very successfully, a replay of that paradisiacal first night when they pleasured each other.

This is how they did it:

Lolita drove to the store just before dark and parked her Zen Carbon a short distance away from the Royal Video Parlour (depending, of course, on where she found parking). She then casually stepped into the store, not wanting anything in particular. Since she was now a fixture there, Ashok Jadhav did not pay her special attention, leaving her to the care of his boys as he did with routine customers. This suited Lolita who did not wish to be fussed over. No longer did she borrow Double X and Triple X DVDs. Instead, she opted for the odd movie, as using the services of the Royal Video Parlour was strictly a pretext. Her real aim was to get Sandesh into bed, and in this she succeeded by merely signalling to him and then hanging around for a few minutes before leaving.

It was two-sided love. Sandesh's heart pounded at the time of Lolita's arrival every evening, and he would anxiously look towards the door each time a customer thrust it open to enter. Luckily, neither Ashok Jadhav, nor Darshan and Aniket ever noticed this. When Sandesh saw Lolita, he would be ecstatic. He looked at her for cues and got them instantly. All she had to do was cock her head slightly and he knew she wanted him over.

In the anarchic set-up that existed in the Royal Video Parlour, getting away was child's play. Ashok Jadhav's boys had the freedom to come and go as they pleased, all in the name of *gutkha* breaks, or more convincing still, delivering or collecting a DVD. In Sandesh's case, the boss made it a point, of course, never to part with his scooter again! He did not invest too much in bicycles for his delivery boys either, his excuse being that Bombay was no cycling city.

Thus, Sandesh trekked all the way to Jannat from the Royal Video Parlour. The exercise took him a good fifteen minutes or thereabouts in the overcrowded landmass that was Bombay, especially in a neighbourhood like Dadar. As he walked, Sandesh developed a habit of swinging his head a full 180 degrees to ensure no one was following him. He was particularly suspicious of his fellow delivery boys, Darshan and Aniket, not because they might report him to Ashok Jadhav who would then sack him, but because jealousy would prompt them to nip his affair in the bud. Why him and not us, they would wonder.

Though security arrangements at Jannat were elaborate, the khaki-uniformed security personnel who manned the electronically operated booths at the building's main gate grew used to Sandesh and let him enter without being frisked. Some of them even shared his *gutkha*, and in this way camaraderie developed. They would ask him for porn DVDs, which he always promised to bring but never actually kept his word.

Once secure in the cosiness of Lolita's flat with the doors fastened, the baby asleep and the maid gone, Sandesh would relax. Lolita would fix herself a Martini and open a bottle of Heineken beer for him with a phallic-shaped bottle opener. They would clink their glasses and begin drinking, saying little to each other for there was little that they had in common. Soon, Lolita would inch towards Sandesh, slip her fair hand into his and squeeze it. At such times, the contrast in their respective complexions alarmed Sandesh. While Lolita's skin had a milk-white sheen to it, his own skin was coffee-black from years of loafing about in the Marathwada sun. But Lolita was no bigot. Dark-skinned working men seemed to be her type, as it became apparent to Sandesh in a matter of days. He knew he was her fantasy.

They drank and smoked and refilled their glasses. They held hands in the mellow light, and as the hours passed, they grew intimate. Lolita would grab Sandesh's hands and put them around her slender shoulders. Sandesh would allow his fingers to travel down till they entered her dress and reached her breasts. These he would fondle, often feeling the dampness there that would give him a hard-on. The passion with which Sandesh caressed Lolita's breasts always made her squeal and this somehow gave him a heightened sense of his own power. Their next step was to leave the drawing room, where they sat, and rush to the master bedroom on the first floor. Here, Lolita would unclothe Sandesh with an urgency that set his body on fire, and once Sandesh unclothed Lolita, they would spring onto the double bed that was neatly done up by Kamalabai with handloom bedcovers and pillowcases in floral designs, Sandesh assuming a bottom position with Lolita astride him.

They preferred it that way. Lolita liked being penetrated from below rather than above (something Aroop never yielded to) and Sandesh loved the idea of lying on the bed during intercourse with his head resting on a fluffy pillow. To him, this was more comfortable than lying atop Lolita's bony body, even though it put his masculinity at stake. At the nth hour, however, Sandesh invariably became the killjoy. His pelvic thrusts abruptly stopped.

'Nirodh,' he said to Lolita. This was a word she had learnt to dread, hoping against hope that he would forget to ask and let his sticky male fluids seep into her. But Sandesh never forgot, and Lolita reluctantly rose and fished out a condom from her stock, bought from the pharmacy next door, and threw it in his direction, watching him wear it like a balloon. His movements resumed after that, till he ejaculated amidst her moans and groans after what seemed to her like ages. But they continued to remain in sexual union as they rolled over each other on the giant double bed. Sometimes, they disengaged with Sandesh's condom still inside while at other times she made it a point, as on that first night, to rip off the sperm-filled contraceptive herself and chuck it down the garbage chute before Kamalabai, or the watchman, or even the neighbours discovered it and spread malice about her.

After they'd dressed, Lolita could peep into Tanu's room to make sure their muffled sounds did not rouse her from sleep.

Then they would both go downstairs hand-in-hand for a final smoke and mouth-to-mouth before she unbolted the front door and let him out. It was close to midnight by then, so there was no question of Sandesh returning to the store. Instead, he took his time to get to his room, strolling along the pavements of Dadar where roadside stalls selling knick-knacks still had a flourishing business.

Darshan and Aniket ragged Sandesh when he knocked and entered the room he shared with them.

'Where have you been?' they demanded. They were certain he was up to some mischief, some shady deal that kept him away from the store night after night. Yet they did not probe. It was a thing between boys, and tomorrow it might be their turn when they would expect him to keep their secrets. But after spending time with Lolita in her plush apartment where everything was picture-perfect, the ambience, the sex, the alcohol, Sandesh grew morose in the company of his fellow workers and couldn't bring himself to engage in good-humoured banter with them. He went to bed almost immediately, covering his head with a tattered sheet, wishing he could find a room to live in by himself, even though he knew it was out of the question. Days when Darshan and Aniket were out half the night, having gone for a late night show to the nearby Chitra or Plaza cinemas, or even to prostitutes on Foras Road, were the ones Sandesh liked best. He had the room to himself as he returned from the warmth of Lolita's home, missing her so much that he felt down in the dumps. Tomorrow he would see her again, but twenty-four hours was a maddening wait.

'Do you have to leave?' Lolita asked Sandesh.

They lay naked in bed, Sandesh's index finger deep inside Lolita's cunt. Minor discord had broken out between them as Sandesh wanted the bedroom door closed, but Lolita was reluctant to oblige because her baby, after all, slept in the chamber next door. This did not deter him from acceding to her request to spend the night in her flat. '*Aaj jaane ki zid na karo,*' she sang. 'We will have the time of our lives.'

'Okay,' said Sandesh, as was his wont. He pretended he was doing her a favour, though in truth he couldn't be happier at the prospect of lying next to her all night in her luxurious bedroom, away from the dinginess of his own lodgings. They made fervent love all night. They'd been together for over two months now and were aware of each other's fetishes well. Sandesh knew, for example, that Lolita loved it when he vigorously caressed her breasts till the milk oozed out and Lolita knew that Sandesh thought of fellatio as heaven on earth. Even as they made out, Sandesh mentally ran through all the excuses he could give to Darshan and Aniket for absconding from the room all night, and decided he would tell them he was with Somnath, his village buddy, who was celebrating his birthday. It was nearly dawn by the time the lovers fell asleep. When Sandesh's eyes opened around noon the next day, Lolita was no longer by his side. She entered the room shortly afterwards, Tanu in her arms, wished him a good morning and asked him to leave before Kamalabai arrived.

'I gave her the morning off,' said Lolita, 'because I did not want her to see you in my bed.'

'Yes, madam,' Sandesh groggily said, as he rubbed his eyes and yawned.

Despite Lolita's express instructions to Sandesh to address her by name, he insisted upon calling her 'madam', his excuse being that she was above him in station. 'We are calling only our equals by name, no?' he once managed to explain to her in English. Be that as it may, Lolita would have been horrified if she had had an inkling of what he called her privately. He called her 'aunty'. It was the fifteen-year-old's ultimate turn-on, sleeping with a woman who was old enough to be his aunt. But Lolita, in a way, had her revenge. As their affair fermented and Sandesh could no longer be kept hidden from little Tanu, she trained her daughter to call him 'uncle'. 'Un-kal,' Tanu would say in baby language whenever she saw him about the house.

A time came when Sandesh began to spend at least one night a week, usually a Saturday, in Lolita's apartment. But after a night of steamy sex, he left before the sun rose, much to her displeasure. This was because he now worked part-time as a newsboy, delivering copies of the *Times of India* along with a whole host of Marathi newspapers, including Bal Thackeray's *Saamna*, to residents in the Dadar – Parel belt. This was early morning work that Sandesh took up to make ends meet, but also because he loved the smell of newsprint.

Aware that his lady-love was pained by his premature exit, Sandesh decided to call her later one day, when all his newspapers were distributed, to ask how she was.

'Don't add insult to injury,' Lolita yelled on the phone.

'Sorry, madam,' he replied. Then, to make amends, he politely asked her if she'd had her tea.

'Tea!' she exclaimed. 'I am having a drink!'

'In morning?'

'Yes.'

Not that it had to be said, but during those early days of their affair, Lolita thought it imperative to warn Sandesh to keep their affair a secret.

'Don't tell anyone,' she frequently advised him as he wore his trousers and left after midnight. She was afraid that teenagers being prone to gossip, he would open his mouth in front of his mates and the cat would be out of the bag. This could wreck her reputation, her marriage. What they did in the privacy of her apartment was strictly between them, and it was important that it stay that way. However, to Lolita's 'don't tell anyone' Sandesh merely nodded his assent, leaving her in grave doubt. She wasn't convinced he understood the gravity of the situation for he was merely a boy of fifteen running sixteen. Nothing would happen to him if they were caught, but she could be booked on several counts: adultery; sex with a minor; introducing a boy less than twenty-one years of age to the thrills of alcohol. Yet her affair with Sandesh liberated her from the tyranny of a patriarchal marriage where the scales were tipped in favour of the male. Who knew, after all, what Aroop was doing that very minute on board his vessel? It was hard to imagine him abstaining from sex for months together.

At first Sandesh did not know what to make of the 'pocket money' Lolita began giving him every Sunday. She went to her cupboard, dug out a crisp 500 rupee note from one of her numerous designer handbags and handed it to him with a smile. 'Keep this,' she said, and blinked. Sandesh hesitated, but found it impossible to resist the temptation to pocket the dough. He took the currency note from Lolita's hands and put it into his cheap wallet, purchased hurriedly from the Dadar overbridge.

The first time he took the cash, he had no idea it would become a regular feature, Sunday after Sunday.

'Madam, why you paying me?' he once asked Lolita, but she did not answer the question.

'Just like that,' she evasively said.

Over time, Sandesh began to look upon the money as his due. If Lolita forgot to pay him, as she occasionally did, he did not feel shy to ask her.

'Madam, what about my allowance?' he asked.

'Oh yes,' Lolita replied, and would dash off to her safe.

Sandesh always stayed over at Lolita's place the night she paid him and made love to her with exaggerated fury. He would do the things he did not routinely do, like assuming position 69 and licking her pussy as Lolita fellated him. I am being paid for a service, he thought to himself, and must work to the best of my abilities. I must please my madam and please myself. In the morning, the alcohol and sex Lolita plied him with gave him a severe hangover which he nursed with lemon tea. Those days, his clients went without their daily newspaper.

Lolita's largesse guaranteed that, unlike before, Sandesh now had enough money in his pocket. The salary he earned from the Royal Video Parlour was his bread and butter while the pocket money from Lolita was the jam. Darshan and Aniket were witness to how Sandesh was dressing better, doing all his shopping at Linking Road where many Bollywood heroes lived. He also spent freely on them, treating them to bottles of beer every other day. But from Lolita's point of view, the best thing about the pocket money was that it enabled her lover to quit distributing newspapers in the early hours of the morning. During his sleepovers, no longer did she have to rise at the crack of dawn to say bye to him. To Lolita, for whom morning sex was the best kind, this meant loads. Sandesh and she wantonly mounted each other by turns before the eastern sky outside her bedroom window brightened, and little Tanu's cries in the anteroom next door obliged them to stop. Lolita would jump out of bed and wear her lace nightgown while Sandesh lay stark naked under the covers, his erection stubbornly refusing to subside.

'*Ek baar phir,*' he would groggily cry out to Lolita, to which she urged him to stop being a naughty boy. 'Too much sex is bad for health,' she said, as she left the bedroom.

Quitting his job as a newspaper boy deprived Sandesh of the smells of newsprint, which he loved only next to the smells of the various body fluids discharged by Lolita and him in bed: seminal fluid, lubricating fluid, lactating fluid. It also prevented him from keeping abreast of the day's headlines, so that he no longer knew what was happening in different pockets of the world.

Aati kya Khandala?

It was the song from *Ghulaam*, starring Aamir Khan and Rani Mukherjee, that gave Lolita a brainwave. One sunny morning in November, Lolita left little Tanu in Kamalabai's care and drove with Sandesh to Khandala, a hill station, nestling in the Sahyadri ranges. They held hands as she drove through the hustle and bustle of the city, before hitting National Highway No. 4, keeping her fingers entwined in her young paramour's even when she changed gears. Once on the highway, Lolita kissed Sandesh in the moving car. Sometimes on the cheek, sometimes on the lips, accelerating to a 110.

Two and a half hours later, they were at Rajmachi, Khandala where they got off the car to view the resplendent scenery. They ate corncobs and cucumbers, and drank tea at the Rajmachi Café where obstreperous monkeys kept them engrossed. Then they drove to a deserted spot in the ghats. Here, Lolita turned off the ignition, rolled up her window, motioning to Sandesh to do the same, and put her hand on his crotch. When Sandesh failed to return the favour by touching her breasts (as she expected him to), Lolita took his hands and ran them all over her torso, nipples to navel. This inevitably led to a bout of smooching which abruptly ended when a policeman tapped at their window to say that they had parked in a 'no parking' zone.

'Sorry,' Lolita tersely said to the cop, hastily starting the engine and zooming off into the wilderness. A few minutes later she stopped at the edge of a cliff and they resumed their kissing. There were other couples in cars doing the same thing, but they were more or less the same age. Sandesh suddenly felt awkward in Lolita's company.

When they first touched the highway, he was apprehensive: where was this woman taking him? The mist and the scenic grandeur of the hills and valleys as they ascended the Western Ghats quickened his heartbeats. Birds chirped. Sandesh had grown hard in his cargoes, unsure if Lolita was aware of his condition.

Now, as Lolita took off her bra, the presence of collegians notwithstanding, Sandesh told himself that this wasn't love. It was just a job for which Lolita paid him. If the collegians did not know how to mind their own business and scoffed at him for entertaining a middle-aged woman, so be it.

Lolita reversed and headed homewards only when Sandesh reminded her of little Tanu.

'Baby must be crying,' he said, 'and it is also time for Kamalabai to leave.'

They had spent a good two hours at Khandala, doing nothing except sit in the car and grope each other. They also finished an entire pack of State Express cigarettes.

On reaching Bombay, Lolita dropped Sandesh off outside the Royal Video Parlour for his evening shift before speeding off towards Jannat.

Ati kya Khandala became a key feature in the lives of Lolita and Sandesh. Every fortnight she picked him up outside a Food World store around the bend and they drove to the hill station, carrying a bottle of scotch, soda and two styrofoam glasses.

Lolita also went to a neighbourhood car accessories store and had dark sun control film fitted on the windows of her Zen Carbon.

'Give me the darkest shade of black,' she told the shopkeeper. When he pointed out that the Greater Bombay Police had banned the use of such products because terrorists misused them, she said, 'I couldn't care less.'

Once in Khandala, the goggle-type glass enabled our Adam and Eve to fornicate in the back seat. 'Aren't we like rabbits?' Lolita often commented during intercourse.

'What you saw in me?' Sandesh asked her.

'Innocence,' Lolita replied. 'I love your eyes.'

There were times when Lolita forgot to replenish her stock of condoms. Once she stopped outside a druggist on their way back from Khandala and asked Sandesh to pick up a whole carton. He stepped inside the crowded drugstore, but was too coy to ask for rubbers in the presence of so many customers. So he returned empty-handed.

'I can't do it,' he told his mistress.

On hearing this, Lolita alighted from the car, briskly marched towards the drugstore, procured her parcel and returned to the vehicle.

'You have to be bold,' she admonished Sandesh. 'You are going to be a man. If you were eighteen, I'd even make you do the driving.'

'Yes, madam.'

Lolita and Sandesh indulged in more romantic tête-à-tête during their sojourns to Khandala than at home, where activity was restricted to movies, drinking and sex. Each time they sampled a new picnic spot, it brought out the Romeo and Juliet in them. They went to the Duke's Nose, the Karla and Bhaja Caves, and the Bhushi Dam. They ate chocolate fudge. Sandesh even possessively asked Lolita if other guys visited her apartment. To this she replied, 'Have you ever seen anyone around, darling?' This made him feel honoured, for it was he whom the charismatic lady had chosen as her companion.

'Come, let's elope,' Lolita said to Sandesh.

When Sandesh figured out what that meant, he grew sullen.

'Why?' he asked his girlfriend.

'Because you turn me on more than my husband.'

Sandesh pondered over this and was flattered. He said nothing while still sober, but after the scotch had inebriated him, he slipped his hand into Lolita's and boisterously asked, 'When do we elope?'

'Tomorrow,' said Lolita, equally drunk. 'We'll get married and live together and have a baby.'

'What about Tanu?'

'Oh, her daddy will take care of her.'

They laughed.

Lolita's next act astounded Sandesh. Without provocation, she took off the twenty-two carat gold chain she was wearing and put it around his neck.

'Never remove it,' she instructed him. 'Think of it as my *nishaan*.'

'I love you.'

As fond as he was of machines, Sandesh took Lolita's off-the-cuff remark about driving her car all too seriously. On one of their weekend drives to Khandala, he tremulously broached the subject.

'Madam,' he said as he bit his nails.

'Yes, darling?'

'Will you teaching me driving?'

'Okay. But you've got to be eighteen.'

'*Gaand maro*. If policeman is catching, we are putting 100 bucks note in his hand.'

'Corruption!'

'Whole world is corruption.'

A lascivious idea came to Lolita just then. They were at the Tungarli dam with almost no one in the vicinity.

'Open your fly,' Lolita said to Sandesh, kneading his crotch.

'Okay.'

A moment later, Sandesh sat next to his beloved in her Zen Carbon, indecently exposed. Lolita held his dick tightly in her hand and moved it with a jerk towards the left and then forwards.

'This is first gear,' she said.

'Ouch,' Sandesh shrieked. 'It is hurting.'

'Doesn't matter,' said Lolita. She next moved Sandesh's male organ backwards. 'Second gear.'

Then, again to the right and forwards.

'Third gear.'

Then backwards.

'Fourth gear.'

Then forwards.

'Top gear.'

Finally, Lolita gave Sandesh's equipment a painful tug that made him howl.

'Reverse gear.'

The first day's driving lesson at Lolita Motor Training School ended with the instructor wanking her pupil till her hands looked as if she'd dipped them in a bowl of yoghurt.

It was Darshan who saw Lolita's photo lying on the floor of the Royal Video Parlour. He picked it up, examined it and hid it in a drawer. The photo had slipped out of the newspaper Sandesh carried it in. Lolita had given it to him a few days ago as they sat in her sepia-coloured drawing room and drank.

'Only for you,' she had said.

'Thanks,' Sandesh replied, taking the photo from her hands and admiring it. Then he had put it inside a newspaper and had forgotten all about it.

The photo intrigued Darshan.

That evening, he stealthily followed Sandesh all the way to Jannat, maintaining a steady distance between them. The streets, as usual, were saturated with pedestrians. It was around 8 p.m. when Darshan saw his mate enter the building and he decided to await his return at a kiosk outside. Until midnight however, there was no trace of Sandesh. At half past 12, Darshan, who'd lost count of the number of cigarettes he'd smoked and the sachets of *gutkha* he'd emptied into his mouth, yawned and turned around to go back home. No sooner did he see Sandesh at the store the next morning than he confronted him.

'I saw you going into madam's building last night,' said Darshan.

'So? I had to deliver a DVD.'

'It doesn't take four hours. Come on. Out with the truth.'

Sandesh laughed, took Darshan aside, put his arm around the latter's shoulder and gave him the low-down.

'Madam and I are having an affair,' he began, and went on to give his covetous co-worker the A to Z of their clandestine relationship. At the end of Sandesh's narration, all Darshan could do was gasp. He asked his buddy if he could accompany him to Lolita's apartment.

'To screw her?' Sandesh retorted.

However, when Sandesh checked with Lolita, she said she'd be glad to meet any of his friends, although she'd implored him to keep their association a closely guarded secret. Thus, on New Year's Eve, Sandesh and Darshan, with their trendy haircuts, dressed themselves in their smartest. They rang Lolita's ding-dong doorbell and were warmly welcomed.

'Here is small present for you,' said Sandesh to Lolita, as he gave her a gift-wrapped DVD. 'It is latest Bollywood film called *Dil Do.'*

'Naughty boy,' Lolita exclaimed, tweaking his cheek.

While Sandesh and Lolita sat together on the long sofa, Darshan was offered a seat on one of the smaller sofas. Sweat gathered on Sandesh's brow when, much to his discomfiture, Lolita put her arm around his shoulder and slipped her hand into his. All in Darshan's presence. The latter tried hard to concentrate on the *Indian Idol* show that was playing on Sony, but couldn't help casting sidelong glances to investigate what Sandesh and Lolita were up to: were they going to kiss?

After a round of drinks, a frowning, scowling Kamalabai served memsaab and her odd guests their dinner.

'You're lucky,' Darshan whispered into Sandesh's ear after the hullabaloo of the midnight hour died down and Sandesh frantically signalled to him to take his leave. 'You've got it all—sex, money and drink. I envy you.'

'Don't tell anyone.'

'No, boss. From today, you're my guru.'

Lolita flabbergasted Sandesh the next day by inviting one of her own girlfriends over while he was around. First, the doorbell startled him because it never rang when *he* was in the apartment. Then Lolita shocked him further because she knew who was at the door.

'Hi, Manisha,' she said as the door opened. 'Happy New Year! Do come in.'

Manisha's familiarity with the set-up made it evident to Sandesh that she'd been to Lolita's apartment a number of times before. She reeked of Evening in Paris, wore indigo-coloured nail polish on her fingernails and toenails and her boobs were larger than Lolita's. The three of them sat down with Lolita and Sandesh on the long sofa once again, with her arms around his shoulders and her hand in his, while Manisha sat on the small sofa at right angles. Drinks were served after Lolita introduced her friends to each other. Two pegs later Lolita and Manisha bickered in chaste English. The quarrel reached a crescendo with Manisha gulping down her drink, getting up and walking out in a huff, slamming the door.

Sandesh looked askance at Lolita.

'The bitch wants to sleep with you,' said Lolita, putting a cigarette to her lips and asking Sandesh to light it. 'And I said no. Her hubby, like mine, is in the merchant navy.'

'But I am ready,' laughed Sandesh, flattered. 'How much she is paying?'

'You male prostitute!'

By the time Lolita and Sandesh began to have their lovers' quarrels, which were often bellicose, their romance was a year old. Lolita had grown so accustomed to Sandesh's presence in her life that if chores at the store kept him back, as they occasionally did, she felt no qualms in calling him up late in the night and throwing a fit. It was a mixture of possession and love.

'So Mr Roadside Romeo, are you dating a younger woman?' she would drunkenly ask. 'How come I have to spend the evening minus your sexy company?'

Such scenes embarrassed Sandesh so much, especially because there were others around who could eavesdrop, that he simply hung up on her saying, 'I will call you later.' But this tormented Lolita all the more and she buzzed him over and over again, and each time Sandesh had no option but to rudely disconnect the line. Yet when he trekked to her apartment the next day, they hugged as if on a dance floor and parted their lips and kissed (with Lolita's lipstick all over Sandesh's mouth), all animosity was forgotten and they became 'friends' again.

Or they fought over the issue of protection. To Lolita, Sandesh's use of flavoured rubbers impeded her enjoyment of the forbidden fruit. Not once did he volunteer to copulate without a condom. His obduracy perplexed her. Why was the teenager so obstinate? Lolita decided to thrash it out of him.

'You think I am a woman of easy virtue,' she began, as they sipped their respective drinks and passed around a single cigarette. It was still early evening. 'You think I sleep around and have AIDS.'

Sandesh kept mum, but Lolita did not let him be. 'Let me tell you, I'm no slut,' she nagged. 'I did not even look at that friend of yours, what's his name, Darshan, when you brought him along to my house. I'm a one-man woman. Don't you see that?'

Here, Sandesh made the mistake of opening his trap.

'What about your husband?' he viciously remarked, smacking his lips.

This question infuriated Lolita and she raised her pitch.

'That's none of your business,' she screamed, and grew hysterical. 'You ungrateful wretch. You forget I've spent a fortune on you so far, you street beggar.'

Sandesh did not give Lolita an eye for an eye, but merely gloated over the missile he had just fired. A married woman who cheated on her husband was no Sita or Savitri. He'd heard the dialogue in scores of Hindi films.

Lolita dried her tears. She wiped her kohl-smudged eyes with a handkerchief. 'You know, you are the only man in my life right now,' she told Sandesh. 'I don't know too many people in this city anyway. This isn't Calcutta.'

'I am not here during daytime to see who is coming and who is going,' said Sandesh. He paused and hesitatingly added, 'I am also worried about *lafda* that is taking place if you getting pregnant.'

Lolita guffawed.

'That is my problem, not yours,' she quipped. 'So what if I get pregnant? Maybe I want your kid in my womb. If not, haven't you heard of abortions? Or of Mala D tablets? Tonight I insist you fuck me without a rubber.'

'No.'

'Then get out of my house right now.'

Sandesh rose and made for the door when Lolita summoned him back.

'I don't believe it,' she said, shaking her head, surprised that he took what she said so literally and was actually ready to leave. Then, after a while, 'Okay, forget it. Peace. We'll do it your way. I'll order a fresh supply of condoms tomorrow. Tonight, it'll have to be oral. In any case, I have my period.'

They hugged, throwing all caution to the winds. Kamalabai peeped in at that very moment to say she was leaving and her photographic memory captured the scene for keeps.

'Oh, shit!' Lolita swore. 'I did not realize she was still around. She purposely stayed back to snoop on us. The fucking voyeur.'

Sandesh, though mortified at being caught in a compromising position by Kamalabai of all people, in whom he saw his mother, nevertheless kept his cool. He was convinced no harm could befall him.

In bed that night, Lolita displayed her sanitary napkins for Sandesh. 'Next time, I'm going to send *you* to the chemist to buy them. Somehow, it's my turn-on.'

'Yes, madam.'

'Your cum is even more bitter than *karela*,' Lolita said, spitting out the semen Sandesh ejaculated into her mouth. He did not press for a condom when they had oral sex. 'How about mixing some sugar in it?'

What neither of them knew was that Kamalabai had decided to sleep in Tanu's room that night. The maid rose at dawn only to find Lolita and Sandesh huddled up under the same quilt. Her photographic memory took in the scene once again and stored it in the album of her imagination.

Kamalabai left before Lolita and Sandesh awoke. Menstrual blood stained the Fabindia bedcovers on which they slept. An early morning telephone call startled Lolita out of her wits. She took the cordless and went into Tanu's room, returning five minutes later.

'Wake up, darling,' she ordered Sandesh. 'It's an emergency. My husband is coming home tonight. Disappear and don't show up until I call to say the coast is clear.'

'Yes madam,' Sandesh yawned, rubbing his eyes.

Aroop rang the doorbell as if he were a fire engine. He held his wife by the hips, tossed her into the air and kissed her on the navel. He then took Tanu into his arms and smothered her with his hugs. He tipped the security personnel of Jannat Rs 500 for bringing up his luggage in the service lift. He pried open one of the bags without even taking off his shoes and showered Lolita with presents: dresses, perfumes, wristwatches, Walkmans, Mont Blanc pens, shoes, slippers, earrings, nose pins, shawls, sunglasses, handbags, chocolates, whiskies, dry fruits and even a battery-operated hair remover. To little Tanu he gave a Barbie doll taller than her in height. He did not forget Kamalabai either, and for her he had brought a portable TV set. For the flat, Aroop carried an especially designed bronze replica of his ship, The Golden Anchor, and placed it on the centre table.

Aroop's joy knew no bounds at being back amidst his family after close to a year. His parents flew in from Jamshedpur that very day to see their granddaughter Tanu, whom they had never seen before. There was jubilation and merriment in the household and that night Aroop threw a gala party for an assortment of guests that included some Bollywood personalities like Govinda, on whom a dance number was once shot aboard his ship. (It was a song called *Goodgoodi* where Govinda tickled shapely item girls on their wafer-thin waists and impelled them to dance.) Lolita busied herself in the kitchen all day, although Aroop had made up his mind to order food from the Taj.

At the height of the party, close to midnight, Aroop was so tipsy that he swung as if on a ship. Lolita, who looked gorgeous in a black dress with silver stars, danced with Govinda who told her it was an honour to have her in his arms. It was dawn by the time the last of the guests started their BMWs and Porsches to leave. Though sex was the topmost priority on Aroop's mind, the party had left him too exhausted to make love to Lolita and to top it all off, the excess alcohol hindered his performance. His sexual grunts were soon replaced by noisy snores as he fell into a dreamless slumber. This suited Lolita, who had gotten so used to Sandesh's touch and the feel of his manhood in her body that she couldn't bear the sight of another man in her bed. Besides, she was afraid that Aroop would discover her telltale vaginal ruptures. The next night the tables were reversed. Guilty at cold-shouldering her husband, Lolita went out of her way to cajole him into sexual submission. 'Come, darling, get on top of me,' she cooed into his ear.

'I'm tired, my love,' Aroop cried. 'Anyway, what's the hurry? I'm here for a whole month.'

'What?' Lolita exclaimed. 'A month?'

This meant her proletarian lover wouldn't be able to visit the apartment for thirty long days and this was a thought that filled our lady with dread.

Noticing a hint of shock in her voice, Aroop sheepishly asked, 'Why, darling, aren't you glad I'm here?'

'Oh. Of course. You don't know how lonely I am without you.'

Aroop's days in Jannat soon assumed an air of monotony. He had the whole day to himself with nowhere to go. In the evenings, he and Lolita sat in their lounge bar and drank. Sometimes they went out to swanky restaurants for dinner and at other times they peregrinated to Khandala. Here too

Lolita was at her wits' end because the picnics reminded her of Sandesh whose presence in her life was temporarily put on hold.

Observing that something in his wife's life was amiss, but not quite knowing what, and all attempts at coaxing it out of her being futile, Aroop busied himself in his paperwork. He sat at his laptop almost throughout the day and often late into the night. When Lolita asked what preoccupied him, he told her he was exploring various business propositions that would allow him to quit the merchant navy and live with his family. This made Lolita sulk.

'Don't quit the merchant navy yet,' she advised her husband. 'The money's phenomenal and both of us need our space.'

Aroop wasn't slow to notice that Lolita disappeared for long stretches most evenings, leaving him and little Tanu to fend for themselves with Kamalabai's aid. She'd devised a bevy of excuses to justify her absence. 'I'm driving down to the grocery store,' she would say or, 'I'm going to pay my electricity bill.'

Kamalabai, who'd developed a loathing for Lolita, came into the living room one day when her mistress wasn't around and chatted with her master about life at sea.

She rocked Tanu's cradle and assured her saab that his baby girl would grow up to be a fine woman.

Lolita took the evenings off to escape the sense of entrapment she felt when her husband was at home. She buzzed Sandesh at the Royal Video Parlour, or went to see him personally when the others weren't around and asked him to meet her at a serene spot (known as Lovers' Paradise) at the Dadar Parsi Colony. He complied, and they cuddled up in her Zen Carbon, holding hands and smooching. Lolita folded Sandesh's ears like a *paan* and put one into her mouth.

'Let's elope,' she said to him again, pressing his crotch.

'I am ready.'

A kiosk nearby sold Chinese food. The flavours teased their nostrils.

'Would you like a plate of chicken lollipops?' Lolita asked Sandesh, giving him his weekly allowance.

'No. A plate of Chicken Lolita.'

'Then touch my boobs.'

Sandesh noticed that Lolita's breath smelt less of alcohol than usual when her husband was around. He lit a cigarette.

'What about drinks?' he asked her.

'I can't drink so much when my husband is there.'

'When he is going?'

'Ten more days.'

'I am counting.'

'Me too.'

'*Ati kya Khandala?*'

'Sure, once he leaves.'

On the eve of Aroop's departure, Lolita merely expressed a token sadness. 'Come back soon,' she told her husband, without actually meaning it, as she helped him pack his bags. 'And thanks for all the gifts.'

No sooner did Aroop's official car take off for the airport than Lolita made an urgent call to Sandesh.

'Leave whatever you are doing and get here at once,' she said. 'He's gone.'

'I am coming.'

As soon as Sandesh arrived, Lolita showed him all the presents Aroop had brought for her.

'No present for me?' he bluntly asked.

Lolita thought for a moment, and gave him Aroop's replica of The Golden Anchor which he'd sentimentally kept on the mantelpiece.

'For you,' she said.

Though Sandesh regarded the replica a worthless gift, he accepted it out of politeness. Why couldn't Lolita give him some of the electronic items her sailor husband had brought for her from different corners of the globe?

Kamalabai entered the living room while Lolita left to fix their drinks and taunted Sandesh in Marathi. 'Why didn't you turn up for a whole month while my saab was around?' she asked. Sandesh kept mum. He reported this to Lolita, who swore it was about time she showed her inquisitive maid the door.

After drinks and dinner, Sandesh stayed over that night to compensate for the continence that had been imposed on him for a whole month. As they lay naked in bed and stimulated one another, Sandesh remarked that he thought of Lolita as nothing less than a wife.

Another year passed. Aroop made his appearance once every three months, but did not linger on in the city longer than a week. Sandesh popped in at the flat everyday and stayed with Lolita half the night before riding back home on a Hero Honda motorbike that he had acquired. They now resolved to have sex every alternate night instead of daily. The raw prurience they initially felt for each other was replaced, over their two years together, by tenderness and Tanu shaped up well under the matronly care of Kamalabai. Life on the forty-ninth floor of Jannat fell into a pattern, with Sandesh becoming a fixture. He was so much a part of the household that sometimes he even went to the windy terrace to fly a kite, or to the clubhouse to swim.

Sandesh assumed position 69 in bed that night and savoured the secretions that oozed from Lolita's pussy while he fingered her cunt and transferred his betel spit into her mouth, sipping her milk before mounting her both vaginally and anally *without a condom*. He could never have known that it was the last time he was making love to her. She did not know it either and it was a happy coincidence that the high voltage sex they had that night distinguished it from the ordinary. There was much after play too, with our lovers continuing to paw each other even after climaxing to round off their escapade into a sort of denouement.

When Sandesh landed up at the flat the next evening, at around seven, it was locked. The Zen Carbon wasn't in its parking lot and he was in a quandary. Where was Lolita? What emergency could have suddenly cropped up in the last twelve hours or so to compel her to leave without sounding him off? He decided to check with the security personnel down below, most of whom were on backslapping terms with him. But they too were in the dark. None of them claimed to have seen her start her car and leave.

Sandesh returned to the Royal Video Parlour, speculating that some pressing exigency may have triggered Lolita's abrupt departure and that she would be back soon. He checked at the flat every other day, but it was always the same story: the door was locked; the Zen Carbon wasn't in the parking nook reserved for it; and when he dialled Lolita's number, no one answered.

Sandesh grew agitated and began to look like a jilted, unshaven lover. At the store, he invariably asked Darshan and Aniket if there were phone calls for him, sickening them with his query. Since Darshan knew of his affair, Sandesh took him out to a beer bar one evening and narrated the story of Lolita's disappearance. Darshan heard him out patiently, but all he said by way of reply was, 'Don't worry, be happy.'

Eventually, Sandesh was so forlorn that he went to Jannat a dozen times a day, praying that Lolita would be there to take him into her arms. But all was in vain. Haunted by memories of her, Sandesh chucked his job at the Royal Video Parlour and began to work for Pigeon Couriers instead. Such was his anguish that he tore up Lolita's photograph and sold the gold chain she had so ardently put round his neck. He gave the money he earned from it to his relative in Parel to send to his mother back in the village to atone for the money he had stolen. He even looked for a substitute aunty, for life was unthinkable without someone to pamper him.

Lolita's exit also deprived Sandesh of the pocket money he was accustomed to, so his Hero Honda gathered dust in a corner of her building for want of fuel.

Precisely two months after she had vamoosed, Lolita reappeared. It was Darshan who called Sandesh at Pigeon Couriers to report that Lolita had dropped in at the Royal Video Parlour that morning, looking for him. She had parted with her mobile number. Sandesh left the customer he was attending to and stomped down the stairs to give his beloved a call.

'Sweetheart, meet me at Lovers' Paradise, Dadar Parsi Colony, in fifteen minutes,' Lolita panted.

'Okay,' Sandesh replied.

When he reached there an hour later, he found that Lolita and Tanu were seated in her Zen Carbon and Lolita was fanning herself with a Japanese fan. She opened the front door for him, put Tanu on her lap and then placed her on Sandesh's lap once he'd entered the car and shut the door. They looked like a family. Sandesh sniffed the air, permeated by the fragrance of booze. They drove in silence and Sandesh knew from the direction they took that the sailor's wife was navigating towards Khandala. All Lolita asked him during the journey was why he'd quit his job at the Royal Video Parlour. When he revealed that it was because *her* memories tormented him and that he'd go to Jannat twenty times a day to see if she was back, Lolita smiled. 'We're crazy about each other, aren't we?' she said.

The real news Lolita had to give Sandesh she withheld till they reached Khandala and parked at an isolated spot where, Tanu notwithstanding, they held hands and smooched and Lolita's mouth reeked of liquor. 'We've shifted to Goa,' Lolita said. 'And would you believe it, I drove all the way from there just to see you.'

Sandesh swallowed the lump in his throat. He was speechless. Seeing the dejected expression on his face, Lolita burst into tears as little Tanu wondered why her mother sobbed. Sandesh had a trying time fighting back his own tears.

After Lolita wiped her eyes and lit a cigarette, she informed Sandesh that the flat in Jannat was to be given out on rent, so there was no question of going there one last time.

'It all happened *achanak*,' Lolita explained. 'My husband arrived that morning and said we were leaving that very day. I had no time to even call you.'

Lolita then opened her Versace handbag, took out her chequebook and wrote out a cheque in Sandesh's name for Rs 10,000. 'It's a bearer cheque,' she cautioned him, 'so make sure no one gets hold of it. It's a gift for you and you alone, for the good time you gave me.'

Sandesh accepted the cheque, his eyes nearly popping out at the five-figure amount.

'Thank you, madam,' he said, both happy and sad at the same time.

They had lunch at a wayside café that they always patronized during their *Ati kya Khandala* jaunts. Then they drove back to Bombay, little Tanu once again in Sandesh's lap.

Lolita dropped Sandesh off at the exact spot where she had picked him up in the morning. Handing Tanu over to her mom, he opened the door and got out, but Lolita summoned him back in.

'One final kiss,' she pleaded, dumping Tanu in the back seat.

'Okay.'

Sandesh hopped into the Zen Carbon, and again, unperturbed by her daughter's presence, Lolita and he indulged in a long and leisurely lip-lock. Then Sandesh alighted from the car for the last time in his life, but not before posing Lolita a question:

'Madam, when we are meeting again?'

'Soon,' said Lolita. 'I promise.'

She drove off and Sandesh couldn't say whether what had happened was for real or merely a dream.

FIVE
Vendetta

Kamalabai, who'd developed a loathing for Lolita, came into the living room one day when her mistress wasn't around, and chatted with her master about life at sea.

'Saheb?'

'Yes, Kamalabai?'

'How does one *contak* you when you are away?'

This, of course, she asked in Marathi.

Aroop guffawed. 'Why, Kamalabai?'

'No, just in case of emergency.'

'It's simple, Kamalabai,' Aroop said. 'Take bus number 66 from Dadar TT and go to the last stop. It's called Ballard Pier. My shipping company, Mariners' Compass International, is on the first floor of a building just next to the bus stop. Leave a letter for me with my name on the envelope and it will reach me.'

'Saheb, I don't know English.'

'But I know Hindi and now I have learned Marathi too. You can write in Marathi, can't you?'

'Yes, saheb. That is a good idea. I will write to you in Marathi.'

This strange exchange intrigued Aroop. What did his maid really have in mind? He decided to report his conversation with

Kamalabai to Lolita as soon as she returned from her 'evening walk'. However, Lolita was so late that day that when she finally opened the front door with her house key and said, 'Sorry, darling, hope you did not miss me,' the matter completely slipped her hubby's mind. He fixed a whisky for himself and a Martini for Lolita. After a takeaway meal of rogan josh, dal tadka and butter naan, they settled down in bed to see the film *Dil Do* which, if recalled, was given to Lolita as a present by Sandesh.

But Kamalabai meant business. Weeks after Aroop had left, she went from pillar to post looking for someone—anyone—to whom she could dictate her letter addressed to her master. She began with people in the vicinity, such as the security personnel of Jannat, all of whom ridiculed her request.

'Please,' she begged them.

'Have you gone mad?' they asked her. 'Why do you want to write to him? Are you having an affair or what?'

Retaliating with a volley of abuses, Kamalabai then went after the khaki-uniformed postman whose beat brought him to Jannat twice a day. In Hindi films, postmen, or *dakiyas* as they were called, wrote letters on behalf of the illiterate. But the postman too brushed her aside, spurning her request. After this she tried her luck with some of the building's numerous drivers. When that failed, an exasperated Kamalabai accosted collegians from the nearby Ruia and Ruparel colleges, whose friends lived in Jannat. One of them, a girl in her late teens, took pity on her and agreed to write Kamalabai's letter, which she dictated in Marathi, but implored the young lady to translate into English. However, no sooner did she pen the first few paragraphs than the contents of Kamalabai's letter so scandalized the young woman that she returned the pen and paper. 'Sorry, bai,' she said. 'I can't write this type of letter. Please ask someone else.'

In the end, it was the dhobi's son, who did not take to his father's profession in this age of washing machines but did his BA (English) from Siddharth College instead, who came to Kamalabai's rescue and took down her letter in toto.

This is what the letter said:

Dear Saheb,

Namaste. Money is not everything. Leave your job and come back soon. Stay in Mumbai with memsaheb and Tanu. Mumbai is big mahanagari. You can find job in Mumbai. You must not stay away from memsaheb. Even Bhagwan Ram taking his Mrs Sita with him to banwas. If you don't want to come back to Mumbai, then take memsaheb with you where you going.

Saheb, forgiving me, small mouth, big talk. But I have to tell you that memsaheb is doing dirty things behind your back. I feel very shameful to say all this, but I having to say it. It is my duty. I have eaten your namak and it is my duty to saving your home. One young boy from nearby DVD store is coming to your house everyday and memsaheb and he are doing what pati and patni are doing in bed. I seeing with my own two eyes, saheb, and I feeling very bad for you. It is not young boy's fault. It is memsaheb who is calling him to house everyday and pilaoing him daru. Then they are playing dirty CD and going into bedroom and closing door from inside.

Sometimes they are not closing because Tanu is in next
room, crying. Saheb, everyday jamadar is finding nirodh
in kachra peti. I cannot stay in your house any more. You
please finding another bai. Take memsaheb with you
where you going. Even Bhagwan Ram taking his Mrs Sita
with him to banwas. Memsaheb is in jawani so if you not
sleeping with her, she is looking for other mans. You come
back to Mumbai, saheb, as soon as you getting my letter.
Don't tell memsaheb I writing you letter.

Yours,
Kamalabai.

On finishing her dictation in Marathi, which the dhobi's son
faithfully took down in English, fancying himself a stenographer
in a multinational, Kamalabai gave the chap a further task. She
told him to buy an envelope from the paanwallah's (for which
she gave him a few coins), write her master's name on it (for
which she passed him his visiting card) and then deliver it to
his office in Ballard Pier, whose address was naturally on the
visiting card.

'Take bus number 66,' Kamalabai instructed the dhobi's son,
remembering the directions that Aroop had given her.

Kamalabai's letter reached Aroop. Initially, it did not shock
him. 'Lolita and her ideology,' he swore to himself, attributing
the allegations in his maid's letter to Lolita's Marxism and
socialism. Why did she marry me and not some Santhal tribal,
he asked himself for the first time since their marriage. His
next impulse was to stealthily look around to ensure no one on

the vessel was close at hand to snoop and read the contents of the letter. The sailors were busy with myriad mechanical tasks on the ship, such as oiling and cleaning, which was about the only work most of them did and for which they were paid hefty salaries.

'Sengupta, everything okay?' some of them shouted out to Aroop, as they noticed his colour and expression change when he read the letter that was delivered to him by an orderly only a few minutes ago. But Aroop did not respond. He kept rereading the letter, transported miles away from the Dead Sea where the vessel had docked.

Pulling himself together, Aroop went into damage control mode. Never did his job bring on such a sense of claustrophobia before. When he would have liked to be by himself and take a long walk, he was confined to his vessel, with his co-workers all about him. In the circumstances, all he could do was ensconce himself in his cabin, with the 'DO NOT DISTURB' sign hanging outside his door.

Aroop's mind wandered. Could he take Kamalabai's words at face value? Could she be exaggerating to settle scores with Lolita, whom she clearly did not like? On the other hand, he could not ignore the letter either. It wasn't Lolita's infidelity that bothered Aroop, for he wasn't the jealous kind, as much as the scandal her misdemeanours might have caused in the neighbourhood. Who was this DVD guy anyway? Did the Vakils and the Chaudhuris and the Ganjawallas and the D'Costas of Jannat see Sandesh come and go, and make him the subject of gossip? Aroop feared he wouldn't be able to live in the skyscraper any more and would have to move house without delay. For how could he face the neighbours and the servants and the drivers and the watchmen of the building? They would call him a cuckold.

The next morning, Aroop SOS'd his headquarters in New York City.

'Need an urgent transfer from base at Bombay, India,' he urged his bosses.

'Why?'

'Personal reasons.'

'Where do you want to be stationed?'

'How about Goa?'

'Let's see. We'll call you back in half an hour.'

In precisely half an hour, Aroop's bosses from Mariners' Compass International called to inform him that since his service record was impeccable, his request had been acceded to. He was granted a transfer to Vasco da Gama, Goa, a city close to the Mormugao harbour. He was free to take up his new assignment any time within the next fortnight. However, the company would give him no more than three days' leave to fly to Bombay and move house.

'Thank you, sirs,' Aroop said to his bosses as he ended the conference call and made instant plans to sail to the nearest airport and catch a flight to Bombay that very day.

'Great posting, Sengupta,' some of his co-sailors enviously said when he told them about his transfer. Goa was a fun place where all of them would have liked to be. It had an abundance of F-things, as one of them put it: feni, fish, firangs and fucking.

On arriving at Bombay's Chhatrapati Shivaji International Airport (formerly known as Sahar Airport), Aroop directed his staff car driver to take him not to Jannat, but to Packers and Shifters at Worli, whom he briefed that his flat, teeming with furniture and effects, had to be emptied in less than half a day.

'I don't care how you do it,' said Aroop. 'But do it you must.'

'Sure, sir.'

Lolita knew the instant her husband abruptly landed at home and announced their departure to Goa that something was fishy. She sensed Aroop's aloofness when he rang the doorbell—very different from his fire engine style of earlier—and stepped into the flat. No hugs and kisses for either her or Tanu. Her husband, Lolita noted with a sense of panic, never appeared more businesslike than he did that morning.

'Transferred to Goa,' Aroop nonchalantly said to Lolita, 'and we've got to be there by nightfall.'

Kamalabai was in the flat too, and Aroop's disposition told her everything: He'd received her letter and come home as a consequence; that he was acting on her advice and taking away his wife and daughter; that she would, from tomorrow, be out of a job and have to look for another. The maid, at the end of the day, was no halfwit.

As for Lolita, there were pulls and counter pulls. She detested being snatched away from the lifestyle she had grown used to. At the same time, she couldn't jeopardize her marriage. She resolved, then and there, to do as her husband implored.

Meanwhile, there was pell-mell in the Sengupta household. Noisy workmen took their possessions downstairs in the service lift, which was as big as a minivan, and loaded them into waiting trucks. From the window of their house, they resembled a column of ants. A couple of fragile articles, such as a marble-topped table bought at a Sotheby's auction, were damaged in the bargain, but neither Aroop nor Lolita were in a mood to reprimand the workers. Kamalabai wept as she held Tanu in her arms. The flat on the forty-ninth floor of Jannat was emptied out in an unbelievably short time and resembled a bird's nest from which all the chicks had flown away. The truckers ignited their engines and took off, with Aroop and his family following them in their Zen Carbon.

'The first thing I'm going to do when we reach Goa is chuck this *khatara* car and get us a new one,' Aroop said while driving. Lolita thought of all the times she had had in the car with Sandesh while her husband was away.

'Okay,' said Lolita. 'Suit yourself.'

The drive to Goa, via Panvel and Mahad, would take over twelve hours, but Aroop decided he would drive through the night, like truck drivers and bus drivers, rather than stop to rest at a wayside inn by the highway. Lolita slept through most of the journey with Tanu in her lap, or in her baby seat at the back.

'It isn't a good idea to fall asleep when you're seated next to the driver,' Aroop admonished Lolita. 'It tempts the driver to doze off himself.'

But the packing and moving had exhausted Lolita so much that she could scarcely heed her husband's advice. Each time he ordered her to wake up, her eyelids popped open, only to close a few minutes later. Aroop could swear his own eyes had drowsily shut at the wheel a couple of times.

When twilight illuminated the sky, and birds shrieked, and the air smelt of the sea, the Senguptas knew they were in Goa with its abundance of greenery. They drove past Mapusa, a town in north Goa, before taking a detour to the right and heading for Vasco da Gama, named after the famous explorer who visited Goa in the fifteenth century.

A bungalow with a sprawling lawn was kept ready for Aroop and his family by Mariners' Compass International. The people from Packers and Shifters, who landed at the address shortly after the Senguptas, provided them with an additional service free of cost: they helped them set up the house. This was a daunting task, considering all the furniture was custom-made to suit their apartment in Jannat. But Packers and Shifters were true professionals. Within a day, the bare bungalow with an eerie echo was transformed into a picturesque dwelling. Instead of a maid, Aroop decided on a manservant, taking special precautions to verify the fellow's antecedents before employing him. His name was Thambi, he was in his fifties, greying and toothless, and was a former merchant navy cook. He was so resourceful that he found Aroop a customer for his Zen Carbon the moment he let him know that he wished to sell it. The buyer was a Goan fisherman whose mouth reeked of liquor. However, just as he was about to drive away with his new purchase, Lolita sobbed and begged her husband not to sell the Zen Carbon. 'I'm so fond of it,' she wept, causing Aroop to relent, even though he had to eat crow before the Goan fisherman.

The next day, the Senguptas bought a sparkling white Skoda Octavia Automatic, recently introduced in India, for Aroop. With it came a free mobile phone.

'She'll suit our bungalow,' Aroop tersely said in the showroom, as his credit card was swiped. Lolita squirmed.

She did not like cars to be referred to as 'she'. A silence had grown between husband and wife which neither knew how to penetrate. Both privately considered divorce, but gave up on the idea, the interest of their little daughter being paramount.

Aroop proceeded to take a long vacation against his bosses' wishes, ostensibly to set up house in Vasco da Gama, but in truth to keep a watchful eye on his wife's movements (which, naturally, he did not tell her). At times he even thought of resigning from his job. He chided himself for being lax and giving his wife too much freedom. He recalled the *Manu Smriti*, the laws of Manu, which curtailed the liberty of women in order to not turn them into libertines.

So suspicious had Aroop grown of Lolita that he hardly left her in the house alone. He accompanied her wherever she went, making the two of them resemble a pair of chaser pigeons. The Skoda, unlike the Zen Carbon, wasn't easy to drive in narrow lanes and bylanes, nor was it easy to park, even in a Portuguese city as sparsely populated as Vasco da Gama. The result of this was that barely a week after its purchase the car already had its first dent.

'Like the dent in our relationship,' Aroop cryptically remarked to Lolita while scrutinizing the damage done to his fender by a passing motorcycle, whose owner, a young man is his twenties, Aroop managed to slap in a fit of road rage. The remark set Lolita thinking, as usual. Though she had a strong hunch that her husband had gotten to know of her licentiousness, she wasn't entirely sure, for he hadn't broached the subject yet in so many words. He was solely responsible for the dent, to the car that is, because Lolita never drove when her husband was around. 'Man's job,' she said, when Aroop asked her if she'd like to experiment with the Skoda. 'Besides, I can't manoeuvre *big* cars.'

Aroop wondered if her statement had any sexual connotation.

Though every passing day made it clearer to Lolita that her husband was aware of her misdemeanours, she decided not to say a word, in self-defence or otherwise, till he made the first move. In Sandesh's language, one might say, Lolita resolved not to take any *pangas* with her husband. Their strained relations notwithstanding, one thing that united them without fail every evening were spirits. Both of them were so addicted, nay accustomed, to their evening drink that life without it seemed impossible. As they sat in their lounge bar from 8 p.m. onwards, which was an exact replica of their bar in Jannat, and sipped their respective drinks, Aroop, with his several large glasses of whisky and Lolita with her several Martinis, they became garrulous. Yet both husband and wife made that extra effort to restrict their conversation to pleasantries and trivialities, and not touch upon what threatened to wreck their married lives. This worked well for the first few weeks of their stay in Vasco da Gama, for the setting, the environment and the ambience were still unfamiliar to them. A television set came to their rescue, as it does in most Indian households, for it fills the silences and communication gaps with its cranky soaps. Lolita and Aroop, each with a remote in their hands, constantly surfed channels and watched nothing in particular. Lolita preferred the DVD player to the television. In a way, it was linked to the memory of Sandesh. And for that very reason, Aroop never once switched on the DVD player.

Then one day, as they drank in the mellow light and little Tanu played with her Barbie dolls, of which she possessed quite a collection, Aroop blurted out what was giving him sleepless nights.

'You cheated on me,' he cried out, stunning Lolita with the directness of his words which hit her like a stone thrown during a riot. No longer could she enjoy the benefit of doubt. It was crystal clear to her now that the cat was out of the bag. Two possibilities unfolded before her at that very moment: admit or deny. She chose the former.

'It wasn't serious,' she replied, unable to look her husband in the eye. 'Just a body thing while you were away.'

'With riff-raff?'

'Riff-raff are here today, gone tomorrow. No strings attached. You wouldn't have liked for me to be involved with a Prem Ahuja, would you?'

This reference was to the famous Nanavati case of the 1960s.

'That gives me an idea,' Aroop said, tears streaming down his face. 'Like Commander Kawas Nanavati, I must pump bullets into the fellow who dared to touch my wife.'

'Forgive him. It wasn't his fault. Besides, he's just a boy.'

'I am ashamed of you. You have brought disgrace and dishonour to the family.'

'I'm sorry. I promise it'll never happen again. We've got to make our marriage work, at least for Tanu's sake.'

'It's you who broke the sacred vows of marriage.'

'I'm sorry. How many times must I apologize?'

'No amount of apology is enough, you adulterous bitch.'

'Please don't be abusive.'

'What about you? You abused me by fucking some roadside Romeo!'

Here the exchange momentarily came to a halt. When it resumed a few minutes later, during which time they refilled their glasses, Lolita said, 'Darling, tell me one thing. Did you never sleep around all those months you were at sea?'

'Never. I swear to God.'

'But they say a sailor has a wife in every port.'

'That's just a myth. Romantic bullshit to glamorize life in the navy.'

'I've heard it said of naval men, that they're also navel men,' she said, drawing a pun on the word 'navel' and 'naval', thus referring to both the body part as well as men in the navy who were after sex.

'Stop trivializing the issue. What you've done is a crime entirely unforgivable. Keep that in mind.'

'I was only trying to ease the tension by cracking a joke.'

'The tension will never ease, as long as you are my wife.'

'Divorce me then.'

'I wish I could. But as you said, Tanu will suffer. We should never have had a child.'

'You know what? You are making a mountain out of a molehill. I've already told you what happened wasn't serious. I've put it behind. Can't you do the same?'

'Not until I've had an extramarital affair myself. That'll make us quits, won't it?'

'Go ahead and have one, then. I promise you, I won't mind. If you want to experiment further, we can even have an open relationship, like Kabir and Protima Bedi. I read about it in Protima's book, *Time Pass*.'

'So that you can get every Tom, Dick and Harry to fuck you?'

'Shut up. You are being abusive again. Let's end this conversation and go to bed.'

'I don't think I can ever sleep with you for the rest of my life.'

'Okay, if that's what you want. I'll have to resign myself to a sexless life.'

Lolita rose and went to Tanu's room, who had by now been sent to bed, to make sure she was comfortably asleep. She missed the services of a maid who could look after the baby. She knew that Aroop's resolve to not have a maid was a sort of punishment that was inflicted on her. If there was no maid, Lolita would have to devote her entire day to Tanu, which would leave her with little time for diversions. Covering her daughter with a soft cotton sheet and singing her a lullaby, although she was already asleep, Lolita went to her bedroom and found that Aroop too had crashed. She lay next to him and attempted to fall asleep, but in vain. She tossed about in bed all night, turning from side to side and at one point, switched on the table lamp and went to the medicine chest to pop a sleeping pill into her mouth. But it did not help. The booze, though she was used to it, made Lolita's head heavy. She wondered if she was beginning to suffer from full-scale insomnia. Suddenly, she felt like her marriage was stifling her. She wanted her old life back.

The next day Lolita drove to Bombay in her Zen Carbon to see Sandesh, with Tanu accompanying her. Aroop had received an SOS from his headquarters to fly to Delhi, even though he was on leave, to interview merchant navy recruits who had just graduated from INS Shivaji and other training institutes. He caught an early morning Jet Airways flight from Dabolim airport, for which an executive class ticket was delivered to him at his doorstep. He would return to Goa, either later that evening or early next morning, depending on how many candidates he had to interview.

Lolita's ride to Bombay was a race against time. She had to reach the city, meet Sandesh, and dash back to Vasco da Gama before her husband was back home. If he arrived before her and found her missing with both the baby and the car, there would be hell to pay. As if what had already transpired wasn't bad enough! The decision to have Tanu in tow was thrust upon Lolita by circumstances. As she drove, she thought of Kamalabai in whose custody Tanu could always be safely kept, thereby liberating her from the fetters of motherhood. Yet she could never forgive Kamalabai for poisoning her husband's ears. Though Aroop never once revealed who it was that told on Lolita, she knew it was Kamalabai. For who else could it be? There were very few people who went up to the forty-ninth floor of Jannat.

Lolita returned to Goa in the wee hours, scarcely an hour before Aroop. She made it by the skin of her teeth. In the car she briefed Tanu not to say anything to Aroop. 'Don't tell daddy we went to Bombay, okay, sweety?' she cajoled her daughter, buying her giant-sized Cadbury bars.

Aroop's day in Delhi and the cheap-fare midnight flight back home exhausted him so much that he went to bed with his shoes on. When he awoke, he startled Lolita by announcing that he was off to Bombay.

'The flat in Jannat has to be sold or given out on rent,' he said, 'and I'm not coming back till I strike a deal.'

Lolita grew suspicious. Was property the only reason he was going to Bombay?

'May I accompany you?' Lolita asked.

'Why?' Aroop sarcastically remarked. 'To meet that urchin again?'

Lolita let it be. She had already received a couple of missed calls on her mobile and they were from Bombay. Did Sandesh intend to get her into more trouble?

Aroop dressed and took off for Bombay in his Skoda Octavia shortly after lunch.

'Drive cautiously,' Lolita said to him, as he left the driveway of their bungalow.

A short distance away from the bungalow, Aroop pulled over to the side to switch on his MP3 player. Most of his music was from Lolita's personal collection which, together with her DVDs and VCDs, had labels bearing the name and address of the Royal Video Parlour. Aroop noted down the address as if he were a sleuth. His reason for going to Bombay was, no doubt, to attend to the flat in Jannat whose value ran into crores. However, to fix the fellow who had had an illicit relationship with his wife was also on his agenda.

Aroop stayed at the Royal Bombay Yacht Club and spent the first few days in Bombay meeting estate agents who promised him the most lucrative deals. He had the option to live in his own flat in Jannat and operate from there, but decided against it as the flat stank of Lolita's treachery. He constantly received calls on his Blackberry from his estate agents and was so floored by their offers that he couldn't decide whether to sell the flat or merely give it out on lease.

'Its value is sure to go up even more,' some agents told him, 'so it's best that you hold on to it for now.'

Other agents advised him to sell the property outright, as no one was likely to offer him more than Deepak Matkar, a shady politician who proposed to buy it for 10 crores.

'But I don't want to sell it to some shady politician,' Aroop protested. The agents laughed him off as impractical.

On his fourth day in Bombay, Aroop walked into the Royal Video Parlour as inconspicuously as he could. Ashok Jadhav, who was alone in the store, obsequiously greeted him.

'Yes, sir? What can I do for you? How may I help you?'

'I'm First Officer Sengupta,' Aroop replied in a clipped accent. 'I believe my wife, Mrs Lolita Sengupta, is a member of your video library.'

Ashok Jadhav grew even more ingratiating upon hearing Lolita's name.

'She is one of our most esteemed customers,' he said. 'But where is she? I haven't seen her for quite some time.'

'Oh, she's away at her mother's place in Calcutta.'

'Any good news?'

It took Aroop a second or two to figure out what Ashok Jadhav meant.

'Oh no, nothing of the sort,' he laughed. 'We have one child already and that's more than enough.'

'You are absolutely right,' Ashok Jadhav quipped. 'Small family is best family. Family planning is good thing. Anyway, when is madam coming back?'

'In a couple of weeks, maybe. Meanwhile, she spoke so highly of your store that I was very tempted to check it out myself.'

'Treat it like your own shop, sir. Choose what you want and I will have it delivered to your address by one of my boys. You are still living in Jannat building, isn't that it?'

The reference to his *delivery boys* made Aroop flinch.

'Yes, we still live in Jannat,' he replied. 'But there's no need to deliver anything to our house. I'll pick what I want and pay you across the counter.'

'As you please, sir.'

'I'm in a hurry now,' said Aroop, looking at his watch. 'But I'll come back another time.'

'Yes, sir. Thank you for visiting the Royal Video Parlour and gracing our shop with your presence.'

Aroop left the store and sighed. Was this Ashok Jadhav as syrupy-sweet with all his customers? Or did Lolita's name do the trick? Maybe both master and servant had had it off with his nymphomaniac wife. The master he had encountered, but who was going to help him nab the servant? Aroop realized he would have to take Ashok Jadhav up on his offer after all and ask the man to have his dummy purchases delivered to him at his flat in Jannat. That would be a foolproof way to lure his wife's delinquent lover into his net and figure out for himself what the teenager possessed that he himself did not.

Aroop checked out of the Royal Bombay Yacht Club and moved back into his flat on the forty-ninth floor of Jannat. He wired his headquarters for indefinite leave, claiming he was suffering from a kidney infection. Lolita called him up on his Blackberry once, twice, thrice, even four times daily. 'Finish your business in Bombay and get back to Goa as quickly as possible,' she scolded him. 'Tanu is sick.' Lolita was very paranoid. She imagined terrible things happening in Bombay that would devastate them. Aroop, in turn, rarely called Lolita. The thought crossed his mind several times that his absence would instigate her to start another extramarital affair. But it was far more pressing to settle scores with that young vagabond. So obsessed was he with the idea of revenge, of vendetta, that he put his plans to rent or sell his flat on hold. On the back burner, so to speak.

'I've changed my mind and wish to keep the flat locked,' he said to brokers and estate agents who continued to pester him, so much so that more than once he thought of writing to his network provider to block their incoming calls or give him a new number. The walls of his flat, in which his wife spent so many sensuous nights with a tramp, which made her out to be like Kamasutra (or Kamatipura) women, mocked him. He took to rabid solo drinking, beginning as early as 5 o'clock every evening and going on until midnight, when he could hardly walk and often peed in his pants.

Days passed before Aroop was able to bring himself to drive to the Royal Video Parlour for the second time. This time, Ashok Jadhav was in the store with one of his delivery boys, Aniket, whom Aroop took to be the culprit he was in search of. Accordingly, Aroop gave the fellow a once-over. Could this dark, skinny, smelly, pimply youth be my wife's choice, he shivered and thought to himself. Such bad taste. Judging by his dwarfishness, the midget was unlikely to have 'good' equipment either.

'Hi,' Aroop said in reply to Ashok Jadhav's 'Good evening, sir,' as he chewed bubble gum to keep his cool. Then, without much ado he said, 'I'm going to choose a set of DVDs and I want your guy here to deliver them to my place post-haste. You see, I've invited some friends over for drinks and dinner.'

'Sir,' Ashok Jadhav smiled, 'your wish is my command (Aroop wondered where the man had learnt the phrase). But sir, this is not the delivery boy who serves your family and I am sending him now on some other urgent business. So it won't be possible for him to come to your flat.'

'Oh,' said Aroop, unable to hide his disappointment. 'By the way, what's the name of the guy assigned to my flat?'

'His name is Sandesh, sir, but unfortunately he has left the job. First thing tomorrow morning, I will send my other delivery boy, Darshan, to your place.'

'Thanks,' said Aroop, and abruptly left the store without selecting any DVDs. He believed half his battle was won, for now he knew the name of the bloke he was looking for. 'Sandesh,' Aroop silently pronounced the name. His favourite Bengali sweet. Thanks, dear wife, he said to himself, for taking me off the sweet forever as if I'm diabetic.

The next morning, Ashok Jadhav called up Sandesh at Pigeon Couriers and tried to persuade him to return to his old job at the Royal Video Parlour.

'Customers have been asking for you,' he said. 'If you come back to the store, I'll increase your pay.'

That evening, Sandesh paid Ashok Jadhav a visit, eager to know what his pay hike would be. Instead of discussing his emoluments, however, Ashok Jadhav informed him of Aroop's visit to the store. This news unsettled Sandesh. Was Lolita back? Why then did her husband, and not she, come to the Royal Video Parlour?

Never in the past had her husband stepped into the store. He probably thought of it as below his dignity. So why did he come here now? Was it likely that he had found out about their affair and was after Sandesh's blood? In which case, he'd have to run for his life.

'Sorry,' Sandesh apologized to his former boss, who was now offering him a token increase in salary. 'I am okay where I am.'

In the end, it was the watchmen of Jannat, the motley crowd of distant cousins from upstate Bihar and Uttar Pradesh who, in another five years, would be hounded out of the city by the MNS, that successfully brought both parties, victor and vanquished, together.

Eager to know if madam Lolita was really back, Sandesh walked right into the trap set for him by Aroop with the connivance of the watchmen. He stealthily crept into Jannat after dark one evening and headed straight for the security booths where he and the watchmen, as usual, shared their Cow Brand tobacco.

'Is madam back?' he whispered to the watchmen as they chewed and spat.

'Yes,' they replied. 'She returned to Bombay a few days ago and was asking for you.'

Sandesh paused before posing his next question. His heart pounded. Mosquitoes hovered all over the place and bit him. A watchman in the society had recently died of falciparum malaria.

'Where's madam's car?' Sandesh nervously asked.

'That *khatara*? She sold it and bought herself a bigger car.'

'Really?'

'Yes.'

One of the watchmen held Sandesh by the hand and led him to the parking lot where he pointed towards Aroop's gleaming white Skoda Octavia.

'See that?' he asked. 'It even has a Goa passing.'

Sandesh surveyed the car and found that it bore the registration number GA-01-AG-7777.

'But madam was never fond of fancy numbers,' he said to the watchman. She thought they were a waste of money because the RTO charged Rs 10,000 for them.

'Who knows the ways of the rich?' the watchman quipped.

It was late. Sandesh wondered whether he should take the watchmen at their word and take the elevator to the forty-ninth floor. But what if Lolita's husband was still around?

'Is saab also at home?' he asked the watchmen, as they strolled around the complex.

'He was there, but has now left,' one of the watchmen replied.

Sandesh was emboldened. Yet he decided against going up just then. He would first call Lolita on her mobile. What he did not know, though, was that Lolita had resolved not to answer any coin box calls that came from Bombay. Sandesh then tried his madam's landline number, only to be told by her answering machine, that too in Aroop's voice: 'We're not there now. Please leave your name and telephone number after the beep.'

When Aroop learned of Sandesh's 'escape', he severely reprimanded the security guards, amongst whom he'd distributed wads of currency notes of various denominations.

'Why did you let the fellow off?' he yelled at the top of his voice, bringing the neighbours out onto their balconies. 'Why didn't you grab him by the collar and haul him up?'

But here, Aroop was in a spot. The watchmen of Jannat possibly wondered what crime their DVD mate had committed that so incurred sarkar's ire. How could Aroop let them know that the lecher had been bedding his wife? Perhaps they knew it already.

'Cash has been missing from the flat,' Aroop lied to the watchmen, 'and I suspect this guy.'

It was decided that the next time Sandesh made an appearance in the building, the watchmen would con him. 'Madam was angry with us for not personally escorting you to her flat the other night,' they would tell him and lead him directly into the lion's den.

They did not have to wait for long. Hungry for Lolita's voluptuous body, her money and her booze, Sandesh retraced his steps to Jannat forty-eight hours later.

'Come, come,' the watchmen said to him in unison. 'We were waiting for you, friend.' They made a mockery of the word friend; the fact that Sandesh was a son of the soil and they were envious outsiders in Bombay city had something to do with this.

Though the over-cordial manner of the watchmen aroused Sandesh's suspicion somewhat, he willingly suspended his disbelief when they told him what *sarkar* had rehearsed with them a dozen times in the past two days. Five of them escorted Sandesh in the *bada* fast lift (named after the famous *bada* fast local that ran non-stop from Virar to Churchgate every morning) and took him to the forty-ninth floor. Aroop's doorbell was rung. When it was finally answered, Aroop being busy in the bathtub, the watchmen said, '*Sarkar, aapke qaidi ko pakad laya.*'

Sandesh tried to scram, but the watchmen and the sailor pounced on him like a tiger pounces on a jackal.

If Lolita turned to page 310 of *The God of Small Things* by Arundhati Roy, one of the books that decorated her bookshelves which won the Booker Prize in 1997, as that was the year independent India celebrated its fiftieth birthday, the following passage, hyperbolically, would apply to her lover who represented to her the forces of liberation.

'*His skull was fractured in three places. His nose and both his cheekbones were smashed, leaving his face pulpy, undefined.*

The blow to his mouth had split open his upper lip and broken six teeth, three of which were embedded in his lower lip, hideously inverting his beautiful smile. Four of his ribs were splintered, one had pierced his left lung, which was what made him bleed from his mouth. The blood on his breath bright red. Fresh. Frothy. His lower intestine was ruptured and haemorrhaged, the blood collected in his abdominal cavity. His spine was damaged in two places, the concussion had paralysed his right arm and resulted in a loss of control over his bladder and rectum. Both his kneecaps were shattered.'

The attack was launched not at home, not in the city, but on the outskirts of Bombay, where Sandesh was bundled into an SUV and driven off. The landscape, ironically, reminded him of his *Ati kya Khandala* excursions with his oppressor's wife. '*Aai ga,*' Sandesh called out to his mother in agony, as the last vestiges of his energy were drained from his body and he collapsed on the ground in an exhausted heap. The infernal violence, needless to say, was perpetrated by the husband and his seamen who, if they had their way, would have sprinkled itching powder all over his body, fastened his hands and then proceeded to sever his head from his body as if he were a Somali pirate.

But the marines did not leave him to kick the bucket in the wilderness. Instead, they drove him back to Bombay where, on Aroop's orders, they opened the doors of their Sumo and threw him out in front of the Royal Video Parlour.

This was where Ashok Jadhav, noticing a commotion outside his shop, found him and rushed him to a hospital.

Did the Good Samaritan know it would be his turn tomorrow? The marines stormed into Ashok Jadhav's store the next day, and though they let him off with only a couple of *fataka* slaps across his face and a punch or two in his belly, they vandalized his possessions. Every single VCD and DVD was pulled out from its shelf, broken in two and chucked out on the pavement. Some of them were flung out intact, and they struck innocent passers-by who hurled abuses at them. The men looked as if they were playing frisbee. Stones were used to shatter Ashok Jadhav's plate glass doors and obscene graffiti disfigured his walls. One classic slogan read: *Mr Ashok Jadhav's servant fucks his wife.* The marines used scissors and blades to slit the telephone wires, fearing that the owner of the store would summon the police. They pulled out the fuses so that all at once the fan, the lights and the air conditioner, which themselves were bent out of shape with cricket bats, conked off. Finally, they grabbed the electronic equipment in the store, DVD players and laptops and television sets, viciously tossing them up in the air and letting them crash on the ceramic floor. When they fled, half an hour or so later, the store looked as if a massive earthquake had rocked it.

It was Darshan who solved his boss's jigsaw puzzle, putting two and two together to link the caveman assault on the Royal Video Parlour to Sandesh's tempestuous affair with Lolita. Ashok Jadhav was speechless when Darshan spilled the beans. He senselessly stared at the ceiling of his wrecked shop.

When Ashok Jadhav rode to the hospital later that day, he had half a mind to instruct the surgeons to discharge Sandesh right away, for no longer would he pay for his treatment. He knew from previous experiences that given the fellow's wretched condition, the surgeons, even if they discharged him, would do so against medical advice (they called it DAMA), and if Sandesh died, they would hold him responsible. So he said nothing. Yet, when he came face to face with Sandesh in his ward, who was so bandaged up that he resembled an extraterrestrial, Ashok Jadhav's reactions were similar to Mammachi's in Roy's classic, when the god of small things goes to see her.

'When Velutha arrived, Mammachi lost her bearings and spewed her blind venom, her crass, insufferable insults … Mammachi continued her tirade, her eyes empty, her face twisted and ugly, her anger propelling towards Velutha until she was shouting right into his face and he could feel the spray of her spit and smell the stale tea on her breath …

"'Out," she had screamed eventually. "If I find you on my property tomorrow I'll have you castrated like the pariah dog that you are. I'll have you killed."'

Unlike Velutha, Sandesh couldn't bring himself to say quietly, 'We'll see about that.' He seemed to have lost his voice.

Aroop disposed of his flat in Jannat to Deepak Matkar after all. Ten crores was a phenomenal amount, he reasoned with himself, and those who live in glass houses cannot afford to throw stones at others. The decision to sell the flat, rather than lease it, was no cakewalk, but in the end Aroop decided in favour of the former because the very sight of their old flat distressed him. An echo arose from the walls and sniggered at him. Who does my wife think she is anyway, Aroop thought to himself. Lady Chatterley, who slept with her plumber? Every book on Lolita's bookshelves must be burned, he decided, in the manner of fanatics: it was books that had corrupted her.

Soon after he struck the deal with the notorious politician with a reputation for usurping land belonging to the meek (who never inherited), Aroop drove back to Vasco da Gama at breakneck speed, after depositing the money in a Swiss bank account he had recently opened.

'What took you so long to get back?' Lolita asked him in the driveway itself, but Aroop was elusive. Though he told her he'd sold the flat (news which Lolita received with a twinge of regret), he did not tell her to whom or for how much.

Nor did Lolita ask. She had learned to leave him alone, to mind her own business, at least for the time being until things improved and they were able to pick up the pieces of their splintered lives again. And if there was one thing that Aroop was extremely tight-lipped about, it was that he had blood on his hands, that he had disfigured the features of his rival in love to such an extent that he'd never be the same again.

Aroop received an SOS from his headquarters over breakfast one morning to 'resume duty as speedily as possible, failing which Mariners' Compass International reserves the right to terminate your contract and to put an end to your services'. He panicked. The thought of having to leave Lolita to her devices again filled him with dread. What if she got in touch with Sandesh, or commenced another affair with someone like him of the Great Indian Underclass? At the same time, he couldn't quit the merchant navy just yet. It wasn't as if another job was waiting for him with open arms, nor did he know how to start a business. There were savings, no doubt, but the time hadn't come to cash in on them yet.

Aroop contacted his headquarters and informed them that he would report for work within the next forty-eight hours. Those forty-eight hours he spent, not with his family, but on his computer. Aroop decided to shop for, of all things, a chastity belt. But though he downloaded pages and pages on a 'device that protected the virginity of women', no amount of clicking of his mouse instructed him as to where he could order one for his wife. Finally, he gave up in exasperation. He left for work abruptly, hastily bidding Lolita and Tanu goodbye, as if he were in a nine to five job that would bring him back to them in the evening. His present stint would be particularly long, for it would be over a year before he was reunited with his family.

SIX

Judgement Day

Good Morning Mumbai, a newly launched tabloid, had staff reporters whose brief was that they had to have a penchant for sensational news, *sansani khez khabar*. Their team of scribes and lensmen, all in their twenties and thirties with degrees and diplomas from Bombay's top journalism schools, hunted the city for controversies that had the potential to embroil their proprietors in lawsuits. The proprietors were Marwari industrialists whose names once appeared in *Forbes* magazine alongside the Tatas and Ambanis for they were amongst the wealthiest people in the country. Their crime reporter-cum-sub editor, Komal Chandran, scoured the police stations night and day, and got hold of the story that her headline called 'Ek Aur Love Triangle'. Though the chief dramatis personae were Aroop, Lolita and Sandesh, Ashok Jadhav's name featured in the story too, since it was he who filed the FIR when the sailors vandalized the Royal Video Parlour. Ms Komal Chandran, who was born several generations after the Nanavati case rocked Bombay, nevertheless went on to compare her story to this famous case which she called 'the mother of all love triangles'. It must be acknowledged that, miraculously, she got most of her facts right, unlike tabloid newspapers anywhere in the world. Her only howler was her reference to Sandesh as a 'boy servant formerly employed in the Sengupta household'. But like most tabloid reporters, Ms Komal Chandran could not refrain from the temptation to editorialize. She took sides. Her sympathies, obviously, were with the heteronormative husband and wife, Aroop and Lolita, who were 'people like us'. Sandesh, conversely, was portrayed as the 'villain of the piece'. He was Mowgli and Caliban rolled into one and she actually used these names in her article, having graduated in English literature, like the dhobi's son who wrote Kamalabai's letter. Lolita, from Komal Chandran's point of view, strayed because Sandesh tempted her. In this, he was no different from Satan in Milton's *Paradise Lost*, who tempted Eve and made her eat the forbidden fruit.

Good Morning Mumbai remained the only newspaper that published Lolita's scandalous story. Its circulation was confined strictly to Greater Bombay (its print run was no more than 50,000 copies), so there was no question of Aroop and Lolita chancing upon the piece in Goa. As for Sandesh, he could not read English. Then, the heavens be thanked for not letting private TV channels get wind of the story. The Hindi news channel *Is Waqt* did spot the article in *Good Morning Mumbai* and attempted, in vain, to get in touch with Komal Chandran. They envisaged a 'Breaking News' expose where none would be spared. They would air it every hour for three days in a row till the case became more famous than the Nanavati case itself.

There were other repercussions. *Straight*, a magazine for women that ran an agony aunt column, plagiarized Ms Komal

Chandran's report in *Good Morning Mumbai* to convert it into a reader's voyeuristic query.

I'm a fifteen-year-old boy from the lower class, a person writing a fake letter said, *and I have desperately fallen in love with a wealthy married woman twice my age. It isn't my fault. The lady seduced me when her husband was away on a posting (he is a fauji), and after that I got so addicted to sex with her that I can no longer think of sleeping with girls of my own age. We now have sex everyday. The woman suggests that we elope and get married, and I am inclined towards marrying her too for I can't imagine a life without her. But I am worried about society and my family. How will a fifteen-year-old boy look with a thirty-year-old wife? Also, when she reaches menopause, I will still be in the prime of my youth [sic] and may even be tempted to harbour unfaithful thoughts. Yet, as of now, I just want to have sex with her all the time. I want to put her n*****s to my mouth and thrust my finger into her p***y. Recently, when her husband returned home on leave, I was so distraught that I wanted to end my life by jumping in front of the Flying Rani. I can't bear the thought of her husband even touching her and I want to kill him for getting her pregnant. Oh, Sister Sheela, please help.* DP.

Sister Sheela, who ran the agony aunt column, was a spinster in her forties with several liaisons similar to the one recounted in Komal Chandran's piece. Her reply was:

Sorry, friend, no matter how hot such an alliance may seem, Indian society does not permit it. This is not the West, the land of savage grace. You can't mess around with a married woman old enough to be your, well,

mom, and get away with it. If her husband finds out what
the two of you are up to, both your lives may be in danger.
The law is entirely on his side because it recognizes the
sanctity of marriage and sees adultery as an offence.
To complicate matters, you are a person below eighteen
years of age, that is, a minor. Your obsession with an
older woman seems perverse. Try to mingle with girls of
your own age and get this woman out of your system.
Besides, this is the time when you should be studying,
not thinking of girls. Act now before it is too late. Abstain
from further sex with the woman. In fact, try to stop
seeing her completely.

The correspondence was titillating. Many sex-starved young men lapped up Sister Sheela's column every fortnight. One of them, whose initials were ZH, wrote to say that he empathized and sympathized with DP because sex with an older woman was much more enjoyable than sex with a peer. An older woman was a *hastini* capable of giving a young man sexual delights of the kind he could only fantasize about. Even the Kama Sutra said so. Moreover, the reverse was also true. Older women enjoyed sex with young men more than with men their age. A young man with an older woman was the most erotic sexual combination and permutation one could think up.

Sister Sheela convinced the editor of *Straight* to publish ZH's letter, which opened up a Pandora's box. It flooded the offices of the magazine with letters, half of which agreed with ZH, while the other half called him a guy with a 'one-track mind'.

Adolescents alone didn't read *Good Morning Mumbai* and *Straight*. A high profile criminal lawyer, Jeevan Reddy browsed through them too; a plethora of carelessly strewn newspapers and magazines adorned his chambers on any given day.

Jeevan Reddy turned to the page that carried Komal Chandran's news report as he had his breakfast of a Spanish omelette and toast with a knife and fork on the sunny terrace of his Cuffe Parade apartment. Her catchy headline caught his eye and he read her story with avid interest, but her partiality so peeved him that he wished to call her then and there. However, it was 9 a.m. and he knew that for newspapermen, it was the crack of dawn. Brushing the breadcrumbs off his silken dressing gown, Jeevan Reddy rose and consulted his electronic diary. Luckily, he did not have to put in an appearance in court that day. He would invite Ms Komal Chandran over for lunch and educate her on the need for news reporters to be objective, to stick to facts the way lawyers did and withhold their own opinions.

Around midday, Jeevan Reddy drove off in his Mercedes-Benz C Class to his chambers in the Fort area. He called Komal Chandran at the editorial office of *Good Morning Mumbai* and unlike the TV channel *Is Waqt* that failed to reach her in spite of obtaining her mobile number, got her on the line instantly. Although Komal Chandran had a tight schedule, Jeevan Reddy persuaded her to have lunch with him at the Taj's Harbour Bar. He knew from experience that journalists invariably succumbed to invitations at five-star hotels, and in this case what also clinched it was the high praise the criminal lawyer dishonestly showered on the crime reporter's article.

Their offices were virtually adjacent, South Bombay being the metropolis's principal business district. Jeevan Reddy picked up Komal Chandran and drove straight to the Harbour Bar where he ordered lager and a variety of continental titbits before getting down to brass tacks. Garrulity came easily to lawyers.

'Hello, I'm Jeevan Reddy. I read your story and it's good to meet you,' he began, and stymied the scribe who scarcely managed to introduce herself, by proceeding to speak non-stop.

The sum and substance of Jeevan Reddy's diatribe was that those who had attitude aligned themselves, not with the capitalist, but with the underdog. It was regressive, nay reactionary, on Komal Chandran's part to depict Aroop and Lolita, the rich married couple, as the Ram and Sita of her story, and the dispossessed Sandesh as the Ravana.

'But, sir …' Ms Komal Chandran attempted to interrupt several times to put forth her take on the subject, but Jeevan Reddy never let her finish. He was teacher-like to the extreme and the fact that he was in his fifties while Komal Chandran was still thirty-two made him certain that she had much to learn from him.

In the end, Komal Chandran threw in the towel. She looked at her watch and got up to leave. 'Sorry, but I've got to be at Worli by four,' she said. 'Thank you for the excellent lunch.'

'You are most welcome, dear,' Jeevan Reddy replied. 'By the way, do you have Sandesh's telephone number?'

'No. But he works for a firm called Pigeon Couriers. You can reach him there.'

'Thank you.'

Sandesh's disfigured face startled Jeevan Reddy.

'Boy, you are beautiful,' he said. 'But these guys have made you ugly. What you need is reconstructive surgery.'

Jeevan Reddy took Sandesh to Dr Hosi Billimoria, the superlatively accomplished plastic surgeon in town, whose case he happened to fight and win when the latter got into the clutches of underworld dons to whom he'd paid protection money.

'Restore him to his original form,' Jeevan Reddy told the doctor who had trained in Argentina and whose diagnosis was, 'difficult, but not impossible'.

The treatment began without delay.

Jeevan Reddy, or JR, offered to file a criminal case against the Senguptas on Sandesh's behalf.

'Why?' Sandesh asked, nonplussed. He couldn't make head or tail of this man who had met him out of the blue and was offering to take him under his wing.

'Because I have an axe to grind with the likes of Lolita,' JR explained.

The lawyer, who'd perfected the art of talking anyone into doing anything, convinced Sandesh that it was in his best interest to let the case be filed.

'We shall ask for lakhs by way of compensation,' he said, which was enough to get the avaricious Sandesh to nod his assent.

Everyday, Sandesh had sessions with Dr Hosi Billimoria, morning or evening, sometimes both, depending on his work shifts. JR met him afterwards and took him home for a drink. Though JR's flat wasn't as tastefully done up as Lolita's, nor was it on the forty-ninth floor, it was, after all, in Cuffe Parade, a

much more upmarket neighbourhood than Dadar. Sandesh
tried to figure out who was richer, Lolita or Jeevan Reddy, but
failed to draw any conclusions. Judging by his powder blue
Merc, which glided through the city streets, JR was richer.
Sandesh also discovered that the price per square foot area in
Cuffe Parade was as high as Rs 50,000, while in Dadar it was no
more than Rs 20,000.

Madam, there are people richer than you, he thought.

What JR said to Sandesh over the next few days flummoxed
him.

'I'm gay,' he said, 'and I have been unfairly accused by
feminists of paedophilia. I have a vested interest in fighting
your case. I wish to prove that women can be paedophiles too.
What was your age when you first had sex with Lolita?'

'Fifteen.'

'See what I mean? That makes you a *minor*. Sex with a minor,
whether the culprit is a man or a woman, is a criminal offence
under Sections 376 and 377 of the IPC.'

The summons served on the Senguptas by the Bombay
High Court threw their household into confusion. As Sandesh
wasn't eighteen yet—his eighteenth birthday was less than a
year away—it was Jeevan Reddy who filed a PIL on his behalf.
The criminal lawyer made sure he implicated both husband
and wife. Aroop was charged with damage to property, as well
as the wrongful assault of Sandesh and the owner of the Royal
Video Parlour, Ashok Jadhav, who was persuaded to become an
'interested party' to the case. The charge against Lolita was sex
with a minor. The notices issued to the Senguptas meant that
Aroop had to dash back to Bombay every so often to confer

with his lawyers. Since he could afford it, he hired a whole host of legal luminaries, although only one of them, a star pleader by the name of Francis Rodrigues would appear on his behalf in court. The others, Ashwin More, Dhruv Malani, Fali Irani and Suhel Shah, would be behind the scenes, in the wings so to speak. When he wasn't catching planes from his various ports of call to Bombay, flying only executive class which considerably depleted his finances, he was on his Blackberry, making international calls to his advocates. More than once, his bosses at the Mariners' Compass International contemplated sacking him for dereliction of duty.

For all intents and purposes, the litigation was a clash of two titans. It was a duel fought by two egoistic gentlemen, Jeevan Reddy and Aroop Sengupta. REDDY VS SENGUPTA would be an appropriate way of documenting it as a case history in the law books for the benefit of posterity, for the law heavily relied on precedents. In between was Sandesh, friend of one and arch-enemy of another. All the rest involved in the matter were against going ahead with it right from the start. Aroop's lawyers were in favour of an out of court settlement. 'Pay the bastards some money and spare yourself the bother,' they advised him. Lolita concurred with them. She was aghast at all the unsavoury publicity the case would bring them, especially her, and tarnish her name. This wasn't what she had bargained for. Though a soft spot for Sandesh still inevitably lurked somewhere, Lolita was irked by his treachery. Weren't the gold chain and the cheque for Rs 10,000 that she gave him enough, she wondered? If he wanted more, why didn't he ask? Was this the way to repay her for all the intimacy they had shared? It amounted to ingratitude.

Sandesh had a soft corner for Lolita too. As the days passed, he was convinced that what he felt for her was nothing less than love. She was my first love, he told himself as he pined for her, and first loves are always the hardest to forget. If he had his way, he would have forgiven her and withdrawn the case. Yet he couldn't go against the wishes of Jeevan Reddy whom he came to regard as a sort of benefactor, having Great Expectations from him. More than that, Sandesh came to see JR as a sort of substitute for Lolita who had given him a taste of the good life before leaving him high and dry. His evenings in JR's apartment were nothing less than a continuation of the good times he enjoyed in Lolita's company at Jannat.

Once it was established that an out of court settlement was ruled out and that the Senguptas would defend themselves in court to the best of their ability, their lawyers spent months before the actual trial began tutoring and briefing Lolita. Though Lolita readily confessed it was she and not Sandesh who initiated sex between them, Francis Rodrigues and his colleagues advised her to forget this point of view.

'Get it out of your system,' Suhel Shah told her.

'Think of it as amnesia, or loss of memory,' Ashwin More said.

The only possible route to victory, the lawyers argued, was to substitute the truth with falsehood.

'What falsehood?' Lolita panicked.

'Rape,' the lawyers answered.

The team then explained to Lolita that the story she would have to tell the judges, from the witness box or wherever, was that Sandesh was a Royal Video Parlour delivery boy who, on the pretext of delivering DVDs to her at home, took advantage of the fact that her husband was away and molested her.

'Given the fact that the fellow belongs to the servant class,' Dhruv Malani said, much to Lolita's chagrin, 'the court will easily believe our story.'

'We will add robbery as a motive too,' said Fali Irani. 'Think of everything that you ever voluntarily gave the boy. We will contend that these things were stolen by him from your apartment.'

Lolita heard her lawyers out as they spoke without butting in. Aroop had instructed them to fly to Goa whenever they needed to brief her, and stay at the best hotels for which he would pay. This was an offer the lawyers couldn't resist.

'I don't want her to go to Bombay at any cost,' Aroop categorically declared.

When the lawyers left, Lolita broke down. How could I get an innocent guy into so much trouble, she wept. Little Tanu wondered, as usual, why her mother was crying. Lolita had half a mind to take a flight to Bombay and advise Sandesh to flee the city for his own benefit. That, of course, was easier said than done. His calls to her on her mobile had abruptly stopped. Her lawyers, she was certain, wouldn't rest till they liquidated her penniless lover.

On impulse, Lolita called Aroop on board his vessel.

'I can't do it,' she said.

'Can't do what?'

'I cannot speak lies in court that will ruin a young man's life.'

'If this marriage means anything to you, you will have to do it.'

'I simply can't. It goes against my conscience.'

'Don't waste my time giving me all that bullshit. It did not go against your conscience to cheat on your husband.'

To this, of course, Lolita had no answer. There was silence, though husband and wife were still on the line. Finally, Aroop said, 'Madam, listen to my ultimatum. Either you do as the lawyers say, or I'll sue you for divorce.'

Saying this, he slammed the phone down.

After much deliberation with their clients, Lolita's lawyers zeroed in on three exhibits to be presented before the court by the prosecution. They were, in order of appearance, a gold chain, a cheque and a ship similar to the one Lolita had once gifted to Sandesh.

The first of these proved the hardest to retrieve, for Sandesh had disposed of Lolita's gold chain in a fit of despair and sent the money to his mother in the village. Now, Bombay has jewellery shops by the thousands and it was anybody's guess which of them Sandesh approached with his treasure. Not till the trial commenced and Francis Rodrigues broached the subject of the gold chain during a hearing, prompting the bench, made up of Justice R.P. Mehta, Justice D.S. Bhandarkar and Justice P. G. Khan to ask Sandesh to produce it, did the defence learn that he had sold it to Gordhandas Jewellers in Pydhonie. Setting convention aside, all five of them then marched to Pydhonie, introduced themselves to the proprietor, Mr Gordhandas, and advised him to part with the gold chain without a fuss.

Mr Gordhandas could not decipher which gold chain these men in black coats spoke about. Nor could he remember who had sold it to him. But when he got his assistants to turn his shop topsy-turvy, almost giving up hope of finding it, one of them chanced upon a 22-carat gold chain and passed it on to the lawyers. They then had to rush to Goa to ask Lolita to identify it, which meant another day or two gone.

On being shown the gold chain, Lolita at first denied that she had anything to do with it. 'This isn't it,' she defiantly proclaimed. But the lawyers, especially Suhel Shah, detected the lies on her face and explained to her, as patiently as they could, that such a stand would needlessly drag the case and complicate matters for all those concerned. It is then that Lolita spoke the truth.

'Yes, this is the damn thing I gave him,' she brusquely admitted. 'What a bloody nuisance.'

Then Suhel Shah said, 'Madam, now please tell us about the cheque.'

Here, Lolita provided the details without a fuss. 'It was a Grindlays Bank cheque for Rs 10,000,' she said.

'Which branch?'

'The one in Dadar. That's where I have an account.'

'Was it a crossed cheque or bearer cheque?'

'Bearer cheque.'

'Good. Thank you.'

The bank took over a week to locate the cheque presented to them by Sandesh. The defence was privately shocked at the bank's inability to recognize that Sandesh was a minor and technically not authorized to cash a cheque, even if it was in his name.

'But he looked eighteen,' the bank manager said, in a cover-up bid.

'Appearances are deceptive, sir,' Lolita's lawyers said. 'As a senior banking official, you should know this better than us. We can have you booked for fraud.'

What saved the day was the bank manager's reasonableness. Where he could have obstinately defended his juniors who erred, he gracefully admitted his mistake and apologized. 'These days, youngsters look much older than they did in our time,' the bank manager laughed, ordering cups of tea for the lawyers.

Lolita was briefed to say in court that she wrote out the cheque in Sandesh's favour under duress. At gunpoint, as it were. The defence was curious to know what Sandesh did with the money. They learned during the trial, as he spoke from the witness box, that he had blown it up on goodies. He bought himself a mobile phone with a camera, Levi's jeans and Nike shoes. In fact, he wore the jeans and his Nike shoes to court, amusing the bench and causing Justice P.G. Khan to remark, 'Well, young men have their desires in this age of globalization, don't they?'

Aroop's replica of The Golden Anchor, the vessel on which he worked and provided for his family, proved the easiest to obtain. Sandesh, who regarded it as a piece of junk, dumped it in a corner of his digs where Darshan and Aniket, with whom he still lodged and boarded, discovered it and innovatively used it as an ashtray. However, the story told in court by Lolita's lawyers was that Sandesh had stolen the ship too, thinking in all probability that he could sell it off as a curio in Bombay's notorious flea market, Chor Bazaar.

For the first time in his life, the hardened Sandesh was wounded by another's treachery. He, who was thick-skinned, grew morose and sullen and JR considered taking him to a shrink. Sandesh, of course, scoffed at the idea outright.

'*Main pagal nahi hoon*,' he emphatically said. 'I am only in tension.'

The versatile JR then decided to play the role of shrink himself. Whenever he drove Sandesh to his Cuffe Parade apartment for a drink after his visits to Dr Hosi Billimoria, he coaxed him into speech to get to know his inner mind. This wasn't cakewalk, given that Sandesh was reticent by nature, especially when the person opposite wasn't Lolita. However, JR knew how to fix and mix his scotch and club soda in such perfect proportions that the fellow ultimately opened up. Sandesh at times bitterly wept at these sessions as he recalled Lolita's love for him and his for her, which Jeevan Reddy called Oedipal, and found her turnaround hard to accept.

'I know she is saying these things in court only because of her *bhenchod* husband,' Sandesh held. 'He is forcing her to speak lies.'

Sandesh confessed that never once did he *ask* Lolita for anything. The pocket money she regularly gave him, as well as the gold chain and the cheque, were given voluntarily, of her own accord, because he filled the void in her life.

'Why did she give you the ship?' JR asked out of curiosity.

'She was showing me presents her husband bringing for her. When I asked her what he bringing for me, she gave me ship,' Sandesh explained.

'She thought of you as a child?'

'Maybe. That is why once she is buying me cricket bat also.'

'Really?'

'Yeah. But after that we are going to see movie in theatre and there in the dark, she is putting hand on my crotch.'

'So you were both her Son and Lover.'

'Maybe.'

The stand taken by the defence convinced Sandesh that victory would be theirs, defeat his. He even feared arrest. During his drinking binges with JR, Sandesh often threw tantrums, declaring that he no longer wished to proceed with the case. 'Withdraw ...' he wept, English words uninhibitedly coming to his lips when inebriated. Sandesh accused JR of conning him into believing that they would extract lakhs from the Senguptas as compensation.

'Not one paisa is coming,' he said. When JR stroked his back and consoled him, Sandesh called him a liar.

'You are just like madam,' he yelled. 'She is speaking lies in court and you are speaking lies at home.'

As the days passed, this became a sort of refrain with him. Yet JR was patient just as a lawyer must inevitably be.

'I assure you, victory will be ours,' he told Sandesh when he was sober, not mincing words.

'How?' Sandesh inquired.

'I will produce such exhibits and such witnesses before the judges that they will be no match for the Senguptas. But for that, you must co-operate with me.'

Sandesh, sober by day, was altogether different from the drunk Sandesh after dark. He told JR he trusted him and promised to do as he said.

Thrice a week, Sandesh religiously made an appearance at Dr Hosi Billimoria's clinic, off Lamington Road. JR would take time off to drive him there personally, certain he would skip visits if told to commute on his own. Dr Hosi Billimoria, in possession of world-class equipment to facilitate plastic surgery and whose patients were fashion models and film stars, painstakingly grafted skin from Sandesh's thighs and buttocks on his face. He performed a hundred other operations that slowly but surely healed Sandesh's wounds and restored the contours of his face. He gave him nutrition supplements that brought out the glow in his complexion. He treated his hair, so that it lustrously grew. He worked on his nose and cheekbones. Sandesh's mutilated lips posed the gravest challenge to Dr Hosi Billimoria, but these too he tackled with the zeal of a sculptor. As for his teeth, the doctor referred his patient to Dr Vispy Merchant, a dentist who specialized in cosmetic dentistry. The man inserted his surgical torch into Sandesh's mouth and told him he was lucky, for although six of his teeth were partially knocked off, their tooth structures were more or less intact. He would thus do root canals on the teeth and fit them with ceramic crowns.

'You will look handsomer than before,' the dentist said.

The damage to Sandesh's other organs, such as his spine, his lungs, his intestines and his knees was taken care of by other surgeons so Sandesh spent most of his afterhours, and all his weekends, in hospitals, dispensaries and clinics before finishing his fatiguing day in JR's drawing room. The cumulative bill for his treatment ran into lakhs. Needless to say, it was JR who ungrudgingly picked up the tab.

'I have no one to spend on,' he told Sandesh to ease the feigned burden on the latter's conscience. 'So I may as well spend on you.'

Ever since they met and began to spend candlelight evenings together, Jeevan Reddy spoke to Sandesh on and off about the nature of his job at the Royal Video Parlour and about Lolita's visits to the store. What he was eager to know was if there were written records to prove that Lolita had indeed borrowed porn. When Sandesh, scratching his head in an attempt to recall, informed JR that the store possessed a register in which client names and disc names were duly recorded every time a transaction took place, his joy knew no bounds.

'This is it!' he exclaimed. 'We have to somehow lay our hands on those registers.'

Sandesh then remembered something else in a flash and shared it with his mentor.

'"*Your red tape will land me in trouble.*" This is what madam is saying to me.'

'Why?'

'Because I am writing down names of Double X and Triple X DVDs she is borrowing and I is asking her to sign.'

'So she obviously knew she was doing something wrong.'

'Maybe.'

'But in the end, did you manage to obtain her signature?'

'Yes.'

In court, Jeevan Reddy promptly called for the registers, flustering the defence.

'Your honour,' he said to Justice R.P. Mehta who headed the bench. 'Those Royal Video Parlour registers are vital evidence that can free my client from the aspersions that have been cast on him. They must be produced before your esteemed selves forthwith.'

The court made it incumbent on Ashok Jadhav, as proprietor of the Royal Video Parlour, to submit the evidence requested for by the plaintiffs. Lolita's lawyers, however, had already advised Ashok Jadhav to say that the registers had been disposed of in the *raddi* and there was simply no way of retrieving them. JR countered this by demanding that he be allowed to visit the Royal Video Parlour to verify facts for himself.

'Objection, your honour,' Lolita's lawyers said in the manner of courtroom scenes in Bollywood films.

'Objection overruled,' the bench replied in an equally *filmy* way.

So JR, with Sandesh in tow who was overcome by nostalgia, took a taxi to the Royal Video Parlour in Dadar and after poring over stacks of dusty registers with a musty smell, unearthed the ones that bore Lolita's signature.

'This is it,' Sandesh excitedly said, aping Jeevan Reddy's style of speech.

The sleazy names of all the Double-X and Triple-X DVDs Lolita had borrowed amused JR. 'We will win,' he guffawed. 'This time madam cannot say that she signed the registers under duress.'

The defence was penalized for lying in court.

'Why did you say the registers were sold in the *raddi* when they were actually in the store all along?' Justice R.P. Mehta sternly reproached Lolita's lawyers.

Ashok Jadhav bore the brunt of their ire for they wondered why he preserved all that useless parchment that destroyed reputations.

'First of all, stocking porn is illegal,' Francis Rodrigues said. 'To make matters worse, you put it all down in black and white. Are you out of your mind?'

Ashok Jadhav, in turn, lambasted Darshan, Aniket and Sharad, a new hand who'd joined in Sandesh's place.

'You *chutiyas*,' he screamed. 'From now on, I want you to make a bonfire of those registers every 31 December. I don't want them in my shop.'

'Yes, sir.'

During hearings, JR, who felt that this was being unjustly overlooked, harped on Sandesh's age.

'He was a minor,' he pointed out to the bench, 'who came to Bombay for work and had not yet attained the age of eighteen when the accused seduced him. In fact, he was barely fifteen when Lolita and he met, and seventeen when they parted.'

The judges took notes and conferred with each other.

'What are you driving at?' Justice R.P. Mehta asked. 'Please don't beat around the bush.'

'If the male is an adult and the female a minor,' Jeevan Reddy submitted, 'there's a name for it. We call it paedophilia. What do you call it when the tables are turned, when the female is an adult and the male a minor?'

Again, there was a stir among the judges. JR realized he had scored a point over the defence. Emboldened, he continued, 'There are anomalies in the law. Can a woman rape a man? Is there some such thing as female paedophilia? I'm afraid the law is silent on these matters.'

'Why would a decent lady, respectably married to a naval officer, want to commit rape?' Francis Rodrigues laughed, demolishing JR's claims.

'Because her naval officer husband was away for extended periods, as all naval officers must inevitably be,' Jeevan Reddy thundered. 'Because she was newly married and badly in want of sex.'

The judges nodded. The argument seemed to work with the all-male bench. Heterosexual men love to believe that it is women, more than themselves, who crave sex. It's their ultimate turn-on.

'Nanavati case,' Justice R.P. Mehta commented in jest, inadvertently echoing the words of reporter Komal Chandran.

There was mirth in the courtroom. When order was restored, Francis Rodrigues said, 'That the plaintiff was a minor at the time of the sexual offence is of little or no consequence. There isn't so much difference between a boy of sixteen and a man of eighteen. The distinction is merely technical. What needs to be given credence is the background of the accused. He comes from a stratum of society to whom crime comes easy. As an adolescent from a lower class, it was he who was in desperate need of sex, rather than Lolita. He once told my client, "*Jab khoon hai garam to kahe ki sharam?*" A cheap Bollywood dialogue, no doubt.'

There was laughter in the courtroom again.

'Order, order,' the bench said, the invoking of Bollywood becoming infectious.

JR coughed and cleared his throat. Taking a sip of bottled water, he said, 'Your honours, it is well known that Lolita was raised in the city of Calcutta which has Marxist, even Naxalite sympathies and leanings. To her, a fellow like Sandesh represents proletarian society at its best. She fetishized him for ideological reasons. Her husband, on the other hand, represents the bourgeois society which she abhors.'

The defence was impressed with JR's research. The judges, however, shot back at him saying, 'If what you say is true, why did Lolita marry Mr Aroop Sengupta in the first place?'

'Because Lolita belongs to bourgeois society too. Most people marry their own kind.'

The criminal lawyer, with a fondness for reading, quoted this last line from a gay novel by a Sri Lankan writer that he had been reading.

All the three judges asked Lolita point-blank if she was a Marxist. The defence raised an objection to this, but once again it was overruled. Lolita was obliged to reply.

'I'm no CPI or CPM member,' she said. 'But yes, I subscribe to Marxist ideology. I've been doing so since my teens.'

Suddenly, the bench was divided. Justices R.P. Mehta and D.S. Bhandarkar saw merit in Jeevan Reddy's arguments. Sandesh's age, they believed, was of the essence and vital to the case. Had he been an adult, over eighteen years of age, the perspective would have been different. But he was a minor. However, the third judge, Justice A.R. Khan, wasn't inclined to side with the prosecution. According to him, Sandesh may have been a minor, but that is what all juvenile delinquents in the remand homes of Dongri were. Jeevan Reddy, he believed, filed the PIL on Sandesh's behalf merely to forestall any attempt by the aggrieved Senguptas to have an arrest warrant issued in his name. Towards working men of Sandesh's ilk, the affluent judge bore a grudge. His boy servants, his drivers and his gardeners had duped him more than once. Justice R.P. Mehta called it prejudice. Justice D.S. Bhandarkar called it bias.

The difference of opinion among them left the bench with no alternative but to adjourn the case.

When Jeevan Reddy, who had been offered judgeship himself, learned that Justice A.R. Khan also called Sandesh ugly, he was livid. 'They *made* him ugly,' he said to his fellow lawyers of the bar council. To this he was told that Justice A.R. Khan believed Sandesh *deserved* the treatment meted out to him by Aroop Sengupta.

The postponement pleased JR, who wished to buy time to present his prize witness before the court: Kamalabai. But the question was, where would he find her?

Sandesh knew exactly whom to approach for Kamalabai's whereabouts: the watchmen of Jannat. However, they were his enemies now.

'We will take revenge on the bastards later,' JR assured him. 'But first let's solicit their help to trace our witness.'

As Sandesh did not wish to see the faces of the traitors from Uttar Pradesh (as he thought of the watchmen) who deserved to be ignominiously thrown out of the land of the Marathi *manoos*, it was left to JR to meet them under the pretext of finding a maid for his home. When the watchmen suggested maids with names like Jijabai, Sheelabai, Nanda and Basanti, all of whom worked somewhere or the other in Jannat, Jeevan Reddy asked, 'What about a woman by the name of Kamalabai, who I am told is efficiency personified?'

'Kamalabai who?' the watchmen wondered. 'The one who used to work for Lolita memsaab?'

'Yes, she's the one I am talking about,' he hastily said.

The watchmen were surprised that JR knew Lolita.

'*Arre usko kaun nahi janta hai?*' one of the guards conspiratorially remarked.

'Give us a day, sir. We will find out where she is,' said the others.

It turned out that Kamalabai worked for a disabled old Parsi lady on the first floor of Jannat itself. The watchmen greeted JR with the good news when he saw them next and he gave them a 1000-rupee-note to share amongst themselves.

It took Kamalabai a while to comprehend what Jeevan Reddy and Sandesh said to her on the telephone, confounding her endlessly. When she gathered that they wanted her to appear in court as a witness, she was shocked.

'*Mala lafdat padayche nahi!*' I don't want to get into *lafdas*, she exclaimed in Marathi.

However, when Jeevan Reddy personally met her at a south Indian restaurant close to Jannat and explained that her testimony could save Sandesh from the gallows (so to speak), Kamalabai resolved with a vehemence to do everything in her power to save the lad who was like her son, even refusing the nine-yard sari JR carried for her as a present.

'*Mi bikaav nahi. Tyala vachwayala mi purna samarth ahe. To majha mulasarkha ahe.*' I cannot be bought. To save him you have my full support. He is like my son.

The next few weeks were spent briefing Kamalabai as to what to say and what not to say when she stood in the hallowed witness box.

'Don't be afraid,' Jeevan Reddy comforted her. 'Speak the truth as you know it.'

The confidence Jeevan Reddy took her into puffed up Kamalabai and prompted her to manufacture exaggerated accounts of her ex-memsaab's immorality. She claimed (in hushed tones) that Lolita was pregnant and since the baby was not her husband's but Sandesh's, she had it aborted before her husband got back. Sandesh and JR had a hearty laugh when they recounted Kamalabai's fantastic tale over drinks that evening.

'I always wearing condom,' Sandesh reiterated, somewhat inaccurately, 'and not once my condom is tearing.'

JR also felt a pang of jealousy whenever there was any reference to Sandesh having sex with Lolita.

The defence grilled Kamalabai as she deposed from the witness box, but the unlettered and unfettered woman, though trembling a bit, did not let them get the better of her. She allowed them to cross-examine her for over thirty minutes, answering all their questions with a precision that the bench found admirable. For example, when Francis Rodrigues asked Kamalabai what her hours of work were in the Sengupta household, she knew what was coming and said in Marathi, 'My hours of work were 10 a.m. to 7 p.m. But once I spent the night in Tanu's room because Tanu was restless. Memsaab did not know this. I caught her and Sandesh red-handed, doing what husbands and wives do.'

When the defence suggested that Sandesh threatened Lolita with dire consequences and forced himself on her, Kamalabai retorted, 'What are you talking, sir? Sandesh is *garib*, sincere. He is a mere child. Memsaab controlled him, as she controlled me, because she has money. Memsaab bought Sandesh with her money.'

Ashwin More said, 'If Lolita wanted to have an extramarital affair, why would she choose someone like Sandesh, from the servant class, younger than her in age and shorter too? Why didn't she choose a handsome young prince of her own background, maybe a few years older than her, and definitely taller?'

Kamalabai fielded this expertly, as JR, certain that such interrogations would come her way, taught her to.

'Sandesh is a *bechara*,' she said. 'Memsaab knew she could get rid of him whenever it suited her, without any trouble. Any other man wouldn't have let her off so easily. He would have blackmailed her and made her life hell. He would have threatened to report their affair to her husband. If she did not give in to his demands for sex and money, maybe he might have even murdered her. Memsaab is very shrewd, sir. She chose Sandesh because she knew he was a baby who would dance to her tune.'

The judges found merit in this reasoning. Even Justice A.R. Khan was beginning to come round. Francis Rodrigues, fighting a losing battle, posed his last question to Kamalabai:

'If, as you say, you knew that Lolita was having an extramarital affair, why didn't you report the matter to Aroop saab when he came home on vacation? Doesn't that make you an accomplice in the crime?'

The prosecution raised an objection to this, but the bench overruled it. Kamalabai was compelled to speak. She referred to the letter she wrote to Aroop, which Lolita's lawyers had no knowledge of since he suppressed it.

The court insisted that the letter be presented as an exhibit.

It had taken Lolita's advocates quite a while to trace the letter, which was in Aroop's custody and had to be couriered from

Marseilles, France where his vessel had docked. But when the letter was finally placed before the judges and examined, there was little doubt left in their minds as to who was guilty and who was innocent.

Kamalabai proudly stepped down from the witness box.

'If the testimony of a humble woman like me can save one life from ruin,' she told JR, 'then I have done my bit and can die in peace.'

She left with a piece of advice to JR:

'Adopt Sandesh as your son, saab. Educate him. Make him a big man like yourself.'

The bench delivered its verdict shortly afterwards. The judgement, written in legalese, ran into fifty pages like a master's thesis. The long and short of it was that all the evidence garnered went against Lolita. The specimen signature on the cheque in Sandesh's possession was undoubtedly hers. It couldn't have been forged, for it was identical to her signatures in the Royal Video Parlour registers. Nor could the court concur with the defence which claimed that Lolita signed the cheque under duress. The defence couldn't furnish enough proof for this and the judges, by a majority, found it improbable that a minor with no criminal history would succeed in getting into the apartment of a lady as self-assured as Lolita and coerce her to draw a cheque in his favour. It was pretty clear that Lolita gave the cheque to Sandesh voluntarily. Then, the Royal Video Parlour lending registers were proof unto themselves that Lolita was an ardent pornography addict. But she wasn't discreet about her addiction. If anything, she used the VCDs and DVDs that she borrowed as a ruse to seduce a minor. That is why she called him over to her place to fix her DVD player, when in point of fact, it had been established that there was nothing wrong with it. The defence's argument, that Sandesh saw the porn-viewing Lolita as a woman outside the triumvirate of mother-sister-wife, and was therefore aroused very much, as a woman who smokes or drinks, or is skimpily clad, invites a certain perception of herself among men, was dismissed by the judges as a figment of the imagination. Sandesh, they pointed out, had come to Bombay to eke out a living and was too nubile to commit a sexual offence so blatant and brazen. That too in the house of the 'victim'. It was Lolita who wanted to have sex with him for a variety of reasons: she was newly-married, her husband was away and boys like Sandesh, from the underprivileged sections of society were her fetish, as they indeed are of several westerners and westernized Indians, not the least because they are gullible and vulnerable. Lolita knew that Sandesh, given his age and socio-economic background, could easily be dumped when the time came. To deal with her pricking conscience, she compensated him with money and gold. This explains the weekly allowance she regularly paid him along with the 22-carat gold chain. She didn't spare even the replica of the ship her husband so lovingly brought home, and passed that on to Sandesh too. This threw much light on the extent to which Lolita cared for her husband and respected his sentiments. In the ultimate analysis, however, it was the testimony of a maidservant like Kamalabai, who had seen adversity, that made it abundantly clear to the bench that Sandesh was innocent. Not just Kamalabai's statements from the witness box, but her very demeanour and body language demonstrated to the judges how outraged she was by what went on in the Sengupta household. Later, when contacted by the prosecution, Kamalabai was even more scandalized to learn that, as if to add insult to injury, Lolita was trying to have him booked for an offence for which she, and not he, was entirely responsible. That is why a woman who had never seen the inside of a courtroom before agreed to come to court and step into the witness box. A woman like Kamalabai, the judges believed, was much more likely to side with another woman than with a man, even if he belonged to the same social strata as she. In other words, gender affinities would take precedence over class affinities. This being the case, if Kamalabai still wholly came out in defence of Sandesh, although it was Lolita who was her employer, it spoke volumes for his innocence. And assuming that the defence was right and that Sandesh molested and raped Lolita, such an offence could happen only once—it couldn't repeatedly happen over a period of two years. Wasn't it obvious, then, that the sexual activity between Lolita and Sandesh was consensual?

Yet, when it came to sentencing the guilty, the court was in a quandary. It simply did not know under what law to punish Lolita since her crime amounted to paedophilia, paedophilia implied penetration and a female could not penetrate a male. It was biologically impossible. Thus, the judges were left with no alternative but to let Lolita off with a warning and a fifty grand fine, which she could easily afford, failing which she would have to undergo six months simple imprisonment.

Aroop, the mastermind behind the attacks, was also fined the same amount and likewise awarded an equivalent sentence if he failed to pay up within one month. His offence was wrongful assault of a minor and damage to personal property.

The judges observed that this was one of the rarest of rare cases they had handled, where a respondent who was an interested party in the defence's case was responsible for penalties imposed on the defence!

Despite attempts by the opposition to frame him for rape, JR's genius ensured that Sandesh was pronounced not guilty. However, his claim for damages (the lakhs promised to him by JR) was rejected.

Aroop, enraged and slighted by the judgement, wished to appeal to the Supreme Court in New Delhi, an option the Bombay High Court gave him, but his lawyers advised him to close the chapter then and there.

'Move on,' they told him. 'The Supreme Court, if anything, is only likely to uphold the judgement of the Bombay High Court.'

Both Lolita and Sandesh were present in court when the judgement was delivered. But they were at extreme ends of the large courtroom, Lolita with Aroop (who clutched her hand), Sandesh with Jeevan Reddy. Neither glanced in the other's direction. Both were in a state of shock, for not once did they imagine as they made love and drove to Khandala and talked of eloping, that this was how their escapade would end. They had believed that what they did was a thing between them, a normal man and a normal woman. But now, somehow, the whole world it seemed, had managed to involve itself in their affair. Yet none harboured ill will towards the other, for neither was responsible for the unfortunate turn of events that put an end to their fantasy. If anything, both felt an ache in their heart as the judges spoke.

If the world was a perfect place, a utopia where equality prevailed, perhaps Lolita and Sandesh could have lived happily ever after, as people did in fairy tales. They could have got married, their age and social position being of no consequence. Lolita, the older and more educated of the two, could have worked and supported Sandesh and no one would have found this a transgression.

Alas, the world isn't a utopia.

SEVEN

Mr Escort

Initially, victory in court did not bring about appreciable changes in Sandesh's life. He held on to his job at Pigeon Couriers and continued to lodge with his former colleagues, Darshan and Aniket. Sandesh was still upset with JR for failing to bring him the windfall he had promised, by way of damages, from the Senguptas. Yet he was grateful to his benefactor for helping him avenge Aroop's insult. He was also aware that had it not been for the flamboyant lawyer whose age, he guessed, was no more than forty, although JR was fifty-one, he would have gone about with a disfigured face for the rest of his life. Even if he knew plastic surgeons like Dr Hosi Billimoria existed, he would not have been able to afford their services in even seven generations. Sandesh shuddered as he recalled the mutilated image of himself that he saw in the bathroom mirror soon after Aroop's goons attacked him. How he had sobbed that day, the sobs leading to convulsions that caused his whole body to shake, as if struck by lightning. He wept in utter anguish. His wounds were excruciatingly painful, but more tormenting was the thought that henceforth, he would look no different from a leper, whose body parts were eaten by disease, leaving only stumps in place of what were once fingers and toes, ears and a nose.

However, thanks to JR, Sandesh's body had been restored to more or less its original shape, making it impossible for anyone to speculate that he had been attacked, as if by wild animals in the jungles of the Sunderbans.

Sandesh continued to pop in at JR's apartment every evening, no matter how late or tired he was. He enjoyed his drink and takeaway meal at JR's flat, as also their discussions in Hindi and English. Sandesh was reluctant to trade these for evenings spent otherwise, ringing JR's doorbell only after freshening up at his digs and daubing himself with deodorant. His sartorial elegance reached new heights, for he had stopped sending money to his mother and spent most of it on his wardrobe, adding F-Street jeans, T-shirts, cargo pants and formals to his collection of clothes every fortnight. The apparel was worn not just by Sandesh, but by Darshan and Aniket as well, who freely helped themselves to whatever they fancied when he was away at work, fights often breaking out among them as a consequence.

'What's written on your T-shirt?' JR asked Sandesh as he entered the apartment one evening, a few days after the judgement.

Sandesh stood before JR and put his chest out so that the latter could read for himself.

'You're massive, I'm passive,' the lawyer read aloud, contemplating its meaning.

'That is a gay T-shirt,' he said at last, smiling.

'Means what?' asked Sandesh.

'Don't you know what "gay" means?'

'No.'

'It means a man who loves another man.'

'Like you?'

'Exactly.'

JR then proceeded to lecture Sandesh on the need to pay careful attention to what was written on his T-shirts before buying them.

'This T-shirt is a present from my *bachpan ka saathi*, Somnath, who I am meeting in Mumbai when I am first time coming here,' Sandesh informed JR. 'At that time, I am not knowing what "massive" and "passive" means. I am still not knowing.'

'Well, massive refers to a man with a large dick and passive is a man who gets fucked during sex,' JR explained.

'Oh shit!' Sandesh swore. 'I am not *chhakka*. Today only I am burning this T-shirt.'

'No, no, don't do that,' said JR. 'Give it to me if you don't want it.'

'You wearing it?'

'No, but I'll preserve it as a souvenir because it's yours and your body smells are all over it.'

As they drank, JR got into a teacherly mode and told Sandesh that all the stuff sold on F-Street were export rejects that imitated the styles and designs of international fashion brands like Versace and Gucci, which cost thousands of rupees.

'They even lift the words off the clothes blindly, without having a clue as to what they mean. The words on your T-shirt are probably copied from Versace. The owner of Versace, who was murdered in Florida some years ago, was known to be gay.'

The topics they discussed as they sipped their whisky differed from day to day. JR made it a point to introduce new subjects every evening, so that their discussions did not become monotonous. The day after they spent all their time talking about clothes, JR announced that the topic for the day was Lolita, which brought a lascivious smile to Sandesh's face.

'You loved her, didn't you?' JR asked.

'*Ho sakta hai wo pyaar tha,*' Sandesh replied. 'She was my first love.'

'Did you find her pretty?'

Sandesh seemed more than ready with his answers. 'Yes, she was pretty,' he affirmed.

'What about her did you find pretty?'

'She was tall, slim and fair. Every boy is liking girl like that.'

'Do you have her photograph? For keeps?'

'No,' said Sandesh, and then narrated the story of Lolita's photo, which he lost.

'But,' he laughed, 'there is girl in my office who is looking like carbon copy of madam. I am satisfying myself by looking at her.'

'I'd love to see her too.'

'Then come to my office tomorrow only in your Mercedes, and I am showing you.'

'Done.'

Although JR did not drive to Sandesh's office at Pigeon Couriers to check out the duplicate Lolita, Sandesh's love life continued to hog the limelight for the next few days.

As they spoke, telephone calls or the doorbell invariably interrupted them. The calls were from clients and acquaintances, while newsboys, cable boys and such like presented themselves at the door to collect their dues and settle their bills.

JR needs a wife, Sandesh often thought to himself at such times. He had never seen a grown man, as old as JR, living as a bachelor. Didn't a man need a wife to cook for him and have sex with him? Though he thought it impolite to say so, Sandesh was convinced that JR was indeed gay because he wasn't married and did not have a woman in his bed at night.

When the phone calls and the doorbell ringing ceased, JR lit up and asked Sandesh why he did not have a girlfriend.

'Lolita …' Sandesh began, but JR cut him short.

'Not an aunty like Lolita, for god's sake. I mean a proper girlfriend, younger than you in age.'

Sandesh took a deep breath and blew rings from the cigarette he smoked.

'I am preferring ladies who are older than me,' he said, and studied JR's face for his reaction.

'Why?' he asked.

'Because,' answered Sandesh, switching over to Hindi, 'if a woman is older, like Lolita, she will look after me. If she is younger, I will have to earn and look after her.'

'So it's responsibility that you shirk?'

'Maybe. But a lady like Lolita who is married and experienced is also more fun in bed.'

'What about the booze?'

'Yes, that too. I was getting it for free, like here, in your house.'

That night JR dropped Sandesh home in his Mercedes, not wanting him to go back by bus.

JR celebrated Sandesh's eighteenth birthday in his house at Sea View Apartments by making him cut a chocolate cake with eighteen candles on it, a cake ordered especially from La Patisserie at the Taj. A few friends of the lawyer, whom Sandesh had never met before, were also invited to the party. Sandesh blew out all the candles in one go and as JR and his friends sang *Happy Birthday* for him while he cut the cake, Sandesh picked up a large chunk and stuffed it into JR's mouth. JR, in turn, did the same to Sandesh and they both stood together between all the guests with cake smeared across their faces. The party then gave Sandesh his customary birthday bumps which he enjoyed so much that he couldn't stop laughing.

Never before in Sandesh's life had his birthday been celebrated.

Bottles of champagne were opened with corkscrews, and the friends drank till the early hours of the morning, draining all the bottles dry. Dinner had been ordered from Hotel President nearby, also run by the Taj. It was a sumptuous fare, made up of mutton, chicken and fish, like a Parsi *navjot*, but the champagne killed everyone's appetite, so most of the food remained uneaten and had to be refrigerated for the next day.

The vomiting guests finally left towards dawn, but JR urged Sandesh to stay back for the night, or what was left of it, and made his bed in the guest room, marked by a huge oil-on-canvas of shirtless men by the late Bhupen Khakkar.

That was Sandesh's first night at Sea View Apartments.

The next morning, he woke up with a severe hangover, threw up in the bathroom sink, and nursed himself with lemon tea to cure his splitting headache. Sandesh telephoned his office to say he wouldn't be reporting for work, as he was unwell, and spent most of the day sleeping in the guest bedroom. By the evening he was more or less okay, and decided to take his leave.

'One moment,' said JR. He walked over to Sandesh and handed him his birthday present, a mobile phone with a camera.

'It's the latest,' JR smiled.

'Thanks,' replied Sandesh's, ecstatic. JR saw that the present revived Sandesh's spirits.

Out of the blue, Sandesh asked JR a question. 'Sir, when is your birthday?'

'Oh,' spluttered JR, 'it's on 29 February.'

'During leap year?'

'Yes,' he answered.

'But which year? I was born in 1986 or 1987. What about you?'

'You are trying to figure out my age, is it?' JR laughed. 'The fact is, I don't know myself.'

'You don't know?'

'No.'

'How it is possible?'

'I'll tell you.'

JR then went on to narrate an improbable story of how his parents, who were both medicos in the Indian Army, eloped and got married, and how he was conceived and delivered in non-family stations where there were no registries for births and deaths.

'The upshot is that my parents couldn't remember the year I was born,' he said.

'I am small kid or what to believe your story?'

'I'm serious.'

JR was an ageist. Although he was past fifty, the hair dyes and age defying creams that he used (they were actually called that) guaranteed that he looked younger. He was self-conscious about his age and manufactured for his friends the fiction of his being born on 29 February (like Morarji Desai) and being twenty-nine-years-old (numerologically, twenty-nine seemed to be his lucky number), which of course invoked mirth and laughter.

'Think what you want to think,' JR shrugged. 'In any case, age is just a number.'

'Shall I guess your age?'

'No,' replied JR.

'Forty.'

'Bullshit.'

When Sandesh arrived the next day, JR asked him point blank if he'd ever had sex with a man.

'No,' Sandesh assertively said. 'Never.'

'Hot property that you are, hasn't a guy ever cruised you in a public loo, or fondled you in a jam-packed bus or train? It happens all the time.'

'No.'

Sandesh then revealed, as he sipped his whisky, that when he was in high school in Paithan, there was a boy in his class who never lost a chance to have a dekko at his dick whenever he unzipped his pants to pee.

'I am finding it so funny,' he said, 'that I am bursting out laughing every time it is happening.'

'Funny?' JR asked, intrigued.

'Yeah, funny. *Maine socha*, why is this guy dying to see my dick when he has one himself? Boys want to see a chick's cunt because they don't own one and don't know how it looks.'

The logic flabbergasted JR.

When JR asked Sandesh if he was bisexual, that is, attracted to both men and women, the latter protested.

'No,' he thumped his fist on the arm of the sofa. 'I am not attracted to guys one bit. I am not understanding how guy can be attracted to guy.'

'Well, I'm attracted to you.'

'Thank you. I am honoured.'

Shortly afterwards, as the alcohol reached their heads, Sandesh passionately flung himself on JR, contradicting all that he'd said earlier. In an instant, he disrobed the startled lawyer and sucked his dick, bit his nipples, and kissed him full on the lips while fingering his backside.

JR couldn't believe his eyes. He almost pinched himself to see if this was for real.

'Wh … what's going on?' he stammered, gasping for breath.

'*Tofa*,' said Sandesh. '*Inaam*. A reward for you for winning my case. I'm a poor guy who cannot afford your fees. So I'm paying you in kind.'

'Thanks. But I thought you weren't gay.'

'I am, just for you.'

That night, after drinking almost till the cocks crowed, Sandesh stayed over at JR's, not in the guest room, but in the master bedroom on the jumbo bed, next to the man who loved him.

'It's been a really long time since I had someone in my bed,' JR drooled. On hearing this, Sandesh turned him on his belly (boy, he was heavy), mounted and penetrated him and both men groaned. Unlike with Lolita, he did not ask for a condom.

Later, JR attempted to return the favour, but was unsuccessful because god had given him excessive foreskin that hampered penetration (as non-Muslims, his parents did not think of circumcising him), and Sandesh had a tiny, really tiny asshole.

'Never mind,' said Sandesh. 'Remember my T-shirt? We'll make it *ulta*. I am massive, you are passive.'

Neither JR nor Sandesh went to work the next day. Sandesh was in a reckless mood. He was already thinking of chucking his job and making JR his sugar daddy. They spent the day drinking and fucking, and by nightfall, JR had a bruised backside. He remembered a meeting he had once attended in New York City, of an underground outfit that called itself NAMBLA. The acronym stood for North American Man Boy Love Association. It even had a branch in Colombo, Sri Lanka, and its members (the late MJ was one of them) argued that men and boys had a mutual need for each other and the state had no business to come in the way of their relationship and call it paedophilia. JR was forced to shell down fifty US dollars as membership fee.

Thereafter, they had sex everyday. Sandesh promptly rang JR's doorbell around 7 p.m., freshened up in his bathroom, and they sat down to drink. Dinner was served just before midnight, JR being a hospitable host who employed a Nepali chef to cook the spicy non-vegetarian meals that Sandesh loved, though he himself had converted to vegetarianism a few years ago. Then, depending on his mood, Sandesh either stayed the night over, or cleaned up and left after they had fucked. Transport wasn't a problem, no matter how late it was. The BEST ran an all-night service from Colaba to Mahim (Route 83) that stopped just outside JR's building and took Sandesh all the way back to his digs at Dadar. Both men suffered from Sleep Deficiency Syndrome (SDS), sometimes crashing for as little as three hours, before the alarm clock rang and startled them out of bed. This took a toll on their performance at the workplace, although their occupations couldn't be more *hostile* to each other.

JR, who in the manner of the Spanish poet Jimenez, was a worshipper of the Exact Name and considered several words that best described Sandesh: boyfriend, partner, lover. He even thought of 'catamite'. But he rejected all of them and decided that Sandesh was just Sandy, nothing less, nothing more.

JR had been in and out of relationships in the past, some with boys as young as sixteen. However, for the most part he had lived alone. Sandy and he were made for each other, he thought, for if Sandy lacked a bank balance, JR lacked youth. He atoned for this by shopping at Charagh Din, and visiting the salons at the Taj every Friday. He paid special attention to his diet, eating less than usual to get rid of his paunch, and jogging every morning on the Cuffe Parade seafront. JR wished to look good, so that Sandy would feel proud to be seen with him in public. Sandy's own features had been restored to a T, save for a scar here and there, and an occasional limp. JR spent a lot of time and money buying him the entire men's range at high-end stores: shirts, trousers, briefs, belts, wallets, shoes, goggles, aftershaves, colognes. His aim was to make Sandy a metrosexual man. He even got him to pierce his ears and eyebrows and adorn them with funky rings that were sold on the streets of Colaba Causeway. In due course, Sandy looked every inch the dude from Cuffe Parade.

Radical moves followed. Sandy quit his job at Pigeon Couriers at JR's behest (this, as we know, was also what *he* wanted).

'It's slave labour,' JR dismissively said. 'I believe in the dignity of labour, but in India, menial jobs enslave people. How much do they pay you anyway? Four thousand? Five thousand?'

'Three thousand.'

'And what are your working hours?'

'Eight to late.'

'There you are.'

JR argued that since Sandy and he were now a couple, they needed to spend quality time together, going on overnight jaunts, going to the cinema, going to parties. 'With working hours such as yours, we can go nowhere,' he ruled.

When Sandy, posing as the devil's advocate, asked JR how he could carry on without an income of his own, even if it was a mere pittance, the latter volunteered to pay him a monthly allowance that would match his earnings at Pigeon Couriers.

'I'll give you Rs 1500 on the first and fifteenth of every month,' he announced. 'You may think of it as pocket money.'

'Okay,' said Sandy, as he thought of Lolita. He then asked JR to help him draft his resignation letter. 'You write in English, and I am translating it into Marathi.'

Pigeon Couriers readily accepted Sandy's resignation.

'No one is indispensable,' his immediate boss curtly said to him. 'Do you know how many *chutiyas* like you have applied to us for jobs?'

For once, Sandy did not answer back. The man was known for his airs, just because he had a B.Com. degree (it was from Amravati University, and all he had managed to secure was a Pass Class).

Sandy's next step was to leave his room at Dadar which had unpleasant memories, both of Royal Video Parlour and of Lolita, and move in with JR. Darshan and Aniket were saddened by his exit. '*Tu amchya mule jaato ka*?' Are you leaving because of us, Darshan sentimentally asked.

'*Nahi yaar,*' Sandy replied. '*Hum abhi bhi dost hain.*' We are still friends.

However, he did not give his buddies his new address. He told them he was going to live with his old friend, Somnath. It was clear that he was closing the Royal Video Parlour chapter of his life, and never again would he be seeing any of the people associated with it—Darshan, Aniket, Ashok Jadhav and especially Lolita.

'*Amhala visru naka.*' Don't forget us, Aniket said, as Sandy stuffed his meagre belongings, made up of a steel trunk and bedding, into the boot of a ubiquitous Premier Padmini taxi.

'I won't. *Kasam se.*'

The taxi sped off. Sandy waved out to his friends through the rear windshield for what he thought was the last time.

At JR's flat in Sea View Apartments Sandy arranged his frugal possessions in the guest bedroom (with the painting by Bhupen Khakkar) which, from now on, would be his.

'Welcome to your new home,' said JR, and kissed him on the cheek.

'Thank you.'

With the guest bedroom temporarily relinquished, JR would have no place to house his overnight guests, many of whom came from abroad, if they unexpectedly made an appearance for a night or two.

'We'll remodel the flat later,' he told Sandy, 'and carve out an extra room for such exigencies. As for now, you use the guest bedroom by day and sleep with me on the jumbo bed by night.'

'Yes, sir.'

Freed for the first time from the rigours of manual labour, Sandy spent his time reading the gay porn in JR's vast collection of books and magazines. He also watched movies. When he was thirsty, he helped himself to chilled bottles of beer and wine in the refrigerator. One rule that JR had imposed was that daytime drinking had to be restricted to wine and beer. Hard liquor was strictly for the after hours. Only *bewdas*, alcoholics, drank hard liquor by day.

'Like Lolita?' asked Sandy.

'You said it,' quipped JR.

However, beer and wine too, when drunk intemperately, could knock a man senseless. JR returned home from work one evening to find Sandy so pissed, he mistook him for dead. When he opened the fridge, he discovered that an entire crate of beer, picked up just yesterday, had vanished. Enough is enough, JR thought to himself, and ordered Sandy to do something with his life, like the writer Christopher Isherwood's teenaged boyfriend.

'What?' Sandy shot back.

'Anything,' JR yelled.

Later, when tempers cooled, the two men sat down and made an inventory of all the things Sandy could profitably do to bide his time. They zeroed in on three: spoken English, computers and driving. After all, Colaba was lined with schools where all three skills could be inexpensively acquired.

Sandy stubbornly insisted that he wanted to start with driving, although JR wanted him to become computer literate and learn spoken English first. But he let the obdurate lad have his way and wrote out a cheque for Rs 5000 in the name of Bharat Motor Training School. Much paperwork had to be done in the offices of the RTO at Tardeo before Sandy could actually commence his driving lessons. Passport-sized photos had to be taken and when asked to write down his address on an application form, he thought to himself, '*Kaunsa*, what address can I write? Royal Video Parlour? Jannat? Darshan and Aniket's room? Or my *baap ka ghar* in Paithan town?' He finally decided to give JR's address as his own.

Sandy realized at that moment that he was a homeless refugee.

Eventually, his driving lessons began and for an hour every morning, and then again in the evening (for which JR shelled out twice as much), his instructor, who reminded him of that charlatan Mr Ali because he resembled him in appearance, took him to the Band Stand and to Cooperage to teach him the ABC (Accelerator-Brake-Clutch) of driving.

'You will pick up fast because you are so young,' the instructor told him as he drove, touching his fingers on the pretext of holding the steering wheel. 'Old men take a long time to learn.'

Sandy, who in recent times had learnt much about gayness, wondered if his instructor too was gay.

He was extremely upset about the car in which he was made to train—a battered old Maruti 800.

'When I am getting licence, I am driving Mercedes-Benz C Class,' he declared, causing his instructor to doubt his sanity.

'Why? Are you going to become Shah Rukh Khan's driver or what?' the instructor asked him.

Later, at home, JR was eager to know if Sandy enjoyed his driving lessons. He also asked him if he'd ever taken lessons before. Here, Sandy gave his old man a graphic account of the one and only driving lesson Lolita gave him in Khandala in her Zen Carbon.

'I am loving it,' he said in the manner of the McDonald's ad and ruined JR's evening.

A month later, Sandy took his driving test and passed in the first attempt.

'Congratulations!' said JR, as they clinked their glasses.

'Thanks. Now give me keys of the Mercedes.'

While JR was pleased that he would at last have a 'driver' who would drive him about town, he also enrolled Sandy at the Shakespeare English Speaking Academy next to his house, and at the Bill Gates Computer Classes a few streets away. Though Sandy was a reluctant student at these institutes, he attended both classes everyday, aware that JR was monitoring his movements.

As JR's live-in companion, Sandy now had full access to his flat and the effects therein. He went in and out of rooms, switched on the TV at will and raided the kitchen whenever he was hungry. There was no part of the flat that was out of bounds for him.

It was inside a chestnut drawer in the study that Sandy first discovered the lawyer's licensed revolver with the initials 'JR' engraved on it. At first he thought it was a toy pistol and then wondered if it was a lighter, like the one he had once seen in an Aurangabad store. When JR told him the revolver was real, Sandy wondered why he needed it.

'You are not politician or an underworld don,' he said, looking perplexed. 'So why you keeping gun?'

'I may not be a politician or an underworld don,' JR explained, 'but I'm a criminal lawyer. I send unlawful people to jail. Any of these convicts may want to take revenge when they're released. I need the gun for self-defence.'

Sandy, who was seeing a gun at such close quarters for the first time, was soon obsessed with it. He went to the chestnut drawer a hundred times a day to see if the revolver was still there, to handle it and scrutinize its feel. He made up his mind to use the gun someday. *Ek din*, one day, I am killing somebody, anybody, with this gun, he said to himself.

On his part, JR noticed Sandy's fascination with the weapon, but took it as no more than a boy's fantasy. Girls are given dolls to play with during their childhood, and boys are given guns. JR attributed Sandy's fondness for his Mercedes and his revolver to his underprivileged childhood where his parents, the Wretched of the Earth, could not give him toys to play with. He was atoning for it at the onset of adulthood, but was too old now to play with toy cars and toy guns.

Meanwhile, in his sleep one night, JR hit upon the Exact Name that described his and Sandy's relationship. On waking up, he hugged Sandy and exclaimed, 'Eureka!'

Sandy, who'd never heard the word 'eureka' before (in school they did not teach him Archimedes) wondered what had come over the man.

'Is mad dog biting you, or what?' he asked.

'No,' replied JR. 'But I have figured out who you are to me.'

'Who?'

'Escort.'

'What?'

JR spent the whole morning explaining to Sandy the business of being an escort.

'An escort is no mere sex worker or one-night stand who is here today and gone tomorrow,' he explained. 'Instead, an escort is no different from a boyfriend or lover. However, there is one crucial difference. While the words "boyfriend" and "lover" imply emotional involvement, an escort isn't emotionally attached to his client. For him, it's just a job and he sees himself as a professional. It is imperative, of course, that he keeps up appearances and *pretends* to be in love with his client. But in reality he's not. In that sense, he's no different from an actor.'

Sandy did not refute the implications of JR's words. In his heart of hearts, he knew he was playing a game. He could never love JR the way he loved Lolita. Moreover, he could never see himself as gay. But the escort's job interested him. JR told him there were agencies in Bombay that trained escorts and found them employment, regardless of their gender and sexual orientation.

'Enrol me,' Sandy said, his eyes lighting up. 'Just as you have put me in Shakespeare English Speaking Academy and Bill Gates Computer Class, now put me in Rakhi Sawant Escort Agency.'

They had a hearty laugh.

Their lives quietly fell into a pattern. By day, JR attended court, while Sandy, except for when he took French leave and stayed home, went to his Shakespeare and Bill Gates classes. The Rakhi Sawant class unfortunately remained a pipe dream and did not ever materialize.

By night, they made love, but here too a pattern emerged. The young Sandy was the archetypal guy on top, while the older JR was the stereotypical bottom guy. Sandy invariably shut his eyes when he screwed JR. He had brainwashed himself into believing that the creature beneath him was no man, but a woman. He imagined he was fucking Lolita, not JR. The difference between vaginal and anal intercourse became apparent to him at once. While the former enabled him to insert his *entire* penis into Lolita's cunt, even as she was close to an orgasm, the latter was marked by JR's annoying sighs. 'You're hurting me,' he screamed, as Sandy pushed deeper. Again, vaginal intercourse made it possible for both partners to simultaneously climax, leading to heightened ecstasy. However, there was no such luck with anal sex. Sandy climaxed way before JR, often discharging his semen outside, rather than inside the man, making him, Sandy, see it as a colossal waste. JR masturbated long after Sandy rose and went to the bathroom to clean up. Their sex was anything but satisfactory.

There were things that JR noticed as they made love. He saw, for example, that Sandy never volunteered to help him masturbate. While he had no qualms about inserting his fingers into the lawyer's backside or fondling his nipples, touching his dick (except for that first time) was an absolute no-no. This, to JR's way of thinking, was behaviour that proved Sandy was straight, but masquerading as gay. Why, otherwise, would he restrict his caresses to the region around JR's tits, squeezing them so hard at times that JR would squeal in pain and go around with a swelling for days afterwards? Why, Sandy even made movements with his fingers that indicated he was 'lactating' JR.

During a drunken spell one evening, Sandy drooled and incoherently rambled, 'Aunty *wapas ayi.*' Aunty is back. The booze stopped the words from clearly forming in his mouth.

JR did not react, but reflected on the subtext of Sandy's words. There was no question of Lolita being back in Sandy's life. But this was clearly Sandy's wishful thinking. He was now seeing JR not as JR, but as a substitute for Lolita.

'A guy speaks the truth either when he's angry or when he's drunk,' JR said after a while, confounding Sandy. They lit a single cigarette, as always, and passed it back and forth between themselves.

'So?'

'So, I'm going to give you a call on your mobile.'

Saying this, JR dialled Sandy's number from his Blackberry, and saw the latter's cell phone as it rang. His ringtone was a song from that year's blockbuster, *Dhoom*. Sandy always kept his cell phone on the centre table next to his glass as they drank, and not in his shirt pocket as he earlier did, after JR told him that cell phone radiation caused cancer. The name that now flashed on his screen was 'Lolita'.

'Why did you save my name as Lolita?' JR demanded.

'Simply.'

'Fuck you.'

JR found a new voyeuristic pastime. Every evening he made it his mission to get his young friend drunk and then ask him to describe, in graphic detail, what Lolita and he did in bed. Sandy had already given him an explicit account of how Lolita had attempted to teach him driving at Khandala, using his dick as a gear shift. Sandy now put on his thinking cap and provided his sugar daddy with the minutiae of how their bodies, Lolita's and his, always touched at three places as they made love: mouth, boobs and genitals.

'She is calling this Triple-X DVD,' Sandy joked.

'But you never put your mouth to mine, or touch my cock,' JR jealously remarked. 'Why, ours isn't even a Double X DVD.'

As these sessions continued, Sandy exaggeratedly recounted how he would insert the entire length of his index finger into Lolita's pussy and then put his finger into his mouth. 'It is tasting like *asli* ghee,' he said. Another time he informed JR that since a woman's boobs were a highly erogenous zone, Lolita forever wanted him to fondle hers.

'Were they wet?' JR asked.

'Yes,' said Sandy. 'Whenever I am touching her boobs, the milk is coming on my fingers and spilling on bed sheet. I am having to wipe it with towel.'

His classes at the Shakespeare English Speaking Academy had added new words to his vocabulary, like 'spill', 'bed sheet' and a host of others.

'And didn't you ever want to drink the milk?'

'I am wanting to, but how can I? It is for her baby, Tanu, and not for me.'

'Did Lolita ever breastfeed her baby?'

'No, she is always making her drink milk from bottle.'

'Why?'

'I don't know. But one time when I am asking her, she is saying, "I have to save my milk for you, my love."'

'Oh.'

Sandy then recalled how, contrary to commercial sex workers, who often bickered with their customers for *not* wearing condoms, afraid they'd contract AIDS, Lolita fought with him for *wearing* one all the time.

'"*Nirodh ke bina karo*," she is pleading with me on daily basis,' he said.

'Why?'

'Obviously, because she is wanting me to make her pregnant.'

'What about her husband and daughter?'

'She is not loving them, but loving me only. She is desperately wanting to elope with me. "*Chalo bhag jayenge aur saath me rahenge,*" she is saying to me so many times.'

'Really?'

'Promise.'

JR was curious to know why Sandy always insisted on a condom when servicing Lolita, but he never wore one while *they* were together.

'I am scared of AIDS,' said Sandy, 'but I am also scared of *lafda* that is happening if madam is getting pregnant. In your case, pregnancy … ha ha.'

It went on like this for days. Sandy reported to his old man that Lolita received no sexual pleasure whatsoever from her husband, who was mostly away at sea. But even when he was in station, he made excuses whenever Lolita, inflamed with desire, dragged him to bed. He said he was exhausted after a hard day's work and deferred their lovemaking to the next day. But the next day, it was the same story all over again.

A doubt crossed JR's mind. He wondered if Aroop was gay, as many sailors are reputed to be.

The sum and substance of what Sandy said to JR then, was that Lolita got all her sexual kicks from him and him alone. '*Jitna mazaa tune diya, utna mere husband se bhi nahi mila,*' she had told him once. She was so in love with him that on days when he couldn't make it to Jannat for some reason or the other, she sulked, threw a tantrum, called him in the office to nag him as if he were her husband, and went to bed sobbing and hungry.

Sandy's disclosures had an effect on JR that neither man could have anticipated. Convinced that the guy who shared his bed night after night was 100 per cent straight, he couldn't climax until he fantasized about Sandy and Lolita, sometimes going to the extent of imagining he was Lolita, and asking Sandy to lactate him. 'Milk me, milk me,' he groaned one night.

Sandy, of course, could not be blamed for the 'psychological damage' he had caused to JR. He had innocently provided his mentor with all the amorous details he had asked for and discovered only much later, when it was too late, that the man had stored them in his unconscious mind to feed his own voyeuristic fantasies.

A stage came when JR couldn't sleep with Sandy, whom he truly fancied, unless it was preceded by hours of dirty talk of the things Lolita and he did in bed. Finally, Sandy saw through his game and refused to open his mouth each time JR probed.

'I don't remember,' he learned to dismissively say, with a flicker of his hand, and changed the topic.

However, all that had already been said couldn't be unsaid and it complicated Sandy and JR's relationship. It was JR's turn now, in the manner of Lolita, to be a spoilsport. He got maudlin.

'You got close to me for my money, for my Merc, for my revolver,' he drunkenly grumbled. 'You got close to me because you needed a roof over your head. You did not get close to me for love.'

Sandy's previous experience with Lolita came in handy here. He knew that the shrewdest way to deal with such a situation was to keep mum till the outburst, like a storm, passed and there was fair weather again. If he retaliated, as he once did, it would backfire. 'Get out of my house,' JR had said to him on that occasion, and Sandy had actually left, till JR tracked him down at Darshan and Aniket's the next day and begged him to return to Sea View Apartments.

'It's your home,' JR had said, leading him by the hand to his C Class.

Of course, Sandy himself was no saint. There were cantankerous nights when he told JR that, as far as he was concerned, what they did in bed was a mere formality and a compromise.

'I am not turned on by you one bit, you old fart,' he cruelly said. 'I am faking it.'

The way JR saw it, this had a miraculous effect on him. It made him a heterosexual by default. A man whose sexual fantasies since puberty hinged around homosexual love, suddenly found himself obsessed with the idea of Sandy penetrating Lolita.

'*Wo mere upar baithti thi*,' Sandy once told JR, and the image froze in his mind.

There were other muddles too. Sandy wanted to experience for himself what Lolita felt when she 'sat' on him and he thought he could achieve this by 'sitting' on JR. But the experiment fell flat on its face, as JR's uncircumcised penis at fifty-one did not have the tenacity of Sandy's at sixteen; conversely, Sandy's anus did not have the malleability of Lolita's vagina.

Sandy turned the episode to his advantage during a drunken brawl, calling JR a hijra.

'Call yourself she and not he,' Sandy abusively told him.

To this JR retorted that some of India's gay icons like Ashok Row Kavi and Hoshang Merchant referred to themselves in the feminine gender.

'Ashok is *amma* to us and Hoshang is Mother Hoshang,' he said.

'So now you be Aunty JR to all the homos of India,' Sandy bitchily remarked.

And so it went on, Sandy habitually tormenting JR by describing Lolita as his first love. At times it seemed as if JR and Sandy, client and escort, were ready to gouge out each other's eyes.

EIGHT

ARSE/Testosterone

Sandy's classes at the Shakespeare English Speaking Academy bore fruit. He was finally able to speak in the lingo sans the use of the present continuous, the irritating 'ing's' as JR called them. Though they had come to his birthday bash, JR felt that only now could he properly introduce his rustic boyfriend to his vast circle of gay friends, all men of distinction. They were architects, journalists, teachers, sculptors, musicians, doctors, dramatists. Together, they formed a club that they called Association for the Rights of the Sexually Exploited, abbreviated to the obscene acronym ARSE. They met by rotation at each other's homes, located in supremely upmarket neighbourhoods such as Pedder Road, Warden Road, Napean Sea Road, Marine Drive, Malabar Hill, Cumballa Hill, and of course, Cuffe Parade where JR himself lived. Sandy conversed with the guests in English whenever it was JR's turn to host a gathering, but his pronunciations often went haywire and led to confusion. Where he meant 'carpenter' for instance, the suave company thought he said 'car painter'.

'JR, you painting your car?' they asked. 'What colour?'

If he used the word 'often', as he was fond of doing, they mistook it to be its very opposite, 'off and on', especially because he tended to mumble.

A typical conversation among them went like this:

'When do you guys have sex?'

'Often.'

'Off and on? Why not daily?'

Of course, when the discussions grew highfalutin in nature, Sandy withdrew, unable to make head or tail of either the issues that they animatedly spoke of, or the bombast that they used. At such times, he would recede into the bedroom with flair and switch on the LCD TV. He was glad to watch soaps in which men romanced women.

Meanwhile, the members of ARSE discussed the various topics on their agenda and had heated debates about them. They spoke, for example, of the need to make one's sexual orientation a part of one's identity. They talked of multiple queer identities such as gay, bisexual, transgender, hijra and koti. They tracked the progress of a writ petition filed in the Delhi High Court that sought to abolish or at least 'read down' an archaic law, popularly known as the anti-sodomy law, that called sex between men 'unnatural' and saw it as a criminal offence. Like murder.

'What's the number of that notorious article?' a pianist by the name of Pheroze asked.

'It's Section 377 of the Indian Penal Code,' replied JR.

'How interesting! That happens to be the number of my car.'

'How can you drive around in a car with a number like that?' Derek the architect remarked.

'I'm fond of irony, you know,' Pheroze retorted.

'With a judiciary as homophobic as ours,' JR said, 'I don't think 377 will ever vanish.'

Someone introduced the subject of gay bashing and everyone had at least one sordid story to tell of how they had been ambushed by policemen or by goondas, and were stripped of not just their cash and valuables, but also of ATM cards and credit cards, besides being beaten black and blue.

'That's the reason I never cruise in washrooms and parks,' said Randhir, a dramatist and French teacher. 'The Internet is much safer.'

To this Hemant, the sculptor, replied that the Internet too had its pitfalls because the wrong kind often stalked one, and then getting them off one's back was a Herculean task.

'Let's camp in the wilderness somewhere,' JR suggested, 'and brainstorm these issues there.' Everyone liked the idea, but when they consulted their calendars, they couldn't zero in on a common date to take off, busy men as they were.

Debashish, who ran an NGO that was situated in the heart of Kamatipura, Bombay's popular red light district, spoke of a new 'cocktail' of medicines that enabled one to live with AIDS for ever.

'Can it be bought off the shelf at a drugstore?' asked Pheroze.

'No,' Debashish explained. 'You have to queue up for it at a government hospital.'

'Such a pain.'

Anand, a journalist with the *Times of India*, boasted that Barkha Dutt had invited him to participate in a *We the People* show on gay rights on NDTV. 'Did anyone see it?' he enthusiastically asked everyone, but no one other than JR had managed to, and that was only because Sandy surfed channels 24/7.

'Oh, TV is so boring,' Ismail, a poet and a college lecturer who taught at St. Xavier's snobbishly said. 'I never watch TV.'

A plump young man in his early thirties, a new member of ARSE, had remained silent so far. When the others asked him what he did for a living, he said he was a child specialist.

'Really?' exclaimed Pheroze. 'Do send me some of your children.'

'He's not a child specialist in your sense,' Debashish said, losing his cool.

Pheroze, everyone knew, had a reputation for paedophilia, as a result of which some members had reservations about admitting him to ARSE.

'He's a paediatrician,' said JR, 'in case you do not know the word. Even Sandy knows it now.'

'Obviously he would,' laughed Anand, 'with his kind of history.'

All of JR's friends were familiar with the case he fought and won on Sandy's behalf in the Bombay High Court.

The plump young paediatrician's name was Mohan. He was attending an ARSE meeting for the first time and he wanted to know if homosexuals and lesbians could come together and fight for their rights on a common platform. Mohan had a sister, Meena, who was lesbian. It was one of those rare cases where both siblings in the family were queer. The reference to lesbians, however, touched a nerve with JR. 'Lesbians have their own agendas,' he declared. 'They can never see eye to eye with us.'

'True,' said Randhir. 'Most women are bitches, but the straight ones at least depend on us guys for fucks. Lesbians don't need even that.'

'Well, the straight ones don't depend on *you* for fucks,' said Debashish.

There was laughter. Sandy peeped in to see what the hullabaloo was all about.

Mohan recounted the story of a lesbian, Chetana, who married a homosexual, Chetan, and had a child with him through extra-sexual means. 'They're still together after five years of married life,' he informed everyone, 'and that's the kind of partnership between gays and lesbians I'm thinking about.'

But Mohan was in the minority. The majority of ARSE members couldn't stand lesbians. Mohan called it misogyny.

Debashish urged everyone to go online and sign a petition for the scrapping of Section 377. 'We've got to do it,' he said, 'so that we bequeath a happier universe to tomorrow's gays.'

When JR reiterated that he was sceptical about Section 377 ever being repealed, Debashish said, 'Our duty is to do everything in our power to change the law. We ought to leave no stone unturned.'

He then proceeded to inform his compatriots that famous men like Amartya Sen and Vikram Seth were signatories to the petition.

On hearing this, Ismail, who taught English literature and had a collection of poems to his credit called *Vignettes from the Vineyard*, said that Vikram Seth was a hypocrite. 'Why didn't he take a stand earlier?' he asked. 'Why does he write fluff like *A Suitable Boy*?'

Anand came to Vikram Seth's defence. 'His poetry, unlike his novels, *does* tend to be gay,' he argued. 'Read *The Humble Administrator's Garden* and *The Golden Gate*. Then decide for yourself.'

But Ismail remained unconvinced. 'Vikram Seth hankers after a mainstream readership and foreign publishers,' he ruled. 'He is squeamish about being cast into the ghetto. A man like that can never do for gay literature what the poet Namdeo Dhasal has done for Dalit literature.'

When the meeting drew to a close, ARSE members drove to Testosterone, a gay bar in Colaba. Testosterone, situated next to the Radio Club on Apollo Bunder, was a hop, skip and jump from JR's house and that was one reason why everyone loved to meet at Sea View Apartments. They also made it a point to get together every Saturday evening, for Testosterone was a gay bar just once a week. However, even on Saturday nights, it was characterized by the presence of skimpily dressed women, and this confused Sandy who reluctantly joined the others at Testosterone.

'What are chicks doing here?' he whispered into JR's ear the first time he went to Testosterone. Ismail heard him and, despite the deafening music, bought him a large beer and explained to him that these ladies were heterosexists, there to prove that homosexuality was perverse and if women were freely available, men would never turn to their own sex for sexual gratification.

'I agree,' said Sandy. The ease with which he slipped into his new role as JR's boyfriend notwithstanding, there was a latent homophobia in him which made him think of ARSE members as nutty. He surreptitiously eyed the women in the bar from the corner of his eye (remember Meryl Streep and Faye Dunaway?) and refused to go to the dance floor with the men. He knew, of course, that the women couldn't be had for free, and to publicly express his desire for them in front of the members of ARSE was like a Marxist wanting to join the Shiv Sena. Hence he silently endured the life that fate had thrust onto him.

'You agree?' exclaimed Ismail. 'Hasn't JR taught you anything yet? What are you doing with a man like him, anyway?'

Ismail joined the others at the table, while Sandy strolled around near the bar with his hands in his pockets.

'Your boyfriend hates queers,' Ismail said to JR.

'I know,' JR replied, surprising everyone.

Pheroze called for the need to ban chicks from entering Testosterone, at least on Saturday nights, so as to lure vulnerable young men whom he called GBCSs or Gay Born Confused Straights, after the fashion of ABCDs or American Born Confused Desis. 'Must complain to the owner, old Mr Pallonji,' he grumbled.

'But it's a free country,' Derek quipped. 'How can you prevent anyone from entering a bar, as long as they pay their cover charge?'

'Ha,' Anand wryly laughed. 'Tell them, "Sorry, miss, you cannot enter because you are hetero, out to woo homos." It's discrimination on grounds of sexual orientation, dammit.'

A dusky hustler eavesdropped on the conversation that the ARSE members were having, and before anyone knew it, joined them at their table.

'Hi,' she said, pulling up a chair. 'May I?'

'Of course,' Debashish politely answered. His work frequently required him to deal with commercial sex workers and the like, and like Mohan, he believed in building bridges between the two sexes.

She introduced herself as Sabina. The discussion she eavesdropped on hassled her, as the creases on her face revealed.

'You guys think only *you* are LGBT?' she peevishly asked, lighting a cigarette. 'You couldn't be more wrong. *I'm* LGBT too.'

Mohan's ears perked up, like a dog or a cat's, for he thought he had found his ultimate lesbian. JR cringed. But Sabina was no lesbian. It turned out that she seriously believed LGBT stood for Lesbian Gay Bisexual Trisexual.

'And I'm the last,' she proudly proclaimed. 'I'm a trisexual. I'll try anything.'

Everyone at the table laughed and, once again, Sandy, who was nearby, looked in their direction to figure out who among these humourless guys (from his point of view) cracked a joke.

'It's not funny,' JR said. ARSE members looked at each other. None, not even Debashish, considered it worth their while to educate the dumb Sabina and inform her that the 'T' in LGBT did not stand for Tri Sexual, or Try Sexual as she inanely thought, but for Transgender. She abruptly left their table when another hustler urgently signalled to her.

The getaway proposed by JR materialized a month or so later, during an extra-long weekend when both Saturday and Monday were holidays.

'God bless India for having so many gods,' said Randhir. 'It ensures that we have a copious supply of holidays.'

This triggered a discussion on the Indian government's brand of secularism, where latitude shown to one religion had to be balanced by that shown to other religions.

'If Ram Navami is declared as a public holiday to please the Hindus,' said Anand, 'then Moharram must be a holiday to please the Muslims, Good Friday to please the Christians, Pateti to please the Parsis and Guru Nanak's birthday to please the Sikhs.'

'What about the Jews?' JR facetiously asked.

'How many man days does that leave us with in a year?' laughed Hemant. 'A hundred and fifty?'

'Man days!' Pheroze interjected. 'What a nice expression!'

'Oh, the English language is full of words like that,' smiled Ismail. 'What about "manhole"? Or "mouthorgan"?'

'Manhole … mouthorgan,' said Derek, smacking his lips. 'I'm horny now.'

'It's called an innuendo, in case anyone didn't know,' Ismail continued. The teacher in him clearly never took a back seat.

'If we ever have a Marxist government at the centre,' said Anand, 'our definition of secularism will change. It will cease to be "equal importance to all religions" and become "no importance to any religion".'

'Well said,' felt Mohan.

'But why are we cribbing?' asked Pheroze. 'Shouldn't we be happy that our beloved country gives us so many paid holidays?'

Debashish, who was a workaholic, said holidays bored him because they were like songs in Hindi films that interrupted the story.

'Good metaphor,' opined Ismail. 'Is it original?'

They left on Friday evening for Alibag in four cars: JR's C Class, Derek's Toyota Corolla, Mohan's Innova, and Pheroze's Scorpio (with the number 377, of course). While Sandy was at the wheel of JR's car, everyone else drove themselves, though they could well afford the services of drivers and chauffeurs. With his young blood, Sandy quickly overtook the others, fancying he was Schumacher himself. 'Slow down, slow down,' a jittery JR kept cautioning him. Ismail, who rode with them, busied himself in the back seat with Mahesh Dattani's *Collected Plays* to take his mind off Sandy's rash driving.

The other cars rode at varying speeds, because of which they did not travel together as the convoy they had started as, but were separated from each other by vast stretches. But their cell phones enabled them to keep in touch. How they loved to unfold maps in their respective cars, to figure out their exact location and the route they would take.

At one stage Pheroze had a flat tyre, and he SOS'd JR who got Sandy to fix it with a jack and stepney.

'Oh, Sandy is so handy,' said Pheroze, not knowing what else to say by way of thanks.

Mohan and Debashish, who were driving together, had a close shave when an ST bus nearly collided with them head on. 'It's only because I swerved at the nth hour that we're alive,' Mohan told his friends, who gave him brandy.

'Debashish would have died with you too,' joked Randhir, who was fond of black humour, 'and that would have been a great loss to humanity, considering the kind of yeoman service he renders.'

At Alibag they checked into the costliest five-star hotel on the beach, the Taj Submarine, which had an underwater pub called the Titanic, where ARSE members, when asked what they wished to drink, answered in unison, 'Whisky and sodomy.' Obviously they meant soda. Derek informed everyone that the celebrated writer Shobhaa De had a villa in Alibag designed by him (which was a lie); at this everyone wondered why, affluent as they were, *they* did not own property in Alibag or Khandala or even Mahabaleshwar. They could drive down every week, just like the Americans who slogged Monday to Friday and then escaped to the countryside during weekends.

First thing next morning, they went to the beach and got into their swimming trunks, each one checking out the others' dicks as they changed. Anand was the only one who did not swim, so apart from minding everyone's clothes, he splashed about in the water up to his knees. JR kept yanking Sandy's shorts off under the water, but Sandy got his revenge by submerging JR's head in the salt water and extracting a promise that he'd never do it again, before letting go of his head. Mohan, who had won swimming championships when he was younger, pushed out toward the forbidden parts of the beach, ignoring the signboards that warned 'swimming is dangerous' till lifeguards in blue and silver uniforms blew their whistles frenetically to hail out to him. Debashish recalled a high school picnic where Mehernosh, a ninth standard student, drowned in the sea off Marve Beach.

'They called it an accident,' he said, 'but I'm sure it was murder. The backbenchers of the class forever bullied him.

They must have dragged him into the deep, knowing he did not know how to swim.'

All this while, Pheroze sat quietly, wondering why there were no nude beaches in India. 'Goa had one, but I believe it does not exist any more.'

Pheroze boasted that he had been to nude beaches in Canada and Spain that were out of this world. 'Even the security personnel were in the altogether,' he said. 'Once, when someone pulled out his camera, the security guards, a man and a woman, started to make their way towards him to warn him of dire consequences. As they ran, the man's dick and the woman's boobs furiously swung.'

'Why?' asked Randhir.

'Because photography is never allowed in nude beaches anywhere in the world.'

'Nor is sex for that matter,' added JR.

'And how! Nude beaches are like Paradise where the forbidden fruit must be seen, but not tasted.'

They lunched at a beachside café, where they ordered fish vindaloo and jugs of beer for themselves. While their cars were covered with sand, Sandy, taking the C Class to be his own, painstakingly washed it with a hosepipe in the hotel's parking lot, although there were workers in the hotel who were assigned the task of washing cars for a fee. But it was princely.

'I saved you 300 bucks,' Sandy said to JR.

ARSE members envied JR for being the only one in the group with a steady boyfriend. Cross-class relationships with young men in their twenties was everyone's fantasy, but none except JR had managed to turn it into reality.

'It's a queer fetish,' ruled Pheroze, 'this business of love affairs with guys beneath us in station. Even a top industrialist like Ratan Wadia has succumbed to the temptation.'

'Whoever is his boyfriend must be fucking lucky,' Randhir enviously remarked. 'A real rags to riches story.'

'Would Ratan Wadia agree to an interview?' asked Anand.

'Not if you are going to write about his love life,' replied JR.

The picnic brought out the adolescents in the middle-aged men. They all went to play billiards at the Taj Submarine's exclusive pool club, with its tinted glass and red carpets. There, Derek asked Mohan, who had his hands in his pockets, if he played billiards or pocket billiards. The reference was to an alumni joke of the sixties, where 'pocket billiards' meant a guy's balls. Again, when Ismail lit his cigarette by touching it to Randhir's, Anand, who hated smokers, commented that this implied the two men wished to touch dicks!

'You've got a one-track mind,' said Ismail.

'Who doesn't?' asked a laughing Anand.

'I don't,' said Debashish, raising his hand, thus putting an end to this conversation.

On the third and last day of their stay at Taj Submarine, they brainstormed the issue of cruising on the net. Ismail, the college lecturer, made a presentation in which he submitted that the five senses—seeing, hearing, smelling, touching and tasting—were central to both art and love.

'How?' asked Anand.

'No art is possible unless the senses are evoked, and likewise, love needs the invoking of the senses too.'

There were expressions of intrigue on many of the faces.

Ismail continued, 'Coming specifically to the business of same-sex cruising, I need to *see* the person I cruise with my own eyes, *hear* his sexy voice, *smell* his scent through my nostrils, *touch* him, possibly by slipping my hand into his or grabbing his dick, and then *taste* him as I kiss him on the mouth. The Internet, I'm afraid, makes none of these things possible.'

'But one can see their photo on a website,' protested Randhir, who was Internet-savvy and something of a geek. 'So at least the visual sense is taken care of.'

'But that's not the same as seeing the person face to face,' said Derek, who liked Ismail's analysis. The latter, encouraged by the applause he got from his friends, with the exception of Randhir, who grudgingly joined in, went on to compare the five senses to the five Pandavas, even though he was Muslim.

'Seeing is Arjuna. Hearing, Yudhisthira. Smelling, Bhima. Touching, Nakula. Tasting, Sahadeva.'

This time, however, the audience booed him. 'Now that's far-fetched,' JR dismissively said. 'Don't go over the top.'

Debashish, as was his wont, raised a hand. 'What about the sixth sense?' he asked.

Here, Ismail got a brainwave. 'If there *is* a sixth sense,' he argued, 'why not a sixth element? We all know that air, water, fire, earth and ether are the five elements. According to me, love is the sixth element.'

'You may add truth and beauty to the list as the seventh and eighth elements,' said Derek.

'Why not?' asked Ismail, pleased that the others were catching on to his philosophy. 'In any case, I started out by saying that the five senses are central to the experience of art and love. And art is both beauty and truth as Keats famously said.'

But Anand was still confused. 'Will you please tell me the exact relation between the five senses, the five elements and the five Pandavas?' he asked.

'You are a hopeless case,' said Ismail. 'Why don't you attend my classes in college? I'll explain it to you on the blackboard.'

'Will someone please change the topic?' cried out Pheroze. 'We've had enough of the five senses.'

'I will,' said JR. 'How about our take on the T in LGBT? As we know, that crazy girl in Testosterone thought it stood for Try Sexual!'

'Such a dumbo,' said Randhir.

'Transgenders are our enemies,' declared Derek, offending Debashish who worked with them all the time.

'Whatever for?' he asked.

'Look at it this way,' Derek replied. 'Transgenders dream of becoming transsexuals one day. They are born queer, but they want to have a sex change operation and become the opposite sex so that they can lead a straight life. Doesn't that make them our enemies?'

'I see your point,' said JR. 'Transsexuals, or whatever we might call them, have more in common with heterosexuals than with us, at least ideologically.'

'I beg to differ,' said Debashish. 'Transsexuals are born queer, and that is what we have in common with them.'

'But they do not have the guts to stay that way,' Derek said. 'Their desire is for normalcy, just as a man with a temperature wishes that it would return to normal and that's why would take medicines. The sex change operation is like their medicine.'

'I saw a documentary on a lesbian who had a sex change operation, became a man, and hated being a lesbian any more,' said JR. 'That's homophobia.'

'You said it!' Derek jumped in. There was a great rapport between the lawyer and the architect. 'Homophobia is what all transsexuals suffer from. If we hate straights for their homophobia, why make transsexuals an exception?'

'Homophobia is linked to the guilt cultures of the West, while heterosexism is linked to the shame cultures of the East,' said Ismail.

Everyone then urged him, with folded hands, to stop complicating matters.

More than a couple of months went by before the members of ARSE had their next meeting at JR's. And from there, as usual, they went to Testosterone. They occupied a corner table as always (corner tables were in demand and they had to wait for one to be free) to continue with their deliberations over beer, occasionally jostling through the crowds to the dance floor to let their hair down.

Like the dozens of times before, Sandy was only tangentially involved with the group with whom he had tagged along. He seated himself on a high revolving stool at the bar and ordered one beer after another with the dough JR always gave him as they alighted from their C Class. Today as he downed enough beers to make his vision blurred and hazy, he couldn't be sure if the middle-aged man who passionately smooched another at the far end of the pub was Aroop. Yet he resembled him all right, for he had the sailor's height, the gait, the paunch, and above all, the sailor's haircut. Sandy rubbed his eyes over and over again till they were bright red, but his senses were failing him. Now he saw them, now he didn't. To worsen matters, the crowd at Testosterone that Saturday night was unprecedented, making it impossible for him to lift himself off his butt to go in search of the couple he had just spotted.

Eventually, however, Sandy managed to rise and he teetered up and down the jam-packed place, knocking a man's glass of lager out of his hands in the process, thus inviting his murderous glares. Others accosted him as he ambled along, and asked if he was 'single, ready to mingle'. Someone offered to buy him a beer, and he very nearly succumbed, but in the end spurned them with a polite 'no, thank you'. He was determined to investigate whether it was indeed Aroop, Lolita's husband, whom he had seen in the hallowed precincts of Testosterone.

But Aroop seemed to be nowhere in sight. Nor was the hunk in orange bermudas around anywhere, and Sandy knew that *he* couldn't be missed, for he was the only one who had dared to indecently enter the disco in shorts. Meanwhile, Sandy also lost contact with his own group, the members of ARSE, but this did not worry him because he still had enough in his wallet to pay for the cab ride to Sea View Apartments.

When yet another sculpted-bodied bloke, more mannequin than man, asked Sandy if he was single, ready to mingle (was this Testosterone's mantra?), he was able to say, 'No, thanks, I've got company.'

'What's your name, anyway?' the man asked.

'Sandy.'

'And I'm so randy.'

This one foxed our protag, and he rushed to the washroom where he opened his pocket OED (a birthday present) to look up the meaning of 'randy'. His dictionary told him that the word meant 'full of sexual lust', and he was left aghast.

Sandy almost gave up the search for his culprit when all at once he saw the fellow in the orange bermudas again. This time, however, he wasn't with anyone who resembled Aroop even remotely. Instead, surprise of surprises, Mannequin, who had propositioned Sandy only a moment ago, had his arms around Orange Bermudas' waist, and they danced a Bollywood style number that Sandy had seen on TV innumerable times. (The thought crossed his mind then that he must get JR to enrol him in dance classes as well.)

Sandy stood at a safe distance and observed the two for a good ten minutes or so before venturing further, till he was in such close proximity to them that it was impossible for them not to notice him.

'Hi, there,' Mannequin said to Sandy, and motioned to him to come and join them. Sandy accepted the invitation, and now Mannequin promptly put his other hand, the free one, around Sandy's waist. The three of them did a jig that fascinated several drunken onlookers on Testosterone's slippery dance floor.

Sandy slyly observed Orange Bermudas (OB) as they danced. Though he was a muscleman, his dark, tanned complexion made it clear to Sandy that he did not belong to high society. Instead, he appeared to be the gigolo or rent boy about whom JR had spoken so much. It was obvious to Sandy that OB was looking for a moneyed client who would take him in for the night.

Mannequin did not let go of OB for even a second, holding him so tight that twice the guy shrieked. He was the cynosure of everyone's eyes, having two *real* men in his grasp with plenty of testosterone in their bodies. When Sandy looked at OB's shorts, he found that OB had a hard-on. Vulgar, thought Sandy to himself. Why couldn't he wear a pair of Jockeys underneath? Was he that poor?

A round of drinks followed, with Mannequin generously shelling out for large lagers for all of them.

'Hey, come over here,' he shouted out to Sandy from near the bar, remembering neither his name nor OB's. When Sandy reached the bar, Mannequin handed him two frothing glasses, one for him and another for OB, while he picked up his own glass and followed. They went to the place where OB shyly stood, his hard-on refusing to subside. Now they danced, drank and lit up in the psychedelic lighting. Smoke rent the air as Mannequin shared his Mores (ladies cigarette, sniggered Sandy) with his new friends. Mannequin's next question embarrassed Sandy a good deal, though OB was cool.

'Why aren't *you* hard like our friend here?' he audaciously asked.

Because faggots don't turn me on, Sandy thought to himself.

Although Sandy shook a hip with Mannequin and OB, he wasn't quite with them. His thoughts were elsewhere. When Mannequin asked him his name for the second time, despite the din, he managed to scream, 'Sandy'. However, he did not ask Mannequin or OB for their names in turn, as etiquette demanded. He was preoccupied. He could swear he saw an Aroop-like figure smooch OB, but now OB was by himself. Sandy wondered if he was going crazy. He kept glancing towards the swing door, thinking Aroop may have strolled out of the pub for fresh air. But the door opened and closed so many times, to let in and let out hordes of young men hungry for their own kind, that Sandy found it impossible to keep track. He was sure that if he told JR what he'd seen, the latter would laugh it off as a figment of his imagination. You're hallucinating, JR would say.

No sooner did Sandy bring JR into his thoughts than he actually saw the man, who came up to him from nowhere, raised an eyebrow and said, 'You're doing rather well for yourself, my dear. Keep it up.'

'Thanks,' Sandy mumbled, as JR winked and made his way to the bar, only to return with large lagers for Sandy and his friends. He then made himself scarce, keen on leaving his boyfriend to his own devices, as a tigress lets go of her cubs.

The beer and JR's presence revived Sandy's spirits a bit, but he continued to be restive. He couldn't get Aroop off his mind. It was as if his unconscious mind desperately wanted it confirmed whether it was indeed Lolita's husband whom he chanced upon in Testosterone. That would put so much in perspective. It would explain, for one, why Lolita turned to *him* for sex, having been saddled with an AC/DC husband. Sandy had learned from JR to get to the root of every problem, and he decided not to rest till he got to the bottom of the Lolita affair too.

But Sandy also sought Aroop out for vendetta. This was the man who had defaced him beyond recognition for no crime of his own. Should he let the man off just like that? Why didn't he act on his hunch the moment he spied Aroop and OB together, and pounce on the bastard? He would be defenceless since his sailor cronies were not with him now. Even if OB came to his rescue, Sandy could tackle both of them together, Bollywood-ishtyle. He could whistle to ARSE members to come to his aid too, if required. He had thrown away the golden opportunity to humiliate that son of a bitch publicly, in front of so many homos. He could have stripped the man naked and cast him before all those horny hunks to feed on, though it is unlikely he would have any takers.

Then Sandy got a chance to befriend OB and he capitalized on it. It so happened that Mannequin yawned, suddenly losing interest in his plebeian buddies, and slipped away without bidding them good night. Sandy and OB found themselves face to face, with Sandy smiling and taking the initiative.

'Hi, I'm Sandy,' he said, extending his right hand for a handshake. 'Male sex worker.'

'Hello,' OB replied. 'I'm Aaron.'

Sandy quickly switched over to Hindi to introduce an air of informality.

'Do you come here regularly?' he asked. This was a typical Testosterone question.

'Yeah,' Aaron replied.

'Where are you from?'

Sandy expected Aaron to say Andheri or Ghatkopar or Kandivli, or maybe some other suburban neighbourhood of Bombay. But his answer was intriguing.

'Goa,' he answered. 'I'm from Goa.'

'Goa!' exclaimed Sandy. 'And you came here all the way from Goa?'

'Yeah.'

There was a gawky silence during which they danced like zombies. Aaron's reply revived Sandy's hopes, making him certain that the man who had smooched Aaron earlier was Aroop after all. But Aaron was no fool. He wasn't going to volunteer information very easily.

'Did you come here alone?' Sandy asked.

'Nope,' said Aaron.

'Then?'

'With my partner.'

'Who is that?'

'You want me to give you his name? I'm sorry, I can't.'

'Okay, but tell me something about him, no. Is he very rich or what? Is he also from Goa, like you?'

'I'm sorry,' Aaron said again, shrugging his shoulders, chewing gum and lighting a cigarette. 'I can't answer your questions.'

'Why?'

'*Meri marzi.*'

Comical silence again. Sandy broke it like a glass of beer, after a while.

'Where is your partner now?' he asked.

'Oh, he had to leave on some urgent business.'

'*Uska shaadi hua hai*?'

'Don't know,' said Aaron.

'So how will *you* go back?'

'By bus.'

'Without him?'

'Yeah.'

Sandy noticed that Aaron, in turn, asked him nothing. No counter questions. The ludicrous silences, interspersed with titbits of conversation, became a pattern.

'What do you do?' Sandy asked Aaron.

'I work.'

'As what?'

'As a motorbike pilot.'

'Motorbike pilot?' Sandy was overawed. He never knew there was something known as motorbike pilots in the world.

'Yeah,' Aaron answered. 'Only Goa has them.'

'I have never been to Goa.'

'Come, then.'

'But I have no place to stay. Can I be your guest?'

'Okay.'

This spelt hope, though Sandy doubted Aaron meant what he said.

'Really?' he asked, the way JR habitually did.

'Yeah.'

'What bike do you ride?'

'A Splendour.'

'Will you let me ride it?'

'Okay. But do you have a permit?'

'No.'

'The cops in Goa are very strict. They need their cut.'

'How did you get your permit?'

'I bribed them.'

'How much?'

'Ten thousand.'

'Amir baap ke bete ho kya?'

'Nope. My dad is just a lifeguard at Vagator Beach. I took the money from my partner.'

'The same guy who brought you here?'

'Yeah.'

'What's his name?'

'Sorry,' Aaron replied, refusing to give any more information.

'Aroop Sengupta?'

'Nope.'

But Sandy knew the ropes. He had been to Testosterone enough times to know that the way to get a person to open up, literally or figuratively, was to take him to the bar. Accordingly, he excused himself, located JR who was ready to leave, and asked him for 'one grand', which JR, Sandy's ATM, frowningly dispensed.

'You go home,' Sandy told his lover. 'I am staying here until closing time.'

JR looked at his watch: it was a little past midnight and Testosterone did not down its shutters, as the newspapers say, till well after 2 a.m., especially on Saturday nights.

'Open the door with the spare key,' JR instructed Sandy. 'I'm crashing; got to work on a case tomorrow.'

'Okay.'

It was the first time JR and Sandy did not leave Testosterone together.

No sooner did JR and his friends make their exit than Sandy motioned to Aaron to join him at the bar. En route, he bumped into Pheroze, who kissed him on the cheek and said, 'Good night, darling.'

'Good night, Fartmaria,' said Sandy, embarrassing the Zoroastrian by referring to his surname.

'You bitch,' Pheroze laughed and good-naturedly said. 'I shouldn't have given you guys my business card.'

Between 12.30 and 2 a.m., Sandy plied Aaron with a cocktail of alcoholic beverages: beer, whisky, rum and vodka; and large pegs at that, so that by the time old Mr Pallonji announced that Testosterone was closing for the night, he had the answers to all his questions.

He knew, for instance, that Aaron's partner *was* Aroop. The two of them had apparently met at a cruising site near the Mormugao harbour which was frequented by sailors. He knew that they drove to Testosterone all the way from Vasco da Gama whenever Aroop was in town because Aroop missed Bombay, and Goa had no gay bars worth their name. There was one in Panjim, the capital city, but it was mostly empty, its chief patrons being drug addicts who shared needles. Aaron knew that Aroop was married. When Sandy asked him if his wife and he were still together, not revealing anything about his own affair with Lolita, of course, Aaron answered with his characteristic 'Yeah.' But he had no clue if Aroop's wife—he did not know her name—had any knowledge of her husband's secret life.

'Rambo hates questions about his married life,' said Aaron. When Sandy looked perplexed, he explained that Rambo was Aroop's nickname by which he was known in the gay community; it was his alias.

Sandy also learned that night that Aroop, alias Rambo, not only paid for Aaron's permit to be a pilot, but had in fact paid for the motorbike itself. When Sandy, after yet another round of drinking, was emboldened enough to ask Aaron if Aroop was active or passive in bed, Aaron said, 'Of course, passive. He has a big asshole. My whole dick goes into it.'

The only query to which Sandy did not get a satisfactory answer was why Aroop had abruptly left Testosterone. Aaron reiterated that he had left on urgent business. Maybe he spotted *me*, Sandy thought to himself with a smile as Aaron and he stumbled out onto the sidewalk outside the bar and exchanged mobile numbers, and Aaron agreed to give him Aroop's visiting card.

Once he got home, Sandy woke JR up to have sex with a fervency that bewildered the lawyer. He lubricated his partner's backside with margarine, which he found in the fridge. He might have learned this from *The Last Tango in Paris* that the two of them saw together not too long ago. As he penetrated JR, he erotically recalled what Aaron had said about himself and Aroop—'He has a big asshole. My whole dick goes into it.'

As for JR, the pleasure aside, he was glad that Sandy was at last being initiated into the gay life. He attributed it to his being bombarded by gay images night and day—at Sea View Apartments, at Testosterone, and with the members of ARSE.

'Lick it, lick it,' JR groaned from under the blanket Sandy threw over themselves as they made love, the split level air conditioner giving him goosebumps.

What JR referred to was the margarine that made his butt greasy. But this Sandy certainly wasn't going to do. 'You are not

Lolita,' he was about to say. (In the end, of course, he did not say it.) Sandy mounted JR twice that night, all in the space of twenty minutes.

At breakfast the next morning, JR asked Sandy all about his escapades at Testosterone. 'Give me the dope, the low-down,' he said.

Sandy faithfully recounted everything, telling him so much about Aaron that JR wondered if he planned to write his biography!

'You seem to be in love with him,' JR remarked, as he munched his egg on toast.

'No, I'm not,' said Sandy. 'But he is smart. I wish I could be a motorbike pilot like him.'

'They have those only in Goa.'

'I know,' Sandy said, looking dejected.

Then Sandy spoke about Mannequin. But the one piece of vital information that he suppressed was that he had seen Aroop Sengupta at Testosterone. About this, he remained totally tight-lipped, merely referring to Aaron's partner as a middle-aged guy who had no qualms about smooching him in public.

'That's what a gay bar is meant for, isn't it?' JR asked.

'No,' Sandy bluntly replied. JR laughed, and egg yolk trickled down his moustache. He then asked, 'Why was Aaron dressed in bermudas?'

'Because that is the only thing they wear in Goa.'

JR laughed again. 'I love your sense of humour.'

'Thanks.'

'But you didn't have it before, did you? All because of me.'

'Okay, thanks again then.'

They sat in silence and sipped their coffee. The doorbell rang. JR rose. 'Got to go, my dear,' he said. 'Working on a twister of a case.'

With this, he took his leave and ensconced himself in his study with his client who had just arrived.

Sandy dialled Aaron's mobile number and a voice answered, 'Hello?'

'Aaron?'

'Yeah.'

'Sandy *bol raha hoon.*'

'Hi, Sandy.'

After a few pleasantries, they settled down to have a long chat. Incoming calls had just been made free in the country, so Aaron had no issues. As for Sandy, JR had put his number as an 'add-on' number on his own bill. This meant that *he* sponsored his calls.

Sandy was surprised that Aaron was already in Goa.

'It takes twelve hours from Bombay to Goa by bus,' he said. 'How come you are already there?'

'I came by plane,' Aaron replied.

'You went alone by plane?'

'Nope. With my partner.'

'But he left the bar last night before you.'

'I caught up with him at the airport.'

The next segment of their conversation was about Aaron's job. Sandy was very curious about the mechanics of being a motorbike pilot.

'How do you do it?' he asked.

Aaron explained that Goa basically had towns and beaches, so he ferried passengers from the towns to the beaches and vice versa.

'I take them from Ponda, where I live, or from Madgaon, to Colva or Calangute or Anjuna or any other beach.'

'Only one passenger at a time?' Sandy asked.

'Obviously.'

'Lady?'

'Yeah.'

'So romantic!'

'Yeah, it is.'

Sandy wondered what a lady did alone at the beach. Aaron fibbed that she would either invite him to join her in the water, or else handsomely tip him and ask him to buy himself food and a few drinks while he waited.

'I can eat as much fried fish and drink as much feni as I want, for which madam pays.'

'Lucky guy.'

'Yeah.'

Sandy inquired what Aaron charged his customers.

'It depends on the distance,' Aaron said. 'But my minimum fare is Rs 500.'

'You earn a lot?'

'Yeah.'

'Like how much?'

'Twenty thousand a month.'

'That much?'

'Yeah.'

Here the connection got cut. Sandy redialled, but invariably the message that flashed on his screen was: unable to connect.

He put the phone away and decided to go for a shower.

NINE
Bombay to Goa

Yeh hai pyaar ka safar
  There was an ARSE luncheon at Sea View Apartments.

Ismail asked, 'But where do you locate your gayness?'

Pheroze responded by saying, 'That's easy. In my anus.'

Anand looked irritated and said, 'Please, guys … we're eating.'

JR said, 'Derrida asks us to defer judgement. But if judgement is deferred, will utopias ever be realized?'

To this Ismail said, 'Shakespeare said, "All the world's a stage." I say, all the world's a dystopia.'

Sandy broke into this by saying, 'Excuse me, boss.' Boss was how Sandy addressed JR in public. When JR reprimanded him, asking him to address him by name, he asked, 'How can I? You are so much older than me.'

Though JR was in the middle of Derrida and rogan josh, he rose, wiped his hands with a paper napkin, and followed Sandy out.

'Yes, my dear?'

'I want to go to Goa. Can I? Sorry, may I?'

'Permission refused.'

Afterwards, when the guests left, JR relented. He told a sulking Sandy, while tickling him in the ribs, that he was only pulling his leg. In truth, he had no objection to Sandy going to Goa, or even to Timbuktu for that matter, as long as he knew his limits, knew where to draw the line.

'You mean my Lakshman Rekha?' Sandy asked.

'Yes.'

'Don't worry, I promise to behave.'

'Lovely.'

Sandy called Aaron to inform him that he was taking him up on his offer; he would be coming to Goa as his guest. What offer, thought Aaron. I never invited him. He invited himself. Aloud, of course, he feigned joy at the prospect of running into his buddy from Bombay again. *Bombay se aaya mera dost, dost ko salaam karo.* 'Come, come,' Aaron said to him. 'I am there.'

Next, Sandy racked his brains trying to figure out what mode of transport to take to Goa. It was unlikely that JR would lend him his C-Class; he would be left with no other alternative but public transport. Somehow, he got the idea that he would travel by boat to get a feel of life at sea, and with this intent he cabbed it to Bhaucha Dhakka, or Ferry Wharf, to inquire about boat timings. But the boatmen disappointed him. They told him that the steamer that sailed from Bombay to Goa, the M.V. Konkan Kanya, was discontinued after the Konkan Railway Corporation came into being. Now Sandy had only two options, bus or train. He decided by tossing a coin, heads by bus, tails by train, and the verdict was bus. So he told JR to drop him off at the St. Xavier's College on Mahapalika Marg (where Ismail taught) because that is where the buses to Goa were parked.

'Sure,' JR said, as Sandy strapped his rucksack to his back, looking like the perfect hippie from the subcontinent.

As the driver of the bus turned on the ignition and revved his engine, JR kissed Sandy on the cheek and asked him to come back soon.

Once he got home, depressed by Sandy's absence, JR called Derek to have a long chat on the phone.

'What if Sandy has sex with Aaron in Goa?' Derek bluntly asked.

'I guess that's okay by me,' said JR.

'Really?' Derek seemed very surprised.

'Yes, of course. He's much younger than me and he has needs. Besides, if he has sex with Aaron who's a man, it means he's been converted and I see that as a victory.'

'But what if they fall in love?'

'That's unlikely. Theirs is a horizontal alliance. Those don't work. Only vertical ones do.'

'You mean cross-class, or inter-class, or whatever you call it?'

'Yes, exactly. And inter-generational too.'

'But why did Sandy go to Goa in the first place?'

'Well, not for sex. I'm sure of that. He went there for motorbikes.'

'Do you plan to touch base with your harem while he's away?'

'You bet. The same fare day in and day out can be hard on the palate.'

'So who?' Derek asked.

'Well, there's Sunil and there's Vithal. Then there's Mohammad and there's Hanumant. There's also Sagar. Who all can I name?'

'All downmarket?'

'Of course. Motor mechanics, auto drivers, masseurs, cable operators, and such like.'

'Wow! Why not call them all at the same time and have an orgy?'

When the call ended, JR remembered something in a flash: Lolita lived in Goa. But he did not let the thought bother him. Instead, he lost no time and called Deepak, the masseur, to come home and give him a massage.

'I will be there at 7,' Deepak said.

True to his word, unlike high-end masseurs who made false promises and stood up their clients just to prove how much in demand they were, Deepak presented himself at JR's door at 7 p.m. sharp.

'Hi, Deepak,' JR said, and both of them got down to brass tacks without much ado.

Deepak knew that JR liked being stark naked when he was massaged. But he also made Deepak strip, down to his underwear, so that both masseur and client were in the altogether. This was JR's fetish. Invariably, he instructed Deepak to massage the non-sexual parts of his body first and then gradually move to the sexual parts: nipples, balls, lips, dick and asshole. By this time Deepak was as hard as a rock, so that the massage blissfully ended in a round of fucking. Then Deepak packed up, collected his fee and left, while JR rushed into the shower to scrub himself clean of all the cheap scented oil that Deepak used on his body.

The next day JR called Sunil, the motor mechanic who ran a small garage in a cul-de-sac on the street. Sunil's use of metaphors from his trade turned JR on. He spoke of the business of fucking, as 'matching', the way a mechanic matched nuts and bolts. On days when he couldn't perform, he would say, 'Sorry, sir, *match nahi hota.*' JR told him that his inability to perform stemmed from his premature ejaculations that needed to be medically treated. 'Or else, it'll wreck your married life,' JR alarmingly said. This terrified Sunil. But the metaphors came to his lips with imaginative power. He had a way of seeing every tool that he deployed, as he peered into the undersides of cars and bikes, be it a sledgehammer, screwdriver or spanner, as a symbol of the male sexual organ. The dick was also a weapon, and when Sunil voyeuristically wanted to know the dick sizes of JR's other harem boys, his own instrument being on the smaller side, he asked, '*Uska hathyar kitna bada hai?*' The crudity of all this, as opposed to the sophistication and erudition of ARSE members, gave JR a high. He often called Sunil to his flat, not for sex, but just to hear him talk. 'Go on talking,' he ordered him. 'I love to listen to you. Why pay thousands to the 1-800 guys on the phone when one can hear you talk for free?'

After Sunil, it was Hanumant, the cable boy's turn. All JR had to do here was call the fellow to report that his cable services were disrupted. Hanumant arrived within minutes, but did not even switch on the TV set; he knew very well that this was only a ruse.

He came to fix my cable
And we did it on the table.

Hanumant stripped. His dick was like an unripe banana, not just in terms of size but curvature as well. How he loved being fellated! 'Oral, oral,' he groaned in sheer ecstasy as JR played with his dick, ready to swallow it whole, one skin-two skin-three skin foreskin.

'No, written,' JR teased. The joke went above Hanumant's head, for he had not been educated beyond class seven. He had been abused by his teacher somewhere in the rural hinterland of Maharashtra because of which he walked out of school, never to return again. Instead, he travelled to Bombay and found work in Vishnu Cable Vision, owned by a corrupt politician from his village who also happened to be a distant relative. Hanumant's personal history, thus, wasn't radically different from Sandy's.

The beauty of JR's harem was that, like Sandy, it comprised guys from the sexual mainstream. They weren't fundamentally gay, but were open to 'homosex' with men above them in station. JR was perhaps the *only* man they slept with, their other sexual partners being women—maidservants, housewives, prostitutes. While most ARSE members fished in the ghetto, JR, the glib talker that he was, had the whole world, so to speak, to choose from. He regarded this as empowerment.

Meanwhile, Sandy reached Ponda, where Aaron lived, after changing buses at Madgaon. Aaron wasn't at the bus terminus to receive him and Sandy thought of him as inhospitable. But his dwelling place was easy enough to locate, being just a stone's throw from the bus depot.

Aaron lived in a chawl known as Lisbon Chawl which Sandy thought was Lesbian Chawl. The family, which was made up of parents, brothers and sisters, slept in a row in two rooms, and now Sandy would add to the crowd in the tenement. But they welcomed him as a member, Aaron's mother and sisters going out of their way to make him comfortable. As he surveyed the way they made the most of the cramped space that was their lot, their means being limited, Sandy remembered his own childhood home in Paithan. He realized with a sense of grief that his stints at Jannat and Sea View Apartments had spoilt him, made him forget his humble origins. When lunch was served, Sandy saw that, though there were sumptuous helpings of fish curry, the quality of rice used by the Braganzas was distinctly inferior to what he was used to in JR's flat. The lack of air conditioning, too, hit him. Only one room in the Braganza household was equipped with a ceiling fan. The other room had a rickety table fan that sounded like a railway engine whenever it was switched on. But the funniest of all was the television: it was a quaint black and white Crown TV set with sliding doors and it telecast only one channel—Doordarshan India.

Unconsciously, Sandy hummed a song from the blockbuster *Bobby*, which he had seen during his Royal Video Parlour days: *Na maangu sona chandi, na maangu hira moti …*

In the afternoon, Sandy accompanied Aaron on his beat. Aaron, who was dripping with sweat as he'd just returned from the gym, let him ride his Splendour but only on the streets where there was little chance of their bumping into khaki-uniformed traffic constables. But wearing a crash helmet was a must.

'This is Goa, not your Maharashtra,' Aaron said.

Sandy wore a helmet for the first time in his life and all but suffocated. Maharashtra is a hundred times better, he thought, where wearing silly things like helmets wasn't compulsory. He suddenly remembered his own bike in Bombay, Lolita's gift to him that probably lay in a junk heap in Jannat's parking lot.

Their journey wasn't uneventful. On the road to the hippie bazaar at Anjuna beach, their bike had a flat tyre, with no puncture repairer anywhere in the vicinity. Aaron hitched a ride from a passer-by to fix his tyre (unlike Bombay, strangers in Goa were friendly). Sandy stood waiting under a tree for what seemed like aeons, wondering if there was a brothel nearby where he could bide his time. Since Goan women wore skirts, he assumed they were promiscuous.

Another adventure came their way when the Splendour ran out of fuel, and the nearest petrol pump, once again, was scores of kilometres away. 'Hush,' said Aaron, putting his index finger to his lips. He approached a parked motorbike to undo the hosepipe that went into its carburettor to steal petrol. He collected the stolen petrol in an old feni bottle that he always carried with him everywhere. It worked! Within minutes, they were off.

'*Pakda jata toh*?' Sandy asked.

'No problem,' quipped Aaron. 'I would have to just spend a few months in jail.'

Sandy admired Aaron's daring. He also loved his muscles. When the sun set, Aaron fulfilled Sandy's hunger for short-skirted Goan women by depositing him at a brothel in Madgaon, promising to return in half an hour to fetch him.

'Don't you fuck girls?' Sandy asked Aaron without inhibition.

'I do,' Aaron said. Then he joked, 'But today I have my period.'

The brothel owner, a stout matronly woman who had tied her over-oiled hair in a bun, paraded her girls before Sandy, and he chose the one he thought was Goa's answer to Manisha Koirala. As Sandy indulged in foreplay with her, he recalled the film *Ek Chhotisi Love Story*, starring Koirala, and whispered into the girl's ear that this was their own *chhoti si* love story. But the girl, whose working name was Julie, had no time for romance.

'You want to fall in love with me or what?' she sternly asked. 'Madam will chop off your testicles.'

Sandy chuckled.

'I did not crack joke,' Julie scolded him. 'Hurry up. Your time starts now.'

Hardly did Sandy climax that he heard Aaron honking down below.

'Coming,' he yelled, without intending to pun on the word. He left a hundred rupee note with Julie and scrambled down the stairs.

'*Uske saath shaadi kar raha tha, kya?*' Aaron asked. 'Why taking so long?'

'Sorry, yaar,' Sandy said.

Aaron kick-started his bike, and they navigated towards a dimly lit street that housed rows and rows of seedy country liquor bars. They entered a nondescript one, marked nevertheless by a huge painting on the wall, depicting the giant-sized breast of a woman with a giant-sized housefly perched on the nipple. The caption underneath the painting read: Fly Drinking Milk. Another wall had a painting of a round silver moon going into a dark cloud. The caption was: Train Entering Tunnel. Both the paintings were by a French painter who had signed his name at the bottom of his canvases as Andre. Andre evidently frequented the bar regularly.

'Two large cashew fenis,' Aaron said to the waitress, without asking Sandy what he wished to drink. When Sandy protested, saying he'd never drunk feni before, Aaron chortled. 'If you come to Goa, you *must* drink feni,' he ordained. 'You can't leave Goa without drinking it.'

Their drinks arrived. No sooner did Sandy put it to his lips than he wanted to puke. But Aaron advised him to persevere. 'After a while, you will start liking it,' he said.

Which surprisingly turned out to be true. When they left the bar shortly before sunrise, Sandy had downed so many fenis that the world seemed topsy-turvy to him. Aaron was in only a slightly better state. They spent the day lying in the sand on Colva beach, waiting for the nasha, like the fog, to lift. When it eventually did, Sandy saw that a large number of semi-naked white women lay all about them, sprawled on the sand.

'Can I fuck them?' he asked Aaron.

'Your partner did not call?' Sandy inquired of Aaron.

'He is away on the high seas. But, hey, take his visiting card. He has given me so many that I give them to anybody I meet.'

Sandy took the laminated visiting card with white letters on a black background. It bore the name Rambo, together with a residential address and a landline phone number.

'Can I call him?' Sandy asked.

'Yeah. He is forever on the lookout for msms and msws.'

'What is that?'

'Men who sleep with men and male sex workers.'

'Oh. But what if he takes me out on a date? You will not mind?'

'Na.'

When Aaron left for work, Sandy dialled Rambo's number on the off chance that Lolita would pick up. If a man used a false name, it stood to reason that he would use a false address and telephone number too.

'Hello,' a familiar female voice answered and Sandy recognized it at once to be Lolita's. Aroop's cunning impressed him: if a caller asked for Rambo, his wife would say 'wrong number' and disconnect. The husband would be safe.

Nervous, Sandy remained silent for a bit, making Lolita say 'Hello' at least half a dozen times. When she angrily yelped, 'Speak up, damn it,' he said, 'Hello, madam, this is Sandesh.'

'Who?'

'Sandesh.'

'Sandesh! What a surprise? Where are you calling from? Bombay?'

'No, madam. Goa.'

'Goa! How come you're here?'

'I came to see a friend.'

'Your English has improved.'

'Thanks, madam.'

The conversation ended inconclusively. Neither Lolita nor Sandy spoke about meeting, though that was what he had in mind when he called. But he wanted it to come from her—he was too proud to propose it himself. However, Lolita purposely did not ask him over, or set up a meeting somewhere outside, say in one of the numerous clubs where the Senguptas were life members. She had come to regard the Sandesh chapter of her life as closed. Relations between herself and Aroop were already strained and she did not wish to add any more fuel to the fire. Besides, Tanu was in kindergarten now and of an age, Lolita believed, when she would begin to sense things and understand them. All these years, Lolita had behaved like a good girl when her husband was away.

'I sowed my wild oats when I was younger,' she often said on the phone to Manisha, her friend in Bombay who, it will be recalled, was a merchant navy wife herself. 'Now it's time to get serious,' Lolita continued.

In accordance with her resolve, Lolita immersed herself in housekeeping and in her daughter Tanu, buying her all the storybooks she could lay her hands on to read out to her.

Manisha herself had started a 'torrid love affair' as she put it, with her driver, a 'sheer beefcake' who worked out at a local gym in Bombay everyday. Her idea in sharing this information with Lolita was to tempt her, for 'I need company, you see, in my adulterous life.' But Lolita wished her good luck and emphasized that as far as she was concerned, her 'sexcapades' were over.

'I've resolved to be a sati savitri pativrata,' she said, causing Manisha to splutter. Lolita responded to the snub by telling Manisha that she, Manisha, could afford to be wild all her life because she had no 'issues' (meaning, of course, children). Lolita's reference was to Manisha's supposed barrenness and the latter comprehended the insult at once.

'You bitch,' she abusively shrieked, and slammed the phone, as was her wont.

Lolita called Manisha and apologized.

'I did not mean it in that way,' she lied.

'Fuck you.'

Manisha was drunk, and Lolita could almost smell the liquor on her phone. Her own drinking had reduced considerably, though she hadn't given it up altogether, as that would be

equally disastrous. In between, she even did a stint with
Alcoholics Anonymous, but abandoned it because she found
the programme too regimental, like the one at the Vipassana
Yoga Centre in Igatpuri.

'They're concerned about nothing but curing you of your
habit,' she complained to Manisha. 'You could even be dead, for
all they care, and they'll administer their therapies to your corpse.'

But, in abruptly putting an end to Sandy's unexpected call,
Lolita was also nurturing another worry: blackmail. As soon as
Lolita heard Sandy's voice on the phone, apprehension riled her:
Was he here for revenge? What do you want? She might have
ungraciously asked him. Why are you here? Lolita mentally
made a note of all the cash she had in her safe and resolved to
give it to him, if it came to that. A moment later, of course, she
chided herself for harbouring such fears. She wondered where all
her solidarity with the downtrodden had disappeared. The years
had succeeded in making her a thoroughbred bourgeoisie, just as
the pigs in *Animal Farm* became the human masters they once
overthrew. Nothing revolutionary was left in her. She was middle
class to her fingertips. All the trappings of the global world were
a part and parcel of her life now, as indispensable to her as clouds
are to rain. Her bungalow teemed with gadgets—everything
from refrigerators to washing machines to laptops to iPods, and
all in pairs, one for the husband, the other for the wife—but she
did not care for them. Lolita thought of strong women, women
like Medha Patkar, who lived by their ideologies and did not
capitulate to pulls and counter pulls of the material world.

Yet, as these thoughts were triggered by Sandy's unforeseen
call, Lolita was deluding herself for, as JR's arguments in court

indicated, her relationship with Sandy was hardly about fraternity. Instead, it was about exploitation. Rather than calling herself a Marxist or a communist, Lolita might have called herself neocolonial.

On his part, Sandy was confused by Lolita's aloofness on the phone. Could a few years transform a person to such an extent? It seemed unlikely, especially when that person was Lolita. Sandy had rarely come across a human being as self-assured as her, who knew exactly what she wanted out of life. Fickleness, thus, was an attribute he simply couldn't associate with her.

What seemed much more plausible was that Lolita was reticent because her husband was in town. When Aaron returned from work, Sandy buttonholed him.

'Pal, is Aroop Sengupta really on a ship right now?'

'Of course he is on a ship,' Aaron replied. 'He left last Sunday.'

'Did you see him off?'

'Na.'

'Maybe he did not go.'

'Maybe. But then he would call me.'

The real purpose of this exchange was lost on Aaron, who knew nothing about Sandy's history with Aroop or Lolita. He didn't even know of the existence of JR, though JR called Sandy ten times a day. He took Sandy's incessant questioning as a sign of his amorous and material interest in Aroop.

'You want to steal my boyfriend from me or what?' Aaron half-jokingly asked.

'No, thanks. I have plenty of clients.'

'Then?'

'Just asking for kicks.'

Sandy's days in Goa were numbered. He knew he couldn't overtax the hospitality of the Braganzas and would have to head back to Bombay soon. Besides, JR missed him, as he never tired of admitting on the phone. At the same time, he felt his visit wouldn't be worth it if he did not get to see Lolita. He decided to give it another try.

He called her up again and said to her, 'Once you drove all the way to Bombay to see me and now I'm in Goa and you don't want to meet me.'

This time Lolita was more forthcoming. When Sandy telephoned her, she said she was eager to meet him too.

'Please don't get me wrong,' Lolita apologetically told him. 'I *do* want to meet you. Where are you anyway?'

'In Ponda.'

'Well, let's meet halfway. You take a bus to Panjim and I'll come to the Dolphin Restaurant that's just opposite the bus terminus. From there we'll drive to the Miramar Beach and to Dona Paula.'

'Where *Ek Duje ke Liye* was shot?'

'That's right.'

Though they were to meet in the evening, Sandy left home in the morning itself, soon after calling Lolita. He had half a mind to ask Aaron to lend him his bike, but decided against it at the last minute and hopped on to a bus. He located the Dolphin Restaurant with ease and whiled away the hours, loitering in the streets of Panjim, full of undisciplined traffic. He looked in vain for a brothel and gave up in despair, wishing he could call Aaron for directions to the best one in town. But Aaron did not even know that Sandy was in Panjim, drinking coconut feni at a local bar.

Accustomed as he was to the tempo of life in Bombay, time in sleepy Goa seemed to move at a snail's pace. Like the proverbial hare, Sandy decided to take a nap in a public garden, where junkies often congregated, as he waited for Lolita. And like the proverbial tortoise, she arrived at the appointed hour to find him nowhere so she decided to wait for him in her car. Half an hour later, Sandy rose from his slumber, looked at his watch, and rushed to the Dolphin Restaurant.

Sandy searched in vain for the Zen Carbon, but there were only funny-shaped Volkswagen Beetles in sight. Suddenly, a black Swift pulled up to where he was standing and Lolita got out of it.

'Hello, my dear,' Lolita beamed. 'You're looking good.' She had streaked her hair.

'Thanks, madam,' Sandy boldly replied. 'You are looking nice too.'

'And where did you pick up all the English from?'

'I joined a class in Bombay.'

'How wonderful.'

They sat in the car and sped towards Miramar Beach. The road ran parallel to the sea. When they reached the beach, Lolita led the way to a cosy beachside café tucked away among palm trees that, she said, served excellent fish and chips.

'English cuisine?' asked Sandy, stunning Lolita with his knowledge.

'You are not the Sandesh I used to know,' she remarked.

'And you are not the Lolita that I used to know.'

They laughed. It was the first time he addressed her, not as madam, but as Lolita.

As they placed their order and waited, Lolita grew pensive. She put a hand on Sandy's.

'I'm sorry, my darling,' she said.

'What for?'

'For my testimony in court.'

'*Ab kya faayda?*'

'Oh no, please don't say that. You can forgive me, can't you?'

'No.'

The food arrived. Sandy was hungry, so he greedily cut into his fried fish with a knife and fork, dipped the fish and french fries into generous helpings of tomato sauce, and stuffed them into his mouth. Lolita ate with more finesse, wiping her mouth with paper napkins every now and then.

'I was helpless,' she said. 'My testimony was made under duress. That is, I was *forced* to say whatever I said.'

'By whom?' Sandy asked, more for the heck of it than out of any genuine desire for explanations.

'By my husband and my lawyers,' said Lolita.

'Oh.'

'I had to do it for the sake of my daughter Tanu,' Lolita continued, hoping that the reference to Tanu would soften Sandy, make him sympathetic to her point of view. 'Remember Tanu? She's in LKG now.'

'I miss her a lot. Where is she?'

'At the crèche.'

Sandy was about to ask after Kamalabai, but controlled himself in the nick of time. He knew that was one name Lolita did not want to hear. Instead, he asked, 'No ayah now?'

'No. Haven't I had enough of their tribe?'

The waiter kept interrupting their conversation. Sandy opted for another plate of fish and chips, while Lolita ordered coffee. He wondered how she managed to stay away from all the alcoholic beverages listed on the menu.

'What about your drinking?' Sandy intemperately asked.

'I've stopped,' Lolita lied.

'How come?'

'I no longer have a drinking buddy like you.'

'*Bas kya*?'

'Seriously.'

When they were done, Lolita drove to Dona Paula and showed Sandy the spot where *Ek Duje Ke Liye* was shot. She expected him to talk about Sapna and Vasu, the legendary lovers in the film, but he skirted the subject and talked about her car.

'Where is your Zen Carbon?' he asked.

'Oh, I exchanged it for the Swift. The Maruti people gave me a great offer.'

'Why black again?'

'It's my fave colour.'

'It's *abshagun*.'

'But I'm not superstitious.'

Sandy longed to know if Lolita had any inkling of the way her husband and his hooligans had roughed him up in Bombay. He close-read her speech for clues, but found none. Either the lady was truly in the dark, or else she was being super-diplomatic. He was not going to narrate his saga to her; it would amount to self-pity and that went against his scruples. Still, he wondered how Lolita, despite the dark glasses she wore throughout, failed to notice all the plastic surgery performed on his skin. On the contrary, seeing him, all the old fires in Lolita were kindled again. It proved how flimsy her attempt at continence, her determination to abstain, was. Ensconced in her car after their Dona Paula tour, Lolita rubbed Sándy's thighs, caressed his crotch. She put a hand into his light cotton shirt to fondle his nipples. She kissed him, initially on the cheek because he was hesitant to yield, but then, within seconds, it was a full mouth-to-mouth kiss, such was her seductive power still. The next step was to get Sandy to put his hands into her own kameez. He quickly undid her bra and began to play with her breasts. Soon she began to undress him; the Swift, like the Zen Carbon, had black tinted windows. When the foreplay was at its height, Lolita discovered with a sense of déjà vu that the spot at which they were parked wasn't secluded enough. She turned on the ignition of the Swift and headed to another place.

'Remember the driving lessons you gave me in Khandala?' Sandy suddenly asked her.

'Yes, of course,' said Lolita, bringing her free hand to his crotch again.

'But now I have taken real driving lessons. I have a licence too.'

As he said this, Sandy brought out his wallet from his hip pocket to show Lolita his driver's licence.

'Wow!' she cried. 'I'm impressed.'

'So let me drive,' he nervously suggested.

'Okay.'

They got out of the car and exchanged seats.

Sandy started and drove at breakneck speed, terrifying Lolita. It was only when she began to scream that he lifted his foot off the accelerator. As he had no idea where they were going, he looked to her for directions. Lolita guided him as if she were a WIAA manual, till they reached a sandy nook by the sea where there was no one for miles, not even Goa's ubiquitous fishermen. Besides, it was dusk. Here they resumed their lovemaking.

'You're hurting me,' Lolita squealed as Sandy dug his nails into her boobs. 'Don't you possess a nail clipper?'

The foreplay stimulated them sufficiently to start fucking. However, they hit a roadblock when Lolita realized she had stopped buying condoms long ago.

'No problem,' Sandy came to her aid. 'I always carry one in my pocket.'

In reality, he had bought the condoms just before entering the Madgaon brothel, about which, of course, he told Lolita nothing.

They made out in the back seat of the Swift which was roomier than the Zen Carbon. Neither of them were worried about Aroop. Upon climaxing and wearing their clothes, they regained their position in the front seats, with Sandy at the wheel. Afterplay followed, during which they also made small talk. Lolita chucked Sandy's used condom out of the window of the Swift.

'How's Manisha?' Sandy asked without warning.

'She's good. You remember her still?'

'She called me in Bombay once.'

'You're kidding.'

'No.'

'Did you service her?'

'Yeah.'

'For how much?'

'One thousand.'

'You slut!' gasped Lolita.

Sandy's sartorial elegance lent credence to his lies. The trendy shirt and cargoes that he wore, complete with gold earrings and patent leather shoes, intrigued Lolita. To top it all off, he spoke English like a collegian and had already acquired a driver's licence though he was just over eighteen. All this was radically different from the days when he slogged for a living at the Royal Video Parlour.

'Tell me about yourself,' Lolita said, unable to mask her curiosity, as she licked his fingers.

'I am in love,' Sandy ventured to say.

'In love!' Lolita exclaimed in treble. 'With someone other than me?'

'Yeah.'

'And who's the lucky chick? Manisha?'

'It isn't a chick,' Sandy dryly said. 'It's actually a guy.'

'A guy! But you're not queer.'

'No.'

'Not bisexual either.'

'No.'

'So what are you talking about? And who's this punk anyway?'

'You have seen him. In court,' Sandy quietly said.

'In court?'

'Yeah. The man who fought my case.'

'That old fart! How disgusting! I can't believe my ears. I

didn't know he was gay, or I would have exposed him. And he talked of exploitation! What's he doing then, if not exploiting you? Why, he's old enough to be your dad. Or grandpa. What do you call him? "Daddy?"'

Sandy kept mum. He had a vested interest in telling Lolita about JR: he wished to investigate, as if he were from the CBI, whether she knew anything about her husband's bisexuality. But her words and her facial features betrayed nothing. It looked like this would remain a conundrum.

'Believe me,' Lolita continued, 'you are made for the opposite sex and not for your own, you who are capable of giving a woman so much pleasure.'

'Thank you.'

'Tell me, how can you say you're in love with a man and then deny, in the same breath, that you are gay or bisexual? It's absurd.'

'Love is more than just sex.'

'I don't believe it,' Lolita shook her head. 'That creep has brainwashed you thoroughly. That's what lawyers are about, aren't they? They have the gift of the gab, which they misuse. I'm going to take the son of a bitch to court.'

'Don't. Please.'

'I've got to get even with him—give him a tooth for a tooth, and an eye for an eye.'

'No. Don't.'

Lolita left in a state of indignation. Sandy was about to blurt out that he wished to see her house in Vasco da Gama so as to compare and contrast it with the flat in Jannat, of which he was so much a part. However, seeing how agitated she was, he chose not to open his mouth to rub salt into her wounds. He took a bus back to Aaron's, and though it was past midnight when he rang their doorbell, they unlatched the door and served him his dinner.

'Where did you disappear, man?' Aaron rubbed his eyes and asked. 'We were so worried.'

The next morning, as Sandy trudged to the bus terminus to book his ticket to Bombay, his mobile beeped. He thought it was JR, who was justified in being sore with him for hanging around in Goa for so long. But when he picked up, it was Lolita.

'Are you still in Goa?' she asked.

'Yeah.'

'Then let's meet today, at the Dolphin Restaurant again.'

'But …'

'No ifs and buts. Just come. For old times' sake.'

'Okay.'

This time, Sandy asked Aaron for his bike in no uncertain terms.

'Take it,' Aaron said, without grumbling for once about escalating fuel prices, or about Sandy not possessing a permit. 'I'll spend the day at the gym.'

'Thanks.'

Aaron's Rod prominently stood out in his bermudas.

When Lolita saw Sandy arrive on a motorbike, she thought it was the one she had given him. Sandy informed her, however, that it belonged to a friend who was a motorbike pilot.

'That gives me an idea,' Lolita said, snapping her fingers.

'What?'

'You can be a pilot too. I'll buy you the latest motorbike.'

Sandy pondered over Lolita's words. But there was more to come.

'Leave Bombay,' Lolita said, 'and come and stay in Goa.'

'Where?'

'I'll buy you a studio somewhere. Goa, unlike your Bombay, is cheap. And since you'll soon be in your twenties and I will be in my forties, I can be your official cougar.'

Sandy stood up.

'Where are you going?' Lolita asked him.

'To Bombay,' Sandy replied. 'To get my things.'

'How long will that take you?'

'Three days.'

Lolita telephoned an estate agent in Sandy's presence to ask for a 'one BHK apartment'.

When the realtor inquired what part of Goa she wanted the flat in, she rattled off the names of all of Goa's cities: Panjim, Madgaon, Mapusa, Vasco da Gama. 'But I prefer Vasco da Gama,' she hastily added.

Towards the end of Lolita's conversation with the realtor, Sandy decided to take his leave. 'Goodbye, madam,' Sandy said.

'Bye bye. Come back soon.'

Sandy kick-started his bike and sped off. En route to Aaron's, he called JR as he rode and wailed on the phone. Fortunately, he happened to be on a deserted stretch of road where there wasn't a soul for miles.

'I am homesick,' Sandy cried. 'I want to come back home.'

'What's stopping you?' JR asked. 'I'm miserable too.'

'But I have run out of cash. Can't get home unless you send me some here.'

Sandy dictated Aaron's address which JR scribbled out on the cover of a wedding card that lay nearby. He decided to surprise Sandy by couriering him an air ticket. Private airline companies in the country were bending over backwards to woo prospective customers, offering discounts that barely enabled them to break even, thus making air travel cheaper than ever. It was the new global India of the twenty-first century, and the captain of the ship was India's economist prime minister, Dr Manmohan Singh. The only catch was that the tickets had to be booked on the Internet, and paid for with credit cards which were possessed by few. But there was a plethora of airlines to choose from, and each boasted of unique packages. Some, in a bid to cut costs, went to ridiculous lengths. They declared that no food or drink would be served on their flights. If passengers were hungry during the journey, they were free to open the overhead luggage racks in the aircraft and dig into their hand baggage for sandwiches or samosas that they may have thoughtfully picked up on the way to the airport.

And so Sandy undertook his first ever journey by plane. Aaron went to see him off at the airport. Unlike Sandy, flying wasn't new to him.

As the plane took off, Sandy felt a wheezing sensation in his head and stomach for a few seconds, but then it was okay. He quickly acclimatized to his surroundings and became engrossed in the TV screen in front of his seat that mapped the course of their flight. The demonstration given to them by the air hostesses prior to take off seemed hilarious to him—the ladies looked as if they were engaged in a tribal dance. Soon it was lunchtime: Sandy ate his non-vegetarian meal with gusto. Knowing how Sandy loved to eat, JR ensured that he wasn't on one of those Bring-Your-Own-Sandwiches-and-Samosas-type flights, with names that coincided with the colours of the rainbow, where all they gave you was bottled water. Since he had a window seat, he peered out of the little window of the Boeing, and saw houses, roads and trees. Never in his life had he imagined that one day he would fly—planes were things that he saw as a child high up in the sky. They were so infinitesimal that it was hard to believe there were people in them! Sandy dozed off and dreamt that the plane flew so high it left the Earth's gravity and got lost in space.

Then they began their descent; the wheels of the plane popped out of its belly, like a bird's legs, and they landed on solid ground with a thud. Sandy was amazed that he made it from Goa to Bombay in less time than it took JR to drive from Cuffe Parade to Santacruz's Chhatrapati Shivaji Airport.

Back home, or 'home sweet home' as he called it, not tutored at the Shakespeare English Speaking Academy to shun clichés like the AIDS virus, Sandy chanced upon a shimmering red-and-gold wedding card on the table, the very card on whose envelope JR had scribbled out Aaron's address. It read: KIRAN WEDS KIRAN. He thought it was a gay wedding. But when he asked JR, he was told that Kiran was a unisex name that belonged to both men and women.

'We have a man like Kiran Nagarkar, who is a distinguished novelist,' said JR, 'and we have a woman like Kiran Bedi who is India's most formidable police officer.'

'So, in this case,' asked Sandy, referring to the wedding card, 'both husband and wife have the same name?'

'Yes,' said JR. 'Funny, but true.'

He went on to provide examples of other unisex names.

'There's Shashi Kapoor, the male actor, and Shashi Deshpande, the woman writer.'

Sandy looked very amused.

'Your own name,' JR continued, 'is unisex too. I mean, there are both guys and girls whose name is Sandy.'

On impulse, Sandy got it into his head to propose to JR that they get married.

'Marriage!' JR exclaimed. 'For that we will have to migrate to the Netherlands.'

He hurried into his study and returned with a book entitled *Love's Rite*. It was by Ruth Vanita, whose work JR regarded as more significant than the New Testament. He flipped through its pages and read aloud, more to himself than Sandy.

'"Many kinds of marriage have been outlawed in different societies; among these are widow and divorcee remarriage, inter-caste and inter-racial marriage and same-sex marriage. Marriage has varied so widely over time and space that its only core component is commitment.

'"Commitment between two persons of the same sex is not inherently different from commitment between persons of different sexes. 'Gay marriage' is a misnomer. A marriage is not gay (though the two partners may define themselves as gay). Being gay is just one dimension of a person, and marriage encompasses the whole person. Most of the same-sex couples who married in India did not define themselves as gay. When people claim the right to marry, their sex or sexuality is not intrinsic to that right, although social prejudice makes it appear so.

'"Some people say that same-sex commitment is not possible; they insist that governments, religious organizations and social communities should not perform, witness or bless rites that unite two persons of the same sex. They would have us believe that marriage has always, in all civilizations, been between a man and a woman. If they are right, then the idea that two persons of the same sex may marry one another suddenly appeared in the twentieth century, *ex nihilo*, out of nothing. But ideas do not appear out of nowhere. The Bible states, 'there is nothing new under the sun', and the Mahabharata declares, 'that which does not occur here occurs nowhere'. These claims, if read metaphorically rather than literally, indicate that phenomena grow out of earlier phenomena. They may take new forms, but are never entirely new.'"

After all of this, Sandy yawned. 'Sorry my dear,' JR apologized, as he snapped the book shut and put it away. 'I know that was a bit tedious.'

Did Sandy tell JR that he met Lolita in Goa? Of course not.

Nor did JR ask, though he might have. Instead, Sandy fished out a dog-eared photograph from his wallet, and showed it to JR, who had never seen the photo before. He put on his reading glasses and looked at the black-and-white picture closely, at the back of which was stamped the date June 1992.

'That's you?' JR asked Sandy in amazement.

'Yeah.'

'And who are the man and woman flanking you? Your parents?'

'Yeah.'

'Well, you must have been just five-years-old when this picture was taken. How innocent you looked then, unlike now!'

'Yeah.'

The photo moved JR to tears. He wept for the prodigal son abandoned by his parents, but he also wept because Sandy thought him fit to share the timeless photograph with. It was a singular honour. On the spur of the moment, JR resolved never to dump Sandy, come what may.

'I pledge myself to you, dear,' JR said, blowing his nose into his handkerchief. 'I promise to stand by you through thick and thin. And that's much more than a marriage can mean.'

Sandy kissed JR's hand. He took out his mobile to click a picture of them both.

'For keeps,' JR remarked when the flash came on. He then gave Sandy a bear hug. 'I will tell you something funny,' he said. 'A gay couple in America got married. But later, when they wanted a divorce, they couldn't get one. Why? Because the court recognized gay marriage, but not gay divorce. Only heteros can get divorced, the court ruled. So our gay couple were stuck together for life.'

One day, Sandy was busy, as usual, watching TV while an ARSE meeting was in progress. *Indian Idol* on Sony was on and a memory was triggered. Three years ago, it was this very show that played the day Darshan accompanied him to Lolita's flat in Jannat. But that was *Indian Idol*, Season One and this was Season Three, with a different set of singers, and he was seeing it in a different place too. The winner then was the debonair Abhijeet Sawant, but Sandy had no idea who the winner would be this time, though he had voted for a handful of them from his mobile.

Voices pierced the silence, and when Sandy looked up he found that some of the ARSE members had emerged from the meeting to snoop on him.

'What are you watching, boy?' Derek asked him.

'*Indian Idol,*' Sandy replied.

'Oh, that's a patriarchal show,' Anand dismissively said.

'What do you mean?' asked Mohan.

'Well, all the Indian Idols will always be men. The women will inevitably be eliminated before the finals. Can you ever imagine a female Indian Idol?'

'But isn't talent gender-neutral?' Derek remarked.

'Not really,' said Anand.

'What are you guys bickering about?' Pheroze said. 'We want to see more dicks on the show, not pussies. I'm glad if all the Indian Idols are men.'

'That's so politically incorrect,' said Debashish.

'Balls to political correctness,' snapped Pheroze.

'Peace,' cried Derek. 'Thou shalt not disturb our friend Sandy here. Thou shalt let him watch the show in peace.'

They made good their exit.

TEN
Murder Most Foul

The time spent with Aaron in Goa rekindled Sandy's passion for bikes. So much so that, braving all odds, he actually ventured into Jannat, where his own bike, now possibly fit for the scrapyard, was parked. The odds had to be braved since it was those very watchmen from UP and Bihar, known for their exemplary loyalty, who'd delivered him into the hands of the enemy, Aroop Sengupta. What if those bastards captured him a second time? Sandy toyed with the idea of enlisting the support of Darshan and Aniket, and their friends from the newly formed Maharashtra Navnirman Sena (MNS), whose presence would cause the watchmen to defecate in their underwear. In the end, however, he decided to go alone. What was the point in politicizing the issue, he thought. Even if the watchmen attacked him, there was no question of their handing him over to the man he hated from the bottom of his heart. The niggard no longer lived in Bombay, but had escaped to Goa instead. Still, he resolved that if the blighted watchmen tried anything, he would instantly send an SOS to Darshan and Aniket, and request that a contingent of MNS hoodlums be deployed to Jannat to beat these men up. In return, they would ask him, at the most, to become a member of the MNS as well, for which he was more than ready, for the philosophy of its leader, Raj Thackeray, made sense to him.

UP and Bihar to him, and to MNS members, were not states within the union of India. They were an enemy country, like Pakistan.

When Sandy reached Jannat and intrepidly walked past its imposing wrought iron gates, he was pleasantly surprised to note that the watchmen, far from pouncing on him, cordially called out to him from their security enclave.

'Sandesh saab,' they said, as if to atone for their sins. 'Where were you all these days?'

'I'm no saab,' Sandy wryly remarked, and deliberately wore a hurt look on his face. The watchmen registered this and went on to profusely apologize for what they had done.

'You are our bother,' they said. 'We shouldn't have taken you to that motherfucker's home. We had no idea he would assault you so savagely.'

Sandy saw that the watchmen were genuinely repentant. If they betrayed him, he reasoned that they must have done it for the money, for they obviously lived in abject poverty, like his own parents back in Paithan. He decided to forgive them.

The watchmen asked Sandy what *seva* they could do for him.

'I have come to collect my bike,' he informed them. 'Is it still in one piece?'

On hearing this question, some of the watchmen led him to a corner of the building's parking lot, where the bike lay. A tarpaulin sheet had been thrown over it to protect it from the dust.

'We covered it,' the watchmen claimed, 'because we knew you would come here one day to get it. Consider this our gesture of friendship.'

'Thanks,' said Sandy, as he surveyed the bike. Everything seemed to be in order; none of the parts had been stolen or vandalized, though things like rear-view mirrors, or the sari guard, could be stolen in a matter of minutes and disposed of at Chor Bazaar.

The watchmen definitely deserved some credit. Without their help, it would have been well-nigh impossible for Sandy to retrieve his motorbike. The residents of the building, and those of other high-rises in Bombay, had grown so paranoid that they were suspicious of anyone who entered their premises. Had any of them spotted Sandy fiddling with a bike in the parking lot, which they had no idea was actually his, they would have immediately raised the alarm. The upshot would be messy. Instead of proudly riding away on his bike, fancying he was Aaron and Bombay was his Goa, Sandy would find himself in jail, and unable to secure his release without JR's intervention. But now, thanks to the comradely watchmen of Jannat, no one raised an eyebrow as Sandy tampered with his bike in a bid to start it. No one, not even the secretary of the building, asked who this chap was or what he was doing there, taking him to be the kith and kin of the watchmen themselves. No one knew he was Lady Lolita's Lover, who at one time visited the building everyday. Why, no one knew who even Lady Lolita herself was, for memories faded, and it had been a while now since the naval officer's wife had ceased to be a resident of Jannat.

When the bike stubbornly refused to start after a hundred kicks, Sandy called JR to sound off Sunil, the mechanic, who was part of the lawyer's harem. Sandy was aware of Sunil's existence, but this did not threaten him because, the way he saw it, JR was acquainted with Sunil long before he came knocking on the door of his life. What was more, JR's association with Sunil was restricted to the physical, a 'body thing' as he called it.

It took Sunil more than a couple of minutes to gather that JR had called him, not to be serviced himself, but to service a bike. This puzzled him, for he knew JR owned only a car, a Merc to be sure. Two-wheelers were below his dignity. Without going into trivialities, JR explained that a bike that belonged to one of his friends had stalled somewhere in Dadar and had to be fixed. Upon hearing this, Sunil dropped whatever he was preoccupied with in his makeshift workshop on the street, and immediately took off for the site with his young assistant, Babu, leaving several of his customers fuming. There was a time when almost no one rode scooters and motorcycles in Bombay, preferring only cars. But now, in the twenty-first century, a conglomeration of factors, such as rising fuel prices and insane traffic, caused many a family to opt for two-wheelers instead. As a consequence, mechanics like Sunil were in form. But Sunil, who slogged from morning to night, saw JR's call as a chance to take that much needed break from nagging customers, which he pined for. So Babu and he, before riding off to Dadar, entered an Irani restaurant and ate and drank to their hearts' content. They did not forget to ask the manager for a copy of the bill, which would be duly forwarded to JR, and while they ate their food with gusto, Sandy waited.

When our mechanic duo eventually reached Jannat and saw the bike that required their attention, they were shocked that its owner, whom JR had described as a friend, looked no different from themselves. But then Sunil quickly put two and two together and decided that Sandy was no more than one of JR's harem boys, just like himself. This led to a sense of camaraderie among them. Sunil inspected the bike's ignition key and found that it was faulty. He was already carrying a duplicate key which had been made at a local key maker's. He then opened the bike up as a scientist dissects a frog, or a literary critic deconstructs a poem. While he worked, ordering Babu to tighten a nut or pass on a spanner, Sandy awkwardly hung around, feeling inferior and superior at the same time—inferior because he wasn't a skilled worker like Sunil and had no idea how to fix a bike; superior because he was, after all, a rich man's boyfriend, who did not have to soil his hands like Sunil.

Three hours later Sunil got the bike in running condition. It was, in his words, as good as new. The Jannat watchmen cheered and applauded Sandy as he mounted the bike and rode off, Sunil and Babu following on a Bajaj Boxer, a client's, needless to say. Sunil suddenly grew envious of Sandy, wondering what the bloke possessed that he himself did not. What guaranteed him a hassle-free life where all his needs were taken care of? There was only one conclusion that he could draw: Sandy owned equipment that was branded, while his was 'made in China'.

Halfway between Dadar and Cuffe Parade, the bike stalled. Sandy felt let down and Sunil felt cheated too, for his credibility as Colaba's best mechanic was at stake. He tinkered with the vehicle for a few minutes, before throwing his hands up in despair. 'I will have to tow it to my workshop,' he announced. 'I can't repair it here.'

Sandy had no idea how a bike could be towed.

'I will show you,' Sunil said, ordering Sandy to sit on his bike. He started his own Bajaj Boxer with Babu riding pillion, and then went and placed a foot on Sandy's Hero Honda. The Boxer's momentum hauled the Honda; this was physics at its best, but there was something erotic about it as well, the two bikes in motion resembling a pair of mating dogs. It took them twice the time to reach their destination, but in the end they made it. Sunil dragged Sandy's bike into his garage, promising to examine it before coming up with a diagnosis. The diagnosis arrived within a few days, with Sunil prescribing a whole lot of parts that needed replacement.

'Buy them off Lamington Road. Or wherever you find them,' JR instructed him on the phone, 'and send me the tab.'

'Okay, sir,' said Sunil.

A week later, Sandy's Hero Honda, his present from Lolita, was truly in showroom condition. This time Sunil wasn't fibbing. No one could have guessed that the bike once lay abandoned in the parking lot of a residential complex for months.

Sandy's next brush was with the traffic police. First, they stuffed his bike into a tow-away van for parking in a 'No Parking' zone. Second, when they released it, after they fined him, of course, they caught him for riding without a licence for a two-wheeler. Here, the money that changed hands could not be called a fine, for the cops did not give Sandy a receipt for the five hundred bucks they pocketed. Instead, it was a bribe.

'My job is to uphold the law,' JR sarcastically remarked over dinner that night, 'and yours is to break it.'

Those ominous words hung in front of Sandy.

The next day, JR took away the keys of the bike and declared he wouldn't return them until Sandy procured his rider's licence. Sandy sulked and threatened to leave home, pointing out that the bike was given to him by Lolita and not JR, but in the end good sense prevailed over him.

'Fine. I'll get my licence,' he affirmed, 'but you will have to come with me to the RTO, because ...'

'Because paperwork baffles you.'

'Exactly.'

'All right. Done.'

But the paperwork at the RTO exasperated JR as well. They spent a whole day at the chaotic office, resisting the offers of touts who promised to get their work done in thirty minutes flat, but at the end of it all, they came away without a damn licence.

'I give up,' JR swore. 'This country is going to the dogs.'

Reluctantly, he conceded that a licence in India couldn't be obtained without the intervention of middlemen, thanks to the nexus between corrupt agents and government officials. So he sent Sandy to the Bharat Motor Training School to solicit their help. They taught Sandy the ABC of driving a two-wheeler. Here, Sandy met his instructor who looked more like Mr Ali now than ever before. He confirmed that the man was gay because each time Sandy handed him his forms or photographs (of which there were a dozen), he did not lose the opportunity to let their fingers brush. But the man knew his job. He first got

Sandy a learner's licence, and then a permanent one a month later, after Sandy successfully made a figure of eight with his bike while an inspector watched.

'Good show,' Mr Ali applauded him, holding his hand for one last time. 'And congratulations.'

'Thanks.'

As Sandy paid his instructor the fees, he had a good mind to ask him for some of the money back for touching him inappropriately.

Traffic constables continued to corner Sandy on the streets even after he'd obtained his licence, but now he faced them, man to man, empowered. They tried to find other loopholes so that they could extract their pound of flesh, but Sandy did not let them get the better of him. Always he won and zoomed off without parting with any money. He accelerated to a hundred and zigzagged his way home among cars, buses and lorries.

Sandy's motorbike brought him closer to JR's queer circle of friends too. He broke into ARSE meetings that were held in the study and offered to take everyone on joyrides by turns. All except JR fell for the idea. Because of this, the ARSE members saw Bombay as never before. JR vehemently refused to ride pillion with Sandy, though Sandy insisted on taking him to office each morning, because he perceived Sandy as a rash driver.

'Bier-pyre-fire' JR bizarrely reminded him every time he picked up his bike keys from the table, which was his way of suggesting that bad motorcycle riding was a way of courting death. Honestly speaking, Sandy never wore a helmet and did have a couple of accidents on occasion, but luckily they were not of the bier-pyre-fire variety. He liked the bandages on his head after the mishaps. He thought they made him look macho.

How perverse can one get, JR wondered.

The flat had come alive. There were friends and food and drinks. There was pandemonium, with snatches of conversation on diverse subjects simultaneously taking place in different corners of the apartment, while Sandy and some of the ARSE members continued to talk about bikes.

Sandy fancied he was a motorbike pilot and that Bombay was Goa. Everyday, he left home around noon, started his bike, and aimlessly ambled all over Bombay. Bored, he pulled up at bus stops and offered lifts to commuters who waited for buses in serpentine queues. Most commuters ignored him, his personality in general making them highly suspicious of his intentions. To them, he came across as a hoodlum who, if they hitched a ride with him, would waylay them at a secluded spot and strip them of their cash and valuables. Perhaps, he had accomplices who were waiting for him somewhere. Bombay-ites were not used to being solicited by Good Samaritans, and the people at the bus stop were justified in spurning Sandy's advances.

But then there were those who succumbed to the temptation of a free ride. Most of them were single, unattached young men who knew they could overpower someone if required. When they told Sandy to drop them at such-and-such place, he would say, 'I am going there only.' At the end of the ten or fifteen minute ride, with numerous halts at the traffic signals, the people he gave lifts to got off his bike, said 'thank you' for the sake of formality, and disappeared among the city's multitudes.

Sandy felt like strangulating them for getting away without tipping him. If Aaron is paid for his services, he thought, why not me? However, he knew he couldn't openly demand money from his pillion riders, and this made the enterprise frustrating. Yet it was an interesting way of killing his time.

When the bus stops failed to yield the desired results, Sandy made for the taxi stands. Here, he blatantly propositioned men—never women—who were hailing taxis and whispered into their ears, just as the taxi drivers were about to flip down their meters, that he would take them to their destination for half the fare. Once again, most people turned a deaf ear to Sandy's offer, but once in a while a passenger or two relented and sat astride his Hero Honda. The taxi drivers who lost their customers to him felt repudiated, and had a good mind to get together and thrash him, but luckily for Sandy this never happened. At the end of the journey, his passengers duly paid him half the taxi fare, giving Sandy's self-esteem a boost. Once again, as in his Royal Video Parlour and Pigeon Courier days, he was making an honest living. At times, however, he was burdened with cantankerous customers who haggled over the fare, arguing that the taxis charged much less than what he claimed. To tackle such tricky situations, Sandy acquired a tariff card and kept a logbook, noting down speedometer readings at the time of departure and arrival.

Of course, all of this was illegal. Anyone could run a parallel transportation service in the city and make money on the side if it were that easy. But there were laws, especially in a big metropolitan city like Bombay. Sandy's foolhardy idea could have landed him in jail if the traffic wardens on the street got a whiff of what he was up to. It's a different matter that they did not call his bluff.

Then, he got his share of gay passengers who ran a racket of another kind throughout India. They either asked for, or gave lifts on two-wheelers, ostensibly because no buses or taxis were available. Their real intention, however, was to get physical with the young men they rode with and ultimately take them to bed. Their modus operandi was simple. The pillion rider clung to the driver, pretending he was afraid he would fall off, clutched his waist and slowly worked his hand towards the driver's crotch. Soon, the driver would have a hard-on as he rode. After that, getting him into bed, either in an apartment or a cheap lodge, was cakewalk. Or, the driver initiated sex by asking his pillion rider to inch closer, saying his rear tyre did not have enough air. Nine times out of ten, the reasoning worked: the pillion rider edged so close to the driver that he appeared to sodomize him!

When Sandy came across a gay passenger who wanted to hitch a ride, he knew of his sexual orientation in the first minute. However, his association with JR and his circle of friends had sensitized him to the plight of homosexuals. Earlier, he might have stopped his bike and asked the offender to piss off, or worse, assaulted him. But now he did nothing. He let his co-passenger have his fill, drawing the line only when the fellow unzipped him. At such times, he simply brushed away the roving fingers with a jerk and continued to ride. The person would get the message and withdraw.

To complement his biking image, Sandy went to Chor Bazaar where, among rows and rows of roadside shops that

sold just about everything under the sun, from antiques
to shoes, from vintage cars to clothes, he picked up a black
leather jacket that fitted him to a T. Though there were no
long mirrors in which he could narcissistically see himself, he
perceived that the jacket suited him—as the shopkeeper kept
telling him—and decided to buy it, even if it meant selling off
his valuables. The shopkeeper asked for Rs 5000, but Sandy
knew that Chor Bazaar was a place where one could bargain
like crazy. Then, the shopkeeper invented another lie. The
leather jacket, he claimed, once belonged to Shah Rukh Khan
who wore it for a film shoot and then discarded it. He even
showed him the initials 'SRK' engraved on the collar. 'Which
film?' Sandy asked the shopkeeper, who was nonplussed for
an answer. 'I know,' said Sandy, answering his own question.
'*Baazigar*.'

Sandy knew that the shopkeeper had spun a yarn, but he
let him be. What he especially liked about the jacket were its
pockets. They were so large that anything could fit into them.
In the end, the shopkeeper slashed the price to one-tenth and
gave Sandy the leather jacket in exchange for a crisp 500-rupee-
note, which the shopkeeper held up to the light to check
whether it was a fake. That's okay for Chor Bazaar stuff, Sandy
said to himself. Aloud, however, he rubbished the shopkeeper's
actions, arguing there was no need to check the note and that
he'd withdrawn it from an ATM nearby.

'That ATM's also made in Chor Bazaar,' the shopkeeper
laughed, pocketing the dough.

As Sandy left with his acquisition, wearing the leather jacket
over his printed cotton shirt there itself, unperturbed by the

heat that caused him to sweat, the shopkeeper hailed out to him.

'Come here,' said the shopkeeper. When Sandy went, thinking the mad shopkeeper wasn't finished with his 500-rupee-note as yet, the man showed him a pair of leather boots that went well with the jacket. 'Perfect matching,' he said. 'And who does this belong to?' Sandy asked him. 'Salman Khan?'

The shopkeeper laughed and offered the boots to Sandy for another 500 bucks. This time, Sandy really wished he could lay his hands on some fake currency notes, or better still, print them himself. He wanted to buy all the goodies that were available in the world. He asked the shopkeeper if note-printing machines too were available in Chor Bazaar which, but of course, made the man laugh again. But Sandy liked the boots and saw the shopkeeper's point about matching them to the leather jacket. So he decided to buy them, no matter what. He used the cash JR had given him to pay the electricity bill, deferring thoughts about the fight they would have later.

Sandy wore the boots, asking the shopkeeper to wrap up his old running shoes in a thin polythene bag, the sort that had badly clogged Bombay's storm water drains a year ago and caused the city's worst-ever floods in which many died.

Now Sandy looked like the perfect stuntman as he kick-started his bike and rode off, wheelie style.

What's the first thing Sandy did on getting home? He went into JR's study, where his revolver sat, and put it into one of his giant pockets. The sleek revolver went deep inside the pocket, disguising itself completely. Sandy sat at home all day just like that—in his black leather jacket and black leather boots, with JR's pistol in his pocket. As for JR, who was away in court all day, he had no idea that when Sandy served him his masala chai that evening, his revolver was sitting in Sandy's pocket the entire time.

'Very smart,' he said, when he saw Sandy in his new attire, and asked, 'Isn't Bombay a tad hot for such clothing?' But Sandy had an answer for that as well—he turned on the air conditioner at full blast, causing JR to grumble about inflated electricity bills. This in turn reminded Sandy that he'd spent the electricity bill money on his boots! But no, he wasn't going to confess to this now. He'd leave it for later, when JR was in a better mood and would not resent Sandy's errors, for to err, after all, is human.

When Sandy finally undressed at night, the revolver continued to sit in his pocket.

On days when he did not sport his leather jacket and leather boots, kick-start his bike and take off, Sandy stayed home and returned to his childhood pastime—sketching. At first, he sketched on A4 sized sheets that JR kept next to the printer, using whichever pens and pencils he found in the flat. Later, he went to the Bombay Stationery Mart at Fort and bought the best quality art paper, sketching pencils and drawing boards that were available. Sandy was proud of his art. He thought of himself as a professional artist, not an amateur. If encouraged, he could outdo great masters like M.F. Husain, whose work adorned the walls of JR's house. He would start sketching the moment JR left for office and sit in the study, which he thought of as his studio, and would be there till late in the afternoon. So absorbed was he in his work that he often skipped lunch. At times he tore up his sheets, unhappy with the results, and chucked them into the dustbin. At other times he liked his creations so much that he wanted to frame them and hang them up on the walls. Sandy recalled that the last time he drew was in his rented room at Dadar, soon after he met Lolita. So much had happened since then. Why, if only he'd documented his journey in pictures, depicting the different way stations through which he went, there would be enough to fill up an art gallery.

Sandy liked to draw what he was obsessed with. When he first met Lolita and was captivated by her charm, all his portraits were of her. Now, although he did the odd landscape, enchanted by views of Bombay as seen through JR's apartment, majority of his drawings were of Aroop Sengupta. Rambo, as he was also known, was drawn as he looked in reality, and also as he did not. Rambo in his sailor's haircut, and Rambo with long, hippie hair. Rambo without spectacles and Rambo with spectacles. Rambo with a moustache and Rambo without a moustache. Side profiles and frontal views. The saint with a beatific smile, and the sinner baring his fangs. Without earrings, and with earrings. There was even a sketch of him dancing with Aaron at Testosterone.

JR returned from work to find sheets of paper strewn all about the house, and when he examined the portraits Sandy had drawn, holding them close to his eyes, he found them to be those of Aroop. He collected them all, put them in a folder and advised Sandy to continue drawing. 'You are a dynamite,' he flattered his boyfriend.

JR displayed Sandy's portraits at ARSE meetings. When the members expressed intrigue at his choice of subject, Ismail explained that the drawings were cathartic.

'They are meant to purge the ghosts of a man who haunts him night and day,' he said. Then he went into classroom mode again.

'Aristotle speaks, specifically, of two emotions—pity and terror. It is these emotions that tend to dominate our psyche, and so have to be dealt with. A good play, by invoking pity and terror, helps the audience purge themselves of these undesirable states. It is likewise with a good sketch.'

'I can understand why terror grips Sandy at the thought of Aroop Sengupta,' said Anand. 'But why pity?'

'Don't take it literally,' Ismail held. 'Pity and terror are paradigmatic emotions that represent other emotions.'

'So what you are saying is that in sketching his portraits, Sandy is really dealing with a gamut of emotions that have been plaguing his life.'

'Exactly.'

Never in his dreams would Sandy have imagined that his drawings could provoke art criticism of this type. However, he was unaware that his work was being put to such scrutiny. While JR and his friends fervently discussed Sandy's use of lines and texture, he was busy in the other room, immersed in his art, working by lamplight.

Yet Sandy's life was, in the main, characterized by boredom. Riding his motorbike and sketching weren't adequate ways of expending his youthful energy.

'How about another holiday?' he asked JR over drinks one evening, and JR jumped for joy, like a child. 'But,' continued Sandy, '*sirf hum tum*, not your whole gang.'

'Agreed,' JR clapped his hands.

Together they decided to go on a tiger safari. Accordingly, they went to the railway station the next morning to book their tickets and waited in a never-ending queue.

'Stand in *that* queue,' Sandy told JR, pointing to a queue to the right. 'There's no rush there.' When JR looked, there was a sign at the window that said *Senior Citizens Only.*

'Stand in *this* queue,' JR told Sandy, pointing to a queue on the left. 'There's no rush here either.'

The sign at this window read: *Handicapped Persons Only.*

'But I'm not handicapped,' Sandy laughed.

'And I'm no senior citizen,' JR quipped. Then he said, 'And who said you aren't handicapped? Aren't you mentally?'

Once they obtained their tickets and were driving back home, they came by a road sign this time which said *Yield to Straight Traffic.*

'Means what?' Sandy asked.

'It means heteros have right of way, the bastards,' JR explained.

Their affair with signboards did not end in the city. It followed them all the way to their tiger safari, deep into the jungles of central India. After a tedious rail-cum-road journey, as they drove to their hotel in a taxi, one of the first things that greeted them was a sign that read, *Love tigers? Well, they love you too!*

'That sign is bound to put tourists off,' JR felt. 'It's alarming in the extreme!'

But the sign wasn't without significance. The tiger reserve in question had acquired a notorious reputation for tiger attacks. Over sixty people, villagers mostly, had been killed in the past five years. JR couldn't have known then, as he read the sign and a shudder passed through his spine, that one day, when things were different, his work would bring him back to this very forest to fight a case. Sandy, on the other hand, was excited and hoped they would see a tiger.

'I can fight a tiger single-handed,' he boasted.

Of course, when their safari began and they actually came across a tiger just a few feet away, Sandy's bravado deserted him.

'Shoot,' JR whispered into Sandy's ear.

To his horror, Sandy pulled out JR's revolver from the pocket of his leather jacket, which he continued to wear. JR learned for the first time that day that Sandy's jacket pocket was now the permanent home of his licensed revolver. The revolver went wherever the jacket went, and the jacket went wherever Sandy went.

'Shoot with the camera, not the gun, you Neanderthal,' JR screamed at him.

Their guide hushed them. Human voices were anathema to the tigers, and there were people in the safari that had travelled thousands of miles and waited for days on end, just to glimpse the lord of the jungle.

JR shut his mouth, but later, when they were back in their hotel suite, he exploded, almost as if he were the revolver itself.

'How dare you touch my gun without my permission?' he yelled. 'Do you know you can't be seen in a tiger reserve with a gun? It's the surest way to invite arrest!'

'I know. I was just playing the fool.'

'That joke of yours could have landed me in jail. That gun, after all, is registered in my name. Why did you bring it along anyway?'

'Because it goes well with my jacket.'

'That's your excuse?!'

Truthfully speaking, Sandy's actions really gave JR the jitters. In recent times, even ministers and celebrity film stars weren't spared if they hunted for big game in India's depleting forests. Environmental awareness and animal rights were political issues that had the support of NGOs from all over the world today, not to speak of women like Maneka Gandhi. These things had changed from the days of the British Raj and the maharajas.

But there was more to come. That night, the events of the day gave JR nightmares. He dreamt that a tiger had smashed through the windowpane of his room, caught him by the scruff of his neck, and vanished with him into the thick of the forest. The fact that JR went to bed reading a book about Jim Corbett perhaps brought on his nightmare with greater ferocity.

JR woke up with a start which startled Sandy out of sleep too. 'As soon as we get back to Bombay, I'm going to deposit that revolver in a bank locker,' JR announced, as Sandy brought him a glass of water to calm him down.

Sandy worried, not about his partner's health, for yes, they had grown to be partners, but about the prospect of life without the gun for he had become so obsessed with it.

The following Wednesday, Aaron telephoned Sandy from Goa, surprising him to no end. Sandy truly believed that the Aaron chapter of his life was temporarily on hold, at least for now, if not downright closed.

'We are coming to Bombay,' Aaron said. 'Let's meet.'

'"We" who?'

'Rambo and I are coming, you madman.'

'But isn't he at sea?'

'He's quitting the merchant navy.'

'What?'

'Yes, he is setting up his own business.'

'Where?'

'Don't know. Goa, maybe. Or Bombay.'

'When?'

'I don't know.'

'I mean when are you coming to Bombay?' Sandy asked again.

'Tonight itself.'

'Where do you want to meet?'

'Testosterone. On Saturday night. We are coming there to shake a leg.'

'Okay, fine.'

'You'll come?'

'Yeah.'

'See you, then.'

'Bye.'

JR was at the dining table, waiting for Sandy to join him for supper. Sandy did not tell him about Aaron's call. He planned to go to Testosterone alone.

'The fowl smells foul,' JR said, as he opened the lid of a steel dish to serve his boyfriend. 'Must change the cook.'

Meanwhile, another man and another boy, Aroop Sengupta alias Rambo and his boyfriend Aaron, were having dinner at the Royal Bombay Yacht Club, opposite the Gateway of India. As they stepped out of the taxi that brought them there from the airport, a memory stung Aroop. He remembered, with a twinge of pain, that this was where Lolita and he had stayed when they first arrived in Bombay soon after their wedding, as their flat in Jannat was not yet ready to live in. He had loved his wife so much then. Did he know that a day would come when things would sour between them to such an extent?

Aaron's news about Aroop's plans to leave the merchant navy was correct: Aroop intended to set up a car shop with the money he had made in the merchant navy. That was one of the reasons which brought him to Bombay.

The pair took a post-dinner stroll along the Gateway of India promenade and were amused by the spectacle of ageing Arab men looking for catamites. When they reached the Radio Club end of the promenade and saw their favourite pub, Testosterone, they regretted it was a gay bar only on Saturday nights.

'I've been to gay bars in all the ports I've sailed to,' Aroop informed Aaron, 'and they're never gay bars just on Saturday nights. India is ridiculous.'

Aaron responded to this with his trademark 'Yeah'. He wasn't equipped to give his partner sermons on patriotism.

The next morning, after a colonial-style breakfast made up of cornflakes, poached eggs, bacon, orange juice, fruit and coffee, they took a taxi to Lamington Road where Aroop surveyed the rows and rows of shops that dealt in automobile spares and accessories. He spoke to scores of traders, mostly Sikhs from Punjab whom he addressed as 'Sardarji', to know what profits they made.

'A Bengali isn't cut out for this business,' some of them jocularly told him. 'You will have to wear a turban and pose as

a sardarji if you want to succeed.' Aroop chortled, wondering if
the Sikh gentlemen were being racial in their remarks. After all,
the hatred that the Punjabis and Bengalis had for each other was
well-known. In the early 1970s, Prime Minister Indira Gandhi
cleverly cashed in on this hatred and freed East Pakistan from
West Pakistani tyranny. That was how Bangladesh was born.

While Aroop hobnobbed with the sardarjis, Aaron sat in a
corner and yawned. He was bored to bits, though he did not
openly show it. Then he discovered that there were shops in the
area that also sold motorcycle parts and this cheered him up.
He would buy some of their wares to deck up his bike, and that
would fill him with pride. He nudged Aroop as a child nudges a
parent when he discovers a toy in a toyshop.

Afterwards, Aaron, whose pace slowed down because of the
bag loads of merchandise that he carried in both hands, asked
Aroop *where* he would be setting up his business.

'Bombay, of course,' Aroop replied.

'That means you'll leave Goa?'

'Not at all,' said Aroop. 'I'll employ a manager to run the
store. I wasn't born to be a shopkeeper.'

Saturday came. As luck would have it, the ARSE meeting
that night wasn't at Sea View Apartments, but at Derek's newly-
acquired suburban villa in distant Vasai. JR had assumed all
along that Sandy would be accompanying him to the venue,
and was so peeved by his vehement refusal to be part of the
crowd that they weren't on speaking terms the entire day. Sandy
had promised to meet Aaron at Testosterone round about ten,
and he did not wish to renege on his word. Of course, touching
base with Aaron was only a ruse. It was a vital mission that held

Sandy back that night, and nothing, not even JR's tantrums, could prevent him from accomplishing it. Sandy was absolutely sure about one thing: It was now or never.

Aroop and Aaron were already on the dance floor when Sandy paid his cover charge and pushed open Testosterone's swivel doors to enter, dressed as usual in his black leather jacket. From the inebriated manner in which a wizened Aroop clutched Aaron at the waist as they danced, Sandy could tell that they had downed more than a couple of beers. It was Aaron who saw Sandy first, and waved out to him with a 'hi'. Then Aroop noticed him and recognized him at once.

'I know that bloke,' he whispered into Aaron's ear, unnerved by Sandy's menacing look. This came as a shock to Aaron, who until then had no inkling that Sandy and Aroop knew each other.

However, this was no time for life stories.

'The jerk's jerkin',' Aroop diffidently said as he noticed the revolver that jutted out of Sandy's pocket. But it was too late. Sandy whipped out the weapon with flair; walked straight up to Aroop and put it to his forehead. He shot Aroop at point-blank range, rendering Lolita a widow in minutes. Aroop's dying words were, 'The jerk's jerkin'.'

There was complete silence in Testosterone for a few seconds, but it felt like hours. Then pandemonium broke out in the pub. Patrons ran helter-skelter, exiting not just through the front door, where there was a stampede, but from the emergency exits in the kitchen and toilets too. To make matters worse, a fire broke out at the bar as cigarette stubs ignited all the spilt liquor. Women hustlers shrieked in high-pitched voices. The owner, Mr Pallonji, and his bouncers were nowhere in sight.

Amidst all this, Aroop's body lay in an estuary of blood, his eyes still open. The bullet had drilled a hole through his head, entering at the left temple and emerging from the right.

Aaron grabbed Sandy by the hand and started to run.

'No one has seen you doing it,' the panic-stricken youngster gasped, even as he asked, 'Why did you do it?'

But Aaron was wrong. Mr Pallonji, who was missing from the pub, had actually gone to summon the police. They spotted a sprinting Sandy and Aaron on the run near the old Taj and cornered them, putting handcuffs on them both. Sirens blared, and the fire engines that arrived added to the din. But Sandy and Aaron were taken to a police station far away from the scene of the crime. Here, their mobiles were confiscated and they were kept in the lock-up all night. Sandy was only allowed to make a distress call to JR.

Sandy was a novice in crime. The one obvious precaution he should have taken was to wear gloves before shooting. This would have at least prevented his fingers from leaving prints on the revolver. The fingerprints were the giveaway. They proved without a shadow of a doubt that Sandy was the culprit, leading to his arrest. A non-bailable warrant was issued in his name. Aaron, on the other hand, was freed, though he was kept in judicial custody for several days as a suspected accomplice. During this time, his family in Goa moved heaven and earth trying to trace him. Though the cops gave him the option to call upon them to secure his release, Aaron preferred to keep them out of the mess in which he found himself. They'll die of shame, he thought.

Aaron did not grieve Aroop's death. Theirs was a mercenary relationship, all said and done. Tomorrow, another sugar daddy would cross his path.

JR was Sandy's defence lawyer again, though this time he was the offender and the magnitude of his crime was far greater. JR scarcely escaped arrest himself, for the revolver used by Sandy was his. One could deduce, if one so desired, that it was he who was behind the sailor's murder, just as it was Savarkar, not Godse, who was behind Gandhi's murder. Of course, in the twenty-first century guns were like toys that could be procured at the drop of a hat, making issues like the ownership of weapons irrelevant. Yet JR had to face a volley of awkward questions pertaining to his relationship with Sandy, who lived in his house, for which he had to improvise answers. In the end, he got away with a fine and a strict warning to keep his revolver under lock and key at all times.

As for Sandy, he was under trial for several years in various high-profile jails in Maharashtra, such as the notorious Arthur Road Jail in Bombay and Yerwada Jail in Pune, before his case came up for hearing. During this time, JR visited him regularly with food and other basics, humouring him to keep up his spirits.

'Brougnt you custard in custody,' JR would say, as he opened a tiffin box to serve Sandy his favourite sweet dish. Few prisoners anywhere in the world were in Sandy's shoes, with lover and defence lawyer being one and the same man. However, the fact that their relationship had no *locus standi* worked to Sandy's advantage. If the two of them shared any known relationship, such as husband or brother or father, JR would never have been allowed to plead Sandy's case.

The high court awarded Sandy the death penalty; none of JR's arguments worked with the judges. The ghosts of the Nanavati case continued to haunt them, with the judiciary remarking that this was the inverse of the legendary case.

'There, the husband shot the lover at point-blank range,' the learned judges observed. 'Whereas, here, the lover shot the husband!'

There was laughter in the courtroom that got JR's goat.

'How is it that we are unable to forget an incident that took place half a century ago?' JR asked.

Sandy reacted to the verdict stoically. For one, he finally realized his dream of using the revolver some day. He was not repentant for his crime, for he believed that his victim had to be liquidated at any cost. It was he who had thwarted Sandy's love affair with Lolita and it was he who beat him beyond recognition, all but killing him. Besides, Sandy wasn't afraid of death. He thought he had seen it all and there was nothing left for him to get out of life; he was ready to call it quits. If anything, it was the thought that JR would have to do without him in old age that saddened him. I am his crutch, thought Sandy, and without me the man will have to limp. He wasn't wide of the mark. His harem and ARSE meetings notwithstanding, Sandy's absence created a vacuum in JR's life.

'If you are actually sent to the gallows,' JR told Sandy in his prison cell, 'I'll have to take cyanide and follow you to the other world.'

This was followed by silence.

Within minutes their time was up and uniformed prison guards ordered JR to take his leave.

'But I'm his defence lawyer,' JR protested in vain, but that had no effect on the guards.

JR wasn't about to give up that easily. He would live up to the promise he made to Sandy the day the latter showed him his parents' photograph.

'If necessary, we'll write to the president of India,' he assured Sandy. 'We'll write him a mercy petition, asking for clemency.'

The Supreme Court, however, saw merit in JR's reasoning. The case, to its way of thinking, revolved around a key question: Was the murder cold-blooded? If it wasn't, the death penalty wasn't justified.

JR presented exhibits to the court of Sandy's photos taken just before his plastic surgery.

'The murder wasn't cold-blooded, your lordships,' he eloquently argued before the bench. 'It was in retaliation to the way the victim disfigured my client, as these photographs document.'

The court asked if Dr Hosi Billimoria, Sandy's plastic surgeon, would be willing to depose before it as a witness.

'Give me a day,' JR said, and flew the doctor to Delhi by first class.

When the doctor stood in the witness box and corroborated the lawyer's claims, pointing out that a disease like leprosy couldn't do to a man what Aroop's assault had done, the judges changed Sandy's death sentence to life imprisonment, thus dismissing the prosecution's objections that the assault was a fallout of Sandy's illicit affair with the victim's wife.

'Who's the real victim?' one of the judges sardonically asked.

While delivering their hundred-odd page judgement, the learned judges also referred to Sandy's age; they were of the opinion that a man below thirty who had his whole life before him had to be given the opportunity to reform himself.

Victory was theirs a second time.

Epilogue

Aroop's parents would claim his body after his murder and perform his last rites, immersing his ashes in the holy Ganges. They would spend their old age cursing Lolita for bringing ill luck to their family, as if there was *mangal* in her horoscope, and snatching their son away from them. More unbearable than Aroop's death, however, would be the shame and the scandal of having to live in a gossiping, finger-pointing world that called him a cuckold, for his wife, after all, had left him for a younger man, at least in spirit.

One fallout of Sandy's stay in prison would be that he would become a gay activist of sorts, educating all the hard-core criminals with whom he shared cell space about the need to use condoms during homosexual sex. That he was an ARSE member by default would certainly be of help here, but what was more was that his exposure to the rampant same-sex intercourse all around him—in the cells, in the toilets, in the corridors of the jail by sex-starved prisoners—would make him a little more comfortable with his own gay side, and he would learn to be a little less in denial. He would even be in a position to co-ordinate discussions on homosexuality in the prison, and when some of the young inmates convicted for rape or murder would claim that 'homosex' was now legal in India,

Sandy would tell them that it was only legal in Delhi, and that it would become legal in the rest of the country only after the Supreme Court ratified the Delhi High Court decision.

'Why Supreme Court taking so long?' the inmates would ask Sandy.

'Because Baba Ramdev is arguing that if man-man sex was made legal, why not man-animal sex?' Sandy would then respond.

Practice would follow theory and, as he would serve his sentence in jail, Sandy would begin to have sex with men other than JR for the first time in his life.

There would be discord among ARSE members, some of whom would boycott JR for not washing his hands off Sandy, whom they called a murderer.

'You might be next on his list, for all we know,' they would caution him. 'Once a murderer, always a murderer.'

They would all stop going to Sea View Apartments for meetings, because the thought that the apartment housed someone who would one day commit a murder sent a shudder down their spines. The only ARSE member who would remain steadfast in his loyalty to JR, and who would refuse to brand Sandy a serial killer, as the others would begin to call him in jest, was Pheroze.

'Sandy killed Aroop Sengupta out of revenge,' he would tirelessly point out to his friends, and go on to describe the young man as 'down and out'.

But this would not change the mindset of his friends. They would give JR an ultimatum, threatening to expel him from the group if he did not dissociate himself from Sandy straightaway.

'Well, go ahead and expel me,' JR would reply.

Pheroze would meet JR privately and inform him that a faction of ARSE members, including Derek, were still on their side. They would be ready to break away from the parent group and form a rival body. But JR would dismiss the suggestion, pointing out that he was against the splitting of groups in the manner of India's political parties, and that in any case, he had gone beyond activism and was now ready to try something else.

JR would make his will and leave all his movable and immovable property to Sandy. ARSE members, especially the faction that was hostile to Sandy, would come to the conclusion that the old man was losing his mind. They were certain that once JR made Sandy his heir, the next logical step for the delinquent young man would be to eliminate his benefactor as quickly as possible, so that he could claim his inheritance.

'JR, you are a dead man,' they would joke.

When their views would become known to JR, through Pheroze acting as his spy, he would pooh-pooh them and let his enemies know that he believed in the basic goodness of human beings. But his opponents would rubbish his view.

'The twenty-first century does not need another Gandhi,' they would say.

Then JR would ironically concede that even if his detractors were right, he still had a fourteen year or so lease of life because Sandy was busy serving a life sentence in jail. He would not be able to eliminate JR to claim his inheritance at least till he was released. But so cynical was the other side that they shot back in defence that they did not expect Sandy to stay in prison for fourteen years—he would escape much before that by becoming a party to a jailbreak or some such thing.

There would be a sea change in JR's lifestyle at Sea View Apartments too. He would turn monogamous with a vengeance. He would disband his harem and almost completely abstain from sex, resorting only to masturbation once in a while, and that too in order to avoid complications like prostate cancer, about which he'd read so much. Prostate cancer in men is the equivalent of breast cancer in women, he would come to believe, and think of masturbation as a way to reduce the chances of contracting such a dreaded disease. However, while masturbating he would bring all his harem boys into his fantasies by turns—it was his way of enshrining them in his memory forever. The boys themselves would be confused by his behaviour because he would never call them, and if they took the initiative and buzzed him on his mobile, his answer would always be, 'I'm busy, will call you later,' or, 'Sorry, I'm just not in the mood.'

One harem boy in particular, Sunil, who had once fixed Sandy's bike, would be really cut up. He would write a letter to JR in broken English, in which he would accuse JR of using him when he wanted, and then dropping him like a hot potato when it suited his fancy. JR would offer him a wad of currency notes to appease him, but this would offend him even further. Eventually JR would hit upon an idea: He would give Sunil Sandy's bike, the one given to him by Lolita, to keep forever, and it would do the trick.

'I repaired it,' Sunil would proudly say.

Of course, JR would say nothing to Sandy about this deal when they would meet in jail.

Overall, JR's aim would be to make Sandy see his stint in jail as penance and transform himself, at the end of it, into a new man. Likewise, he would see his own life, with Sandy absent from the flat, as his *vanaprastha.* He would practice austerity at home in order to atone for Sandy's sins. He would become philanthropic and fight different sorts of cases in court, where his clients were not rich men living at Marine Drive or Malabar Hill, but poor tribals hailing from India's most backward districts. For example, he would take up the case of a tribal family from Naxalite-infested Gadchiroli on the outskirts of Maharashtra, whose only bread-winning family member was killed by a tiger in adjoining Chandrapur, where Sandy and he had once been, while he was labouring in a field parallel to the highway. As in Sandy's case, JR would first read about the incident in the newspapers and would then take the trouble to contact the family and file a suit against the government on their behalf. All this, without charging them a rupee. In court, JR would cleverly apply Machiavelli's Law of Ends and Means, and argue that the ends did not justify the means. Saving the tiger from extinction was a noble end, but it couldn't be at the expense of villagers whose settlements bordered tiger reserves and wildlife sanctuaries that endangered their lives. He would win the case and the court would not only order the government to pay compensation and guarantee employment to the bereaved family, but it would also ask them to relocate the tiger reserve itself, which had come up around villages that had been there for centuries.

'This is the twenty-first century,' one of the judges would wryly remark, 'and it is strange that tigers should be killing men, as they did in the days of the British Raj.'

Left-wing intellectuals would commend the judgement and JR would receive a congratulatory email from none other than Medha Patkar, who would compliment him for taking up the cudgels on behalf of the tribals, who got it from all sides. However, wildlife enthusiasts would be livid. They would call JR a Maoist and urge him to set the record straight.

'It isn't the wildlife of the region, but the villagers in general and your client in particular, who are the poachers and encroachers,' they would hold. 'Kick them out of the forest if the tiger is not to disappear from the face of the Earth altogether, like the dinosaur.'

The controversy would snowball to such an extent that television channels would get wind of the story and invite JR for panel discussions where he would go armed with facts and figures.

'In the district from which my clients hail,' he would agitatedly point out, 'close to a hundred people have been killed by tigers in the last five years. How long can this go on?'

And, as he would ask the question, JR would thump his left fist into his right palm.

During the course of his jail life, Sandy's parents would pass away. His father would go first, succumbing to cirrhosis of the liver, while his mother would follow a few years later, diagnosed with oral cancer. News of his parents' death would not reach Sandy in jail. As far as he was concerned, they were dead already. His sisters would be married off to distant relatives in their native place, but once again Sandy would know nothing about this.

And what would become of Mr Ali, Sandy's bête noire, the man who duped him and was responsible, in a way, for the dramatic turn his life took? He would die on a railway track in Bombay in an inebriated state, as a fast local train would run over him late one evening and make mincemeat of his body. Sandy would be delighted to hear the news, if only someone would tell him, but then there was none who would. Mr Ali's body would remain unclaimed in the city morgue for days, till the civic corporation would finally dispose of it.

The Royal Video Parlour's business would flourish and they would diversify, starting their own dish antenna service. Darshan and Aniket would still be working there. They would hear of Sandy's arrest and go to visit him in jail, where the presence of convicts on death row would unnerve them.

'Why did you fuck up your life?' they would ask Sandy, as he would rest his head on their shoulders.

Lolita never expected Sandy to return to Goa after their secret meeting—she knew he was spinning a yarn when he claimed he would come back. Had Aroop not been murdered, their divorce would have come through. News of the murder first came to her on the telephone. When she read the newspapers the next morning she learned that Sandy was the culprit. Perhaps that was why she stayed away from the trial and was not present in court when the sentence was pronounced.

Lolita would move on. She would dispose of the house in Goa and go with Tanu, first to her parents' home in Calcutta, and later to the US, where she would emigrate for good when Tanu would become a teenager.

Fourteen years would pass. Sandy would be released from jail. Why is a life sentence in India fourteen years? Because Lord Ram spent fourteen years in exile.

Sandy would return to his kingdom of Ayodhya in Sea View Apartments after fourteen arduous years. He would be thirty-five-years-old. JR would be over sixty-five, and would have retired from active legal practice. They would leave Bombay and begin a new life, in a remote, peaceful, idyllic, pastoral, prelapsarian place where JR would try his hand at farming and landscape gardening.

At first, that place would be Meghalaya in India's Northeast, where they would drive from Guwahati to Shillong and Tura in a hired jeep, enjoying the scenic drive. Soon, however, they would tire of the Northeast, separated as it was from the rest of India by Bangladesh, and moreover, the political upheavals of the Northeast would also scare them.

'What if the ULFA abducts me, holds me to ransom and kills me, as they did my classmate Sunjoy Ghosh decades ago?' JR would ask Sandy.

Our duo would then return to Bombay and head for Kodaikanal in the Palani Hills of south India, where they would finally settle down. Their arrival would coincide with the blossoming of the purple-coloured *kurinji* flower, which blossoms once in twelve years, just like the Kumbh Mela. JR would regard this sign as auspicious.

Sandy would complete his education in Kodaikanal, famous for its public schools, through correspondence courses offered by an open university in Delhi. Thereafter, he would join art school and become a successful artist. A day would come when he would exhibit his drawings and sketches in art galleries. Some of them would be sold for decent amounts and the art criticism pages of Sunday newspapers would carry his photograph. He would feel empowered.

'I have given you wings, as Icarus gave his son Daedalus,' JR would tell Sandy. 'But you must not fly too close to the sun, or your wings will melt and you will come crashing down.'

Their story would have a fairy-tale ending. JR would live on, considering he was very particular about his diet and his exercise, and that the climate of Kodaikanal was much more salubrious than that of Bombay. Sandy would be by his side at all times, but as a fellow traveller, not as an escort. They would transcend bodily passion and achieve a state of nirvana that would enable them to see, several times over, the blooming of the *kurinji* flower, which blossoms once in twelve years.

Printed by RR Donnelley at Glasgow, UK